HARRISON
SQUARED

Also by Daryl Gregory and available from Titan Books

Afterparty

HARRISON SQUARED

DARYL GREGORY

TITAN BOOKS

HARRISON SQUARED
Print edition ISBN: 9781783297641
E-book edition ISBN: 9781783297658

Published by Titan Books
A division of Titan Publishing Group Ltd
144 Southwark Street, London SE1 0UP

First Titan edition: March 2015
10 9 8 7 6 5 4 3 2 1

Names, places and incidents are either products of the author's imagination or used fictitiously. Any resemblance to actual persons, living or dead (except for satirical purposes), is entirely coincidental.

Daryl Gregory asserts the moral right to be identified as the author of this work.

A CIP catalogue record for this title is available from the British Library.

Printed and bound in Great Britain by CPI Group (UK) Ltd

What did you think of this book?
We love to hear from our readers. Please email us at readerfeedback@titanemail.com
or write to us at the above address.

To receive advance information, news, competitions, and exclusive offers online,
please sign up for the Titan newsletter on our website:
www.titanbooks.com

Author's Note

All chapter epigraphs are from "The Rime of the Ancient Mariner" by Samuel Taylor Coleridge.

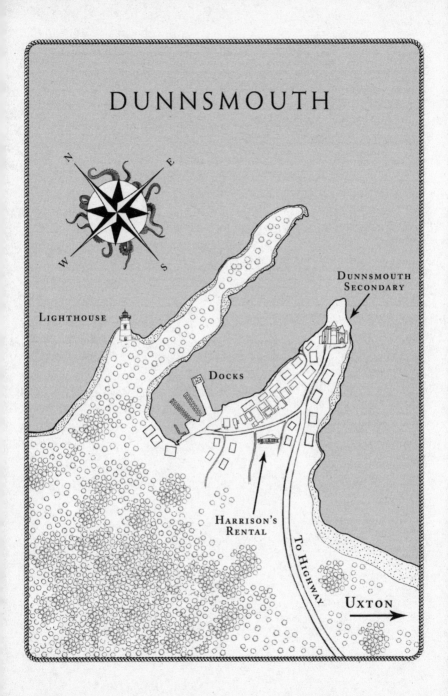

Since then, at an uncertain hour,
That agony returns:
And till my ghastly tale is told,
This heart within me burns.

Samuel Taylor Coleridge,
"The Rime of the Ancient Mariner"

PROLOGUE

What I remember are tentacles. Tentacles and teeth.

I know that those memories aren't real. I was only three when my father died, too young to understand what was happening. So later I filled in the gaps with snippets from monster movies and nature documentaries, with half-forgotten visits to dim aquariums, with illustrations from my mother's grad-school textbooks.

This is how the brain works. It makes up stories out of whatever odds and ends it finds. Sometimes they're scary stories.

But there are gaps I can't fill. Like, the sound of my father's voice. I can't remember what he sounded like, even though I can picture him calling to me. In my memory I simply *know* that he's yelling my name. He's lifting me up out of the water, and there's something trying to pull me back down. It's black as oil and I can feel its teeth digging into my leg. In my memory I'm screaming, but I don't hear that either.

We're in the ocean, and it's night, and the waves are lifting us and throwing us down. Somewhere nearby, a boat is upside down, showing its white belly. We're getting farther and farther from it. (How would a toddler know this? Well, he wouldn't. These are "facts" I've layered on over time, like newspaper on a papier-mâché piñata.)

Some images, however, are so clear to me that they feel more true than my memory of yesterday's breakfast. I can see my father's face as he picks me up by my life vest. I can feel the wind as he tosses me up and over the next wave, toward that capsized boat. And I can see, as clearly as I can see my own arm, a huge limb that's risen up out of the water.

The arm is fat, and gray, the underside covered in pale suckers. It whips across my father's chest, grasping him—and then it pulls him away from me. The tentacle is attached to a huge body, a shape under the water that's bigger than anything I've ever seen.

And then nothing. My memories end there, with that frozen moment.

I know there's no such thing as monsters. Yes, we were out on the ocean, and the boat did flip over. But no creature bit through my leg to the bone—it was a piece of metal from the ship that sliced into me. My mother swam me to shore, and kept me from bleeding to death. My father drowned like an ordinary man.

Don't feel bad for me. I barely remember him. I certainly don't remember the infection that nearly killed me, and the series of surgeries, and the months I was in the hospital. T hose memories are gone with the sound of my father's voice.

But I do know this: My parents saved me. My brain can make up all the scary stories it wants to, but I know that much is true.

1

Ah! well-a-day! what evil looks
Had I from old and young!

The building seemed to be watching me.

I stood on the sidewalk, gazing up at it. It looked like a single gigantic block of dark stone, its surface wet and streaked with veins of white salt, as if it had just risen whole from the ocean depths. The huge front doors were recessed into the stone like a wailing mouth. Above, arched windows glared down.

The sign out front declared it to be THE DUNNSMOUTH SECONDARY SCHOOL.

This was like no school I'd ever seen before. I didn't know what it was—a mausoleum, maybe? Something they should have torn down. Yet some lunatic had looked at this hulk and said, I know, let's put *kids* in here!

Except the kids were nowhere to be seen. Nobody was outside, and the windows were dark. I'd suspected that I'd made a mistake coming with my mom to this town, but I now realized that I was wrong: I'd made a *horrible* mistake.

The truck door slammed behind me. Mom hustled around the back of the vehicle. In the bed of the truck were "the buoys in the band": four research buoys labeled E, H, S, and P, otherwise known as Edgar, Howard, Steve, and Pete. The devices, which looked like red-and-white flying saucers with three-foot-high towers attached, were the reason we'd driven across the country.

"Hmm," Mom said, looking up at the building. "It is kind of . . . tomb-y." She touched the back of my neck. From inside the building came the sound of distant murmuring, or perhaps a chant. Maybe they were saying the pledge of allegiance. Or the pledge of something.

"It's not too late, H2." That was her nickname for me: Harrison Harrison = Harrison Squared = H2. It was the kind of humor that scientists found hilarious. "I can call your grandfather tonight. We can put you on a plane—"

"It's fine," I said, lying through my teeth. "*I'm* fine." It had been my decision to come to Massachusetts with her on this research trip. I'd *insisted*. She wasn't going to dump me in Oregon with my grandfather. It was only going to be a month, two months tops, before I got back to my regularly scheduled life. Besides, I couldn't see Mom doing this research trip alone. She'd probably get so obsessed she'd forget to feed herself.

So we'd crossed the continent, four days from ocean to ocean, pushing the pickup as fast as it could go, and rattled into town so late last night that not a streetlight was burning. We'd lost all bars on our phones, and the GPS apps had stopped working, so it was almost by accident that we found the clapboard house Mom had rented, sight unseen, over the phone.

It had looked dismal in the dark, and morning hadn't improved it—or the town. We'd awoken (late!) to find ourselves surrounded by mist, fog, and cold. The Heart of Bleakness. I don't think Mom had noticed; she'd been focused on readying the buoys for deployment. Each tower supported a signal light, a satellite dish the size of a medium pizza, and a solar panel; and each of these components had to be wired to the batteries in the base. That had taken us longer than we'd thought it would. Then we'd loaded them into the truck and driven back up Main Street to the school.

Mom glanced at her watch. She'd chartered a boat to take

her out, and she was supposed to have met the captain at the pier fifteen minutes ago.

"It's okay," I said. I slung my backpack onto my shoulder. "I'll check myself in. You've got a boat to catch."

"Don't be ridiculous," she said. "I'm still your mother."

Together we pushed on the big wooden doors, and they swung open on squealing hinges. The large room beyond was a kind of atrium, the high ceiling supported with buttresses like the ribs of a huge animal. Light glowed from globes of yellow glass that hung down out of the dark on thick cables. The stone floor was so dark it seemed to absorb the light.

Corridors ran off in three directions. Mom marched straight ahead. There were no sounds except for the slap of our feet against the stone. Even the chanting had stopped. It was suddenly the quietest school I'd ever been in. And the coldest. The air seemed wetter and more frigid inside than out.

I noticed something on the floor, and stopped. It was a faded, scuffed logo of a thin shark with a tail as long as its body, flexing as if it were leaping out of the water. Below it were the words GO THRESHERS.

My first picture books had been of sharks, whales, and squids. Mom's bedtime stories were all about the hunting habits of sea predators. Threshers were large sharks who could stun prey with their tails. As far as I knew, no one in the history of the world had ever used one as a school mascot.

Mom stopped at a door and waved for me to catch up. Stenciled on the frosted glass was OFFICE OF THE PRINCIPAL. From inside came a slapping noise, a *whap! whap!* that sounded at irregular intervals.

We went inside. The office was dimly lit, with yellow paint that tried and failed to cheer up the stone walls. Two large bulletin boards were crammed with tattered notices and bits of paper that looked like they hadn't been changed in years. At one end of the room was a large desk, and behind that sat a woman wearing a pile of platinum hair.

No, not sitting—standing. She was not only short, but nearly spherical. Her fat arms, almost as thick as they were long, thrashed in the air. She held a fly swatter in each hand and seemed to be doing battle with a swarm of invisible insects. Her gold hoop earrings swung in counterpoint.

"Shut the door!" she yelled without looking at us. "You're letting them in!" Then *thwack!* She brought a swatter down on the desk. Her nameplate said Miss Pearl, School Secretary.

"Excuse me," Mom said. "We're looking for Principal—"

"Ha!" Miss Pearl slapped her own arm. Her platinum hair shifted an inch out of kilter. She blew at the pink waffle print on her arm, then sat down in satisfaction. I still could not see any bugs. The air smelled of thick floral perfume.

She looked up at us. "Who are you?"

"I'm Rosa Harrison," Mom said. "This is my son, Harrison."

"And his first name?" She stared at me with tiny black eyes under fanlike eyelashes.

"Harrison," I said. Sometimes—like now, for example—I regretted that my father's family had decided that generations of boys would have that double name. Technically, I was Harrison Harrison the Fifth. H^{2x5}. But that was more information than I ever wanted to explain.

"He's a new student," Mom explained.

"Oh, I can see that."

"Principal Montooth is expecting him."

"*Now?*" Miss Pearl said. "It's already fourth period."

"We're running late."

"Did you bring his transcripts?" Miss Pearl asked. "Test scores? Medical records? Proof of residency?"

"No, we just—"

"Not even proof of *citizenship*?"

Uh-oh.

Mom is Terena, one of the indigenous peoples of Brazil.

Which means that her people—*my* people—were nearly wiped out in A.D. 1500 by Europeans who looked a lot like Dad. He was Presbyterian white (like "eggshell" and "ivory," "Presbyterian" is a particular shade of pale). I'm a Photoshopped version somewhere between the two, with Dad's blue eyes but skin a lot darker than your typical hospital waiting room. You grow up in southern California looking like me, a lot of people assume you're Mexican. Some of those people assume you're undocumented, and let their biases spool out from there. Mom got annoyed when people said racist stuff about her, but when somebody started talking stupid about me, her only begotten?

Jaguar claws, my friend.

Mom leaned over the desk. "Does he look like he doesn't belong here?"

Miss Pearl blinked up at her, finally found her voice. "It's standard," she said.

"Look, Miss . . . Pearl, is it?" Classic Mom. "I'm in a bit of a rush. Let's take care of the paperwork later and get my son into class."

It was then I realized that she'd forgotten all the forms I'd filled out back in San Diego. When she was deep into a research project—which was pretty much all the time—she was prone to falling into Absent-Minded Professor mode. When Mom was AMPing, mundane details fell through the cracks.

Miss Pearl was confused. "Are you telling me you don't have any documentation for this child whatsoever?" The cloud of perfume surrounding the woman seemed to expand. My nose itched madly.

"Of course I have *documentation*," Mom said. "Just not with me. If you could just give us some sort of class schedule, we can—"

I sneezed, and Miss Pearl glared at me. "He's what, fifteen years old?"

"I'm sixteen," I said. "A junior."

Miss Pearl sighed. "Why don't you start in Mrs. Velloc's class, then. Practical skills. Room 212."

"*Thank* you," Mom said. It was the "thank you" of a sheriff putting the gun back in the holster after the desperados had decided to move along. Miss Pearl, however, had already returned to fly-swatting. "Close the door behind you!" she called.

Out in the hallway, Mom looked left, then right. She seemed to have already forgotten Miss Pearl. She was like that: Her mind moved fast, and she didn't let anger fester.

"Two-twelve," she said, and glanced at her watch.

"Just go, Mom," I said. "I can find it."

She heard something in my voice and looked up into my eyes. About a year ago I'd passed her in height.

"You're mad," she said. She was worried.

I didn't let things go as quick as she did. And when I was little, I was the King of All Tantrums. Do you know how wild you have to be to be kicked out of elementary school? The answer is: very.

"A little bit," I said.

"Is it about this school?"

"I thought you were taking care of the forms."

"Paperwork is for small minds," she said. But she was smiling as she said it.

"Okay, okay," I said. "I'll take care of it tomorrow."

"Your mind's too big for paperwork too," she said. "How's the leg?"

First the question about being mad, and now the leg. She hardly ever asked about it. When I was little she'd checked in with me all the time, making sure the socket was fitting, and that my skin was okay. But she'd stopped the constant questioning when I became a teenager. I hadn't told her that the leg had started acting up last night. It wasn't socket pain; it was a weird coldness in my phantom limb. I'd chalked it up to the long trip and hadn't mentioned it to her. Had she noticed me limping?

"You're being parental," I said. "Go find that squid."

My mom specialized in finding big things swimming in places they didn't belong. She'd studied whale sharks, sperm whales—the biggest of the toothed whales—and all varieties of squids. Her latest obsession was *Mesonychoteuthis hamiltoni*, the colossal squid. Forty-five feet long, with the largest eyes in the animal kingdom, whose suckers are ringed not only by teeth but sharp, swiveling hooks. It's never supposed to come north of Brazil—but she was sure it did, based on, among other evidence, the beaks found in the guts of certain whales. Down in the abyss it's a dog-eat-dog world, where some of the dogs are the size of city buses.

"*Fique com Deus, querido,*" she said, and kissed me on the cheek. "*Até depois.*"

She ran for the exit. She didn't run in that straight-backed, floor-skimming, not-really-running way adults did—she ran like a kid, all out. She hit the big doors and escaped into daylight.

Science Mom flying off to her next adventure.

. . . while I was left with this: a dark hallway in a school that didn't want me here.

The doors nearest the office were all in the 100s. The doors were all closed, though from some of them I heard voices. Then I found the stairs and went up.

On the landing was a huge aquarium, eight feet long and five feet high. The water inside was green and silt-filled. Something moved within it, but I couldn't make it out. Maybe it was a thresher, and they kept their mascot on the premises.

I reached the second floor to find another row of closed doors. The light seemed even dimmer than downstairs. I bent to look at the number plate next to a door and was relieved to find that at least now I was in the ballpark: 209, 210 . . .

Room 212. I put my hand on the doorknob—and then it swung open, pushed from the inside. A very tall white woman in a very long black dress looked down at me. She seemed to be constructed of nothing but straight edges and hard angles, like the prow of an icebreaker ship. Her black hair, shot with gray, was pulled back tight against her head. Her nose was sharp as a hatchet, her fingers like a clutch of knives.

"Mr. Harrison," she said. "I am Mrs. Velloc." Her lips barely moved.

Behind her, kids my age sat in four rows. Lengths of rope were draped from one desk to another, and the students were tying them together. Or had been, until they'd all stopped to look at me.

They all seemed to be related to each other. Black hair, pale skin, dark eyes. Every one of them Caucasian. I fought the urge to back away.

I said, "The woman in the office—"

"Miss Pearl."

"Right. She told me to come here."

"And you followed directions. Perhaps you'd like a commendation."

Mrs. Velloc made a small gesture, and I found myself walking into the room.

"Class," she said. "This is Harrison. He is from *California*." She enunciated the word carefully, as if it were an exotic country. I wondered how she knew where I was from. Had Miss Pearl buzzed her while I was on my way up?

"Hello, Harrison," the students said in unison. Not just generally at the same time, but in perfect synchrony, like a choir. A choir that had been rehearsing.

I lifted a hand in greeting. They stared at me. They were dressed in blacks and grays, not quite a uniform, but definitely a *look*, as if they all did their shopping at clinicaldepression.com. My tie-dye shirt was like a loud laugh at a funeral.

I let my hand drop.

"It's Practical Skills hour," Mrs. Velloc said. "We're learning how to make a proper net. Do you know your knots, or do you not?"

"Pardon?"

She already seemed put out with me. "This way." She led me to an empty seat in the first row. On the desk was a flat stick almost two feet long with notches at each end. Its middle was wound with rope.

"Lydia will show you the sheet bend. Miss Palwick?"

The girl to my right—Lydia Palwick, I presumed, since I'm smart like that—looked at me with a slightly surprised expression, though that was probably because her eyes were so large. Her long black hair shined as if oiled.

Mrs. Velloc turned and walked back to her desk. She picked up a tiny book and began to read to herself.

I looked down at the section of rope that lay across my desk. Then I picked up the tail end of the rope that was spooled around the big stick. Okay, I thought. Tie this thing to that thing and make a net. No problem.

Except I didn't know any sailor knots. Mom did; she was great at that stuff. But I never went on boats. I didn't know anything about nets or ropes or sheet bends.

Lydia watched me fumble around, then took the stick out of my hands. She moved it in and out of the net, over and around, the rope spooling behind it. Suddenly there was a new diamond in the net.

"Wait, how did you—?"

"Left, loop, right, loop, over, and through," she said. Her voice was flat, bored.

I leaned closer to her and whispered, "Can I ask you a question?"

She glanced to the side but didn't pull away from me.

I said, "How much of Practical Skills hour is left?"

* * *

Forty minutes later the class showed no sign of ending, and my fingers prickled from what felt like microscopic needles. I didn't know that rope could get under your skin like that. Also? I was bored bored bored. My phone was getting zero reception, so there was no one I could text to back home, and no one here was passing notes or even whispering. They simply worked, fingers busy as spiders.

I finally leaned over to Lydia and whispered, "Why is everybody so quiet?"

She frowned. "Why are you always talking?"

"I've said like five words since I got here."

Mrs. Velloc's head whipped around at the noise. I shut up. A few seconds later, Lydia whispered, "Chatterbox."

Somewhere far away, a gong sounded. The students stood as one, and then packed the piles of rope into large wooden trunks lined up at the back of the room. I'd managed to connect three or four lengths of rope. In the same amount of time, Lydia had created a net the size of a queen-sized blanket.

The students began to file out of the room. I walked to Mrs. Velloc's desk. Eventually she looked up from her book.

"I don't know where to go next," I said. "They didn't give me a schedule."

She looked at me as if I were a moron. "Follow Lydia," she said.

"To where? The office? Because I can—"

"Do what she does. Go where she goes. Your schedule is her schedule."

I glanced toward the door. Lydia had already left the room.

"Is that too *complicated* for you, Mr. Harrison?"

I didn't know where my temper came from. Mom didn't suffer fools gladly, but her anger never lasted longer than a minute. My dad supposedly never hurt a fly. But me . . . Calm did not come naturally. Sometimes—like, say, when somebody treats me like I'm an idiot—I could clearly picture my hands around their neck. I could almost feel myself squeezing.

When I was little I didn't know what to do with all that emotion, and I actually did try to strangle people. I punched other kids. Bit teachers. Screamed at, well, everybody, but mostly my mother. Gradually I learned to control myself. My main technique, and still my go-to move when I was feeling the rush, was to simply observe myself. Catalog what was going on in my body and my head. Hey there, look at that fist clenching! Feel that heart beating! Take a gander at that violent movie playing in your head—got any film music to go with that?

I didn't actually step out of my body. I wasn't that crazy. But watching myself did get me to settle down. Rage makes little sense from the outside.

I relaxed my hand and smiled at Mrs. Velloc. "I think I got it," I said.

I walked out, and my right leg was throbbing, right down to my invisible toes. I made sure not to limp.

Students streamed out of the rooms, but it was an orderly stream, without pushing or shoving. Nobody yelled or even raised their voice. Most of them looked younger than me, but they all had that same dark-haired, pale, fishy look as the kids in Velloc's class. From behind I had no idea which one was Lydia, but I finally spotted her as the streams converged on the stairway down.

"Hey, Lydia!"

Scores of faces turned to look at me. The flow of traffic stuttered, then resumed.

Lydia looked up at me. Then she closed her eyes and slowly opened them again, as if hoping she'd imagined me. Nope. Still here. She backed out of the line of students and waited for me on the first landing with her back to the aquarium.

"Thanks," I said when I reached her. "Velloc says I should

shadow you until they give me a schedule."

"Shadow me," she said skeptically.

"It's not my idea," I said. And suddenly it seemed like a very stupid idea. "Listen, never mind, I'll figure this out."

"I doubt that," she said. "Lunch is this way."

She led me downstairs and along a corridor to a cavernous room. The cafeteria. The serving line was on one side, and wooden tables filled the rest of the space. I followed Lydia's lead and picked up a large wooden bowl and tin cup. One by one the students passed the counter, where a pair of lunch ladies filled the bowls with a steaming, chunky stew. The air smelled of vinegar.

I held out my bowl. The lunch lady, a thick-necked woman with horsey teeth, held out her ladle. When she moved I caught a glimpse of the kitchen behind her. A woman who could have been her older sister stood at a metal table wearing a bloody smock. She held a huge silver fish, perhaps three feet long, by its tail. The creature twitched weakly in her grasp. Suddenly she plunged a knife into the belly of the fish and ripped down.

I dropped my bowl.

The serving lady, still holding her ladle aloft, scowled at me over glasses that perched at the end of her long nose.

I raised my hands. "That's it. I'm done."

Lydia frowned at me.

I turned toward the door. Lydia said, "Where are you going?"

"Home," I said.

She followed me for a moment, then grabbed my arm. Her eyes were sea green.

"Truancy is a crime," she said.

"Then I guess I'm a criminal. Besides, who uses the word 'truancy'?"

Something changed in her face. I'd just become marginally more interesting to her.

"See you around, Lydia. It was a pleasure meeting you."

2

Dear Lord! it hath a fiendish look—

Lydia didn't try to stop me again. I walked fast for the door, feeling the eyes of the students on my back, but I didn't care. I was going home. Not to the rental house down the street—all the way back to California, to my friends. My real school. In San Diego, the school hallways were *outdoors*. The sun shined all the time. In class you learned how to do normal things like write essays and speak Spanish—you didn't perform slave labor.

Did I say I'd learned to keep my anger under control? I may have been exaggerating.

I left the cafeteria and marched down the hallway. The corridor turned, turned again—and then dead-ended at a stone wall. I thought I'd been heading toward the front entrance, but somehow I'd taken a wrong turn.

I retraced my steps until I found a hallway that led off to my left. The yellow globes hanging from the ceiling looked familiar, and I hustled toward them. But when I reached the lights I wasn't in the atrium, or anywhere else I remembered.

From somewhere came a moan. A voice pleading. My right leg burned like it was in ice water, but I ignored it.

I slowly walked forward until I came to a set of double doors that hung slightly ajar. The light beyond seemed marginally brighter than that of the hallway. I pushed through.

It was a library. The bookshelves were a dozen feet tall, much taller than seemed practical for a high school. The books, too, were larger and more massive than the books in my old library in California, as if each were an unabridged dictionary. The voice came from somewhere in the stacks.

I edged around the corner of a row. A white-haired man in a gray cardigan sweater stood in front of the shelves, waving his fingers in the air. Though he wore thick glasses, he blinked furiously as if he couldn't get his eyes to focus. "No no no," the man said to himself. "It's got to be here; it *must* be. . . ."

"Can I help you?" I asked.

The man spun to face me, shocked. Then he glanced behind him and said, "Are you speaking to me?"

"I'm sorry, I just thought—"

"What did you mean, *help* me?"

I wasn't sure how I could help, just that he sounded so desperate. Maybe he was so old his vision was failing? I said, "Have you lost a book?"

"What book? Why do you think I'm looking for a book?"

"It's a library?" I said.

"There are many types of items in a library. Maps. Periodicals. Artifacts and artwork . . ." He strode away from me. The floors here were the same dark stone as the hallway. The shelves themselves were thick as ship's timbers.

"You can't possibly be of use," the man said. "I've been combing this library for . . . quite a while. You're a child and I'm a trained researcher, which means that not only do I *search*, I do so *repeatedly*."

I walked after him, curious now. "Maybe if you told me the title."

He wheeled to face me. "The title? You ask me for the *title*?"

"I'm sorry," I said again.

"Ye gods. If I knew the title, don't you think I would have found it by now?"

He pulled at the tufts of gray hair that sprouted from the side of his head. His dusty glasses hid his eyes. "I will not despair. I will not despair." He seemed to be talking to himself now. "It's only a puzzle. A riddle. A mystery. I am a solver of puzzles."

He gazed for a moment at the shelves above us, then forced his eyes away. He shuddered.

"Good luck," I said, and started to leave.

"You've been touched, haven't you?" the librarian said.

I froze. "What?"

"It's the only explanation. You've been exposed, and that's made you *sensitive*."

"I don't know what you're talking about," I said.

"It's all right, my boy. It takes time to adjust to the world you've found yourself in. It's perfectly understandable to engage in denial."

"Right. Well, it's been great talking to you, but—"

"You're searching for something. Of course, why else would you have forced your way in here?"

"I didn't force anything. I just saw that the door was open and I—"

"You had no choice," the librarian said. "I understand. For men such as ourselves, the lure of the stacks is impossible to resist."

"Yeah. Right. So, if you're okay . . ."

"I wouldn't say *that*. How would you describe a man in my condition? No, don't say it. Denial, my boy. Denial is what keeps a soul going in trying times."

"Sure," I said, though I was pretty sure I didn't agree with him. "It was great meeting you, Mister . . ."

"Professor, if you please. Professor Freytag."

A distant gong sounded. I felt it more than heard it.

"I really should get going, Professor."

"What about your book?"

"Maybe later," I said.

Freytag looked disappointed. "Very well. Off you go." He turned away from me. Now he seemed to be mad at me. "Close the door on the way out. I don't like to be disturbed."

I heard the murmur of student voices, the shuffling of feet, but it was impossible to tell where it was coming from. The walls were all damp stone, bouncing sound in tricky ways. There seemed to be no active classrooms in this wing. The doors, when I found them, looked like they hadn't been opened in years. Corridors branched at odd angles. Some of them were only dimly lit, and I had to use my phone's screen like a flashlight. Other hallways were pitch dark; those I refused to go down. My phone was getting no bars. If I fell down some stairs I doubted anyone would find me.

My only strategy was to follow the best-lit corridors. I was surprised when this worked; many minutes later I emerged into a wide hallway and saw a familiar door: OFFICE OF THE PRINCIPAL. The wide staircase was off to my left. There were no students in sight.

My anger had long since disappeared. I might have given up on my escape plan, but I had no idea where Lydia was, or where my next class might be.

I pushed through the big doors and blinked at the gray sky. Still definitely not California.

The rental house was downhill, toward the bay. I started down the sidewalk. The only person out was a man sitting on an iron bench just beyond the border of the school grounds. He was jotting something in a notebook.

As I passed the bench, the man looked up and said, "Tough morning?"

"Pardon?"

He was handsome, with dark hair graying at the temples.

The kind of distinguished gentleman who wasn't a doctor but could play one on TV. His long legs were crossed at the knee, and one long arm spread out along the back of the bench. His suit was black, his shirt white as bone, his tie a sea green. On his collar he wore a silver pin in the shape of a shark. A thresher.

Oh.

He said, "I imagine our little school is probably very different from what you're used to."

"No, it's great," I said lamely.

"It's all right. I know we're a bit . . . rural." He held out his hand. "I'm Principal Montooth."

I'd never had a principal try to shake hands with me. "Harrison Harrison," I said. "Pleased to meet you."

His grip was firm. He held it for a bit too long. "You're not the first person I've met with that name," he said. "Your father was an anthropologist, wasn't he?"

"You knew my dad?"

"*Know* is too strong a word. I met him when he visited the area a while ago."

A while ago? At least thirteen years: Dad died when I was three. I had no idea he'd been here before. Mom had never mentioned it.

A dark car, an old-fashioned sedan with tall rear fins, rolled up to the curb. Montooth stood up. He was tall—taller even than Mrs. Velloc. "This is my ride," he said. "You enjoy your afternoon. I think we can agree that half a day is enough of a start."

"Uh . . ."

"See you tomorrow, Harrison. Bright and early."

Montooth clapped me on the shoulder, then got into the passenger side of the car. The vehicle rumbled away, then turned off halfway down the hill.

I wasn't sure what to do. Was this a trick? Had the principal seriously told me it was okay to skip school?

I glanced back at the wooden doors, then shook my head.

Kidding or not, Montooth was right. A half day was quite enough of Dunnsmouth Secondary.

All I had to do to get home was follow gravity. The school perched on a high, rocky promontory surrounded on three sides by the sea. A single road—the cunningly named "Main Street"—snaked downhill through beautiful downtown Dunnsmouth (a handful of sad stores and a police station), past the town's only stop sign, and ended at the bay. If I'd turned left at that stop sign I would have eventually made it to the highway and civilization. Don't think I didn't fantasize about it.

Our rental was two blocks short of the water, set back from Main Street by a gravel driveway. It was a wooden shack with peeling paint, and seemed intimidated by the surrounding pines. Last night I hadn't been able to see any other houses, but even in daylight they were barely visible through the pines. Every house was an island in an ocean of trees.

I'd made sure to get a key to the rental from Mom. I'd had my own key to every place we'd lived since I was five years old. When she was AMPing, it was good to have my own access to food and shelter.

"Mom?" I called. But I knew she wasn't home yet; the pickup was still gone. She'd probably be out on the water for hours, because the research buoys had to be placed miles apart. There were no messages on my cell phone; not from Mom or anybody. I still had no data or voice. If all of Dunnsmouth was a dead zone, we had to order cable for this house *immediately*.

A bad thought occurred to me. Was this place even wired for cable? I walked around the house, studying the walls. The place was furnished in Early Hermit: a couch framed in dark-stained planks, heavy wooden chairs, an oak kitchen table like a raft. Braided rugs covered wood floors that looked like they'd been warped by water damage. There were not many electrical outlets, and no other wall jacks except for a single line for the phone.

Surely they couldn't expect us to use *dial-up*. That was simply not acceptable. A two-month scientific mission was one thing, but I was not about to get involuntarily Amished.

Almost all of our stuff was still in boxes stacked in the living room. We'd been so tired last night that we hadn't even tried to unpack except to find some bedsheets. Not that there was much to unpack. Because of all the scientific equipment we had to haul, we had to limit the rest of our baggage to the necessities: the waterproof footlocker in which Mom kept her research materials; three suitcases; a cooler of emergency food; half a dozen boxes for household supplies and books; and the few personal items we couldn't bear to put in storage.

I made myself a peanut butter and jelly sandwich, then rooted through the boxes until I found our books, and one book in particular. Out on the back porch were a couple of patio chairs, a wicker coffee table that hadn't stood up to the weather very well, and a wooden barrel that I could rest my water bottle on. The house was surrounded by tall pines. The light was dim, and it was cold, but at least it was peaceful. Far in the background I could hear the ocean, only a couple blocks from here. I put up my feet and settled back with my book: the gigantic hardback of *The 20th Anniversary Treasury Edition of Newton & Leeb*.

Newton was a five-year-old boy genius, and Leeb was his robot dog, and together they made the greatest comic strip ever. The treasury edition collected the best strips, all in color. My dad had owned the book, and it became mine before I knew how to read. Now I didn't have to read them, because I'd memorized them. I ate my sandwich and flipped through the pages, taking in bits and pieces. Newton creating a black hole by putting a star fruit in the trash compactor. Newton and Leeb playing hide-and-seek, showing up in other comic strips like *Nancy* and *Pogo*. Leeb arguing with a real dog about why bones were disgusting (Leeb preferred circuit boards).

After lunch I decided to make myself useful. I put away the food and kitchen stuff, then started in on the other boxes. It was boring, but at least it wasn't making nets.

By seven o'clock Mom still hadn't come home. That wasn't unusual, especially not on the first day of field work. Back in San Diego, some days she was home by supper, but other days, especially when an article was due or she had to be out on the water, she worked until midnight for nights in a row. It wasn't a big deal. I knew how to work a microwave. Mom always called before I went to bed, and I always told her the same thing: I'm fine. Go do science.

I picked up the house phone to make sure it had a dial tone (check). Then I made some canned soup and ate a cereal bar. It started getting dark around 6:30 P.M., which seemed way too early. I turned on the front porch light, then went out back where I'd eaten lunch, figuring it would be good to turn on that light too. I opened the back screen door and stopped.

Something was watching me from the trees.

I couldn't make out the shape. But I knew *something* was there in the bushes between two pines, an extra shadow that didn't belong. I stepped backward, and then noticed something else.

The wicker coffee table was empty. The Newton & Leeb anniversary edition was gone.

From the direction of the bushes came the smallest sound, leaves rasping on leaves. I jerked my head toward the noise. A dark shape darted away through the trees. It looked like an old man, skinny and dark-skinned and bald-headed, but moved quick as a kid, bolting like a frightened rabbit.

This punk stole my book! Suddenly I wasn't scared; I was angry. And when I was angry I did stupid things.

I shouted at it, then leaped off the porch and hit the ground running. The shape dodged to the right. Pine branches blocked my way, so I plunged into them, arms up to shield my face. Then I was through to the other side and the dark shape was in front of me, running fast. He was naked from the waist up, dressed only in shorts. He clutched my book to his chest.

I leaped on his back, but my arms slipped from his shoulders; he was sweating so much he felt slimy. My momentum, though, was enough to push us both to the ground. I fell on top of him, but then he twisted and threw me off like I weighed nothing. I tumbled back into the bushes and came down on a rock. Pain blazed up my spine.

By the time I got to my feet he was gone. I could hear nothing, see nothing but the dark. But I was having second thoughts about chasing him.

When he threw me off, I'd caught a glimpse of his face. The skin was mottled, green and brown. Wide, glassy eyes, two slits for a nose . . . and a mouth full of sharp teeth.

Back in the rental, I walked into each room and turned on every light. There were not, I decided, near enough lights.

I don't get spooked easily. I spend a lot of time on my own. I don't jump at noises; I don't worry about boogeymen. There's only one thing that seriously freaks me out, but it doesn't affect my day-to-day life.

But . . . those teeth. That skin.

I fell asleep on the couch with the lights on. And sometime later, I half awoke to find my mother shaking me.

"You worried about me, H2?"

I let her walk me back to the bedroom we'd decided was mine. Mom's here, I thought. And with that I fell back asleep in an instant.

3

It had been strange, even in a dream,
To have seen those dead men rise.

Sometimes I wake up and I'm still dreaming.

I knew I was in bed. I was equally sure that I was standing in a snowdrift. My left leg was warm inside the blankets, but my right leg was naked and knee-deep in snow, and the cold was driving right into my bones.

I sat up, and the winter dream fell away, even if the cold in my leg didn't. The length of air below my knee throbbed. Worse than yesterday.

Somewhere in the next room, Mom was yelling—but not at me, at least. I climbed out of bed and saw that I was still wearing yesterday's clothes. My prosthetic, also dressed in yesterday's black sock and shoe, lay on the floor next to the beige liner. Mom must have taken them off me last night.

I left the leg on the floor and hopped out to the living room. I'm a really good hopper, even half-asleep. I was surprised to see two of the research buoys, Steve and Pete, sitting in the middle of the living room, Mom's tools scattered around them. Somehow she'd gotten them in here by herself. Mom was talking on the landline phone, pacing as far as the cord would allow. "You know that I need *four* instruments deployed, not—" She listened a second, then said, "I know that's not your fault. I'm not saying it is."

I wasn't sure how long she'd been up. It was possible she'd never gotten to sleep. She'd come home sometime around midnight, and the clock on my phone—pretty much the only part of my phone that was working out here in the eighteenth century—said it was just after seven.

Mom had found the coffee maker that had come with the rental and had made a pot. There were still a few inches of coffee left in it. I found a mug in the kitchen cabinet and took the rest. The coffee distracted me from the not-quite-phantom-enough phantom limb.

"I understand that, Mr. Hallgrimsson," Mom said into the phone. "I know how you make your money. But you understood that when you agreed to take me out. Your father—yes, of course I know that, you don't need to explain that to *me* of all people. But Erik—can I call you Erik?—I think you owe me the courtesy of—"

Mom looked at the phone, and then started cursing. "*Aquele filho da puta sacana!*"

"What did he do?" I asked.

"He hung up on me!"

I thought, Big mistake, Erik Hallgrimsson. "Your lobsterman bailing on you?"

"That . . . that . . . *Viking*. He's refusing to take me out! We only got Edgar and Howard set up yesterday—don't ask, it was a nightmare—and now he says he can't go back out, he needs to check his traps." She slammed the phone down on the ugly, plank-style coffee table that had come with the equally stylish couch. "I've got to get down there before he leaves the pier. Can you help me load?"

I thought, How was your day, Harrison? How awful was that school? What do you think of staying here in the Wasteland? Seen any book thieves in need of orthodontia?

"Let me go get my leg," I said.

I hopped back to the bedroom and scooped up the liner, a high-tech sock with gel on the inside and stretchy material on the outside. I'm supposed to wear a different one every day, but this one smelled okay to me. Well, it didn't smell horrible. I rolled it on, then slipped my stump into the gray carbon-fiber socket. The liner has a black strap glued to the side of it, and that strap feeds through a hole to a ratchet lock on the outside of the socket. The sound of the ratchet tightening and locking into place has a military feel to it, like I'm loading my weapon. Last I slipped a shoe onto my meat foot, just to keep balanced.

When I came back out of the room, Mom was waiting for me by the S buoy. She lifted it and waited for me to pick up the other end.

I hoisted the fat end of Steve. Together we carried it out the front door to the pickup.

"What's that?" I asked. On the hood of the truck, a fist-sized rock was holding down a green piece of paper. While I tied down Steve, Mom went to get the paper. By the time I hopped down, she was angry—angrier than she'd been on the phone.

"What is it?" I asked.

"Nothing." She crumpled the paper and tossed it through the open window into the cab of the truck. "A note from the neighbors."

"Wait, who?" The rental was on a wooded lot, and all the nearby houses were set back from the road. So far I hadn't seen anyone who lived in those houses. "About what?"

Mom does this thing when she's thinking hard: Her eyes flick back and forth as if she's moving puzzle pieces around. Then she looked up at me like I was a piece that Would. Not. Fit.

"When I get back tonight we'll call Grandpa," she said.

"Okay, but why?" Then I got it. "No. No way."

"He'd be happy to have you."

"I'm not flying to Oregon to live with Grandpa. I'm staying here."

"It was a mistake bringing you here," she said. "I can't look out for you while I'm so busy."

"You're always busy," I said. "That's nothing new."

"But this isn't San Diego—there's no one here to back me up. At least at home the school could—"

"I can take care of myself," I said. And thought, There's no way I'm telling her about the book thief now. "I'm fine. School is fine."

We locked eyes. I could see that she'd already made up her mind—but that didn't mean I couldn't unmake it. We rarely argued, but when we did we went at it Samurai Scientist Style. "Opinions" and "beliefs" and "feelings" didn't cut it—only the katana of logic, the plate armor of supporting data, and the dagger of extended metaphor. (Okay, maybe not the last one.) Yelling, though, immediately lost you the duel. I used to lose a lot of arguments that way.

Mom saw I was ready to throw down. She almost smiled. "We'll talk about it when we get home," she said. "Do you want a ride to school?"

"I need to take a shower and change clothes," I said.

"Right. Showering is good." She kissed me on each cheek. "You could shave, too." She climbed into the cab of the truck. "*Eu te amo,* H2."

"Love you, too," I said.

The truck rumbled down the hill, Steve and Pete swaying in the back like happy children.

I got to the school fifteen minutes before first bell. I would have been there earlier if I hadn't taken the time to pack a lunch. There was no way I was going to eat what they were serving in the cafeteria.

The atrium, though, was as empty as yesterday. From somewhere in the distance I could hear voices singing. I didn't recognize the song, or even what type of song it was; the melody moved in mysterious ways. The sound echoed off the stone walls, and I couldn't nail down where it was coming from.

I'd intended to go to the office and see if Miss Pearl had come up with a class schedule for me. Instead I walked toward the sound, passing the office door (closed) and the cafeteria (empty). I paused at an intersection of hallways. The singing seemed louder to my left, so I followed that corridor until it ended in a set of double doors that were slightly ajar.

The singing stopped as I reached the doors. I peeked through the gap and saw an auditorium. At least a hundred students sat in rows on metal folding chairs. Up on the stage, Principal Montooth stood behind a podium, reading in a low voice from a book that was open in front of him. A few feet from the podium was a short, scrawny man drowning in a suit many sizes too big for him. He nodded vigorously as Montooth spoke, clasping his hands with great sincerity.

Montooth paused, and the students chanted back. Neither the words that Montooth said, nor the student response, sounded like any language I'd ever heard.

The chant and response went on for several minutes. Then at once the students rose and began to sing in the same strange language. The melody veered and dipped at unexpected intervals. And when the students held a long note, the chord seemed to vibrate uncomfortably.

"May I help you, Mr. Harrison?"

I jumped. Mrs. Velloc had glided up behind me.

"What's going on?" I asked. "Did I miss an assembly?"

"Voluntary is not for you," she said. "This way, please." She walked toward the big staircase. The singing continued behind me. When she realized I hadn't followed her, she turned. "Off to class, Mr. Harrison. Unless you're planning to leave even earlier than yesterday."

So word had gotten around about me skipping out. I

shouldn't have been surprised. When I caught up to her I asked, "Voluntary what?"

"It's a religious service," she said, and resumed walking.

"Led by the principal?"

"Mr. Montooth is also pastor of our local congregation. Students are allowed to attend Voluntary at the beginning of each day."

"You can do that?"

She hitched her skirt a few inches and started up the stairs. "Do what, Mr. Harrison?"

"This is a public school, right? You can't have a principal who's the pastor too."

"Of course you can. We do."

"But doesn't that put a lot of pressure on the students to conform to—"

"Mr. Harrison." She'd stopped on the first landing, in front of that cloudy aquarium. The creature inside churned in agitation. "We don't worry about things like that in Dunnsmouth. We're a small town. An old town. We do as we've always done. And if you find our traditions *uncomfortable*, perhaps you should move."

I opened my mouth, then shut it. Slow that heart rate down, Harrison.

Mrs. Velloc raised an eyebrow, waiting for me to talk back.

"You know, my mother was just telling me the same thing," I said. "But I've decided I like it here."

"Indeed?"

Yeah, I thought. *Indeed.*

Mrs. Velloc led me into a classroom full of lab tables and high stools. There were no students, but a frizzy-haired man in a white lab coat was hunched over one of the tables, poking at something on a metal tray.

"Dr. Herbert," Mrs. Velloc said. The man didn't look up. "Doctor, I'd like to introduce you to a new . . . Dr. *Herbert*."

The man's head jerked up. Over one eye he wore an elaborate device that seemed to be part microscope, part kitchen appliance. LED lights sprouted from the side, and dangling below it was an articulated arm that ended in a clamp. It was secured to his head by thick black straps and looked much too heavy to wear comfortably. I'd seen people wear goggles, but this was the first time I'd seen someone wear *goggle*.

Mrs. Velloc said, "This is Harrison Harrison. He's new."

Dr. Herbert waved. This gesture was made a bit threatening due to the fact that he was holding a scalpel, and the sleeve of his coat was streaked with blood up to the elbow. His uncovered eye blinked wetly at me. "Have you taken biology?" the doctor asked.

"Freshman year," I said.

"Oh," the doctor said. He sounded disappointed. Suddenly he brightened. "Have you taken *crypto*biology?"

I grinned. "In my family, cryptobiology isn't a course, it's dinner conversation."

"I *like* this boy!" Dr. Herbert said.

He was the first person at the school I felt like I understood. Cryptobiology—AKA cryptozoology—was the study of animals whose existence had not been proven. Think Loch Ness Monster and Sasquatch.

He gestured me toward the tray. On it was a creature in the process of being dissected. The skin was peeled back and pinned, revealing muscle tissue and glistening internal organs. It might have been a salamander, except for the extra set of limbs.

"What is that?" I asked.

"I have no earthly idea," he said. "Isn't it wonderful?"

The class change gong sounded. Mrs. Velloc said, "I leave Mr. Harrison in your hands, Doctor."

"Wait," I said. "I still don't have my schedule."

"I don't know why you keep going on about that," Mrs. Velloc said. "You're in grade eleven. You follow the grade eleven schedule. Wherever Lydia goes—"

"I go. Right. But everybody's not on the same schedule, are they? There's got to be electives."

"This isn't a country club," she said. "We concern ourselves with the fundamentals, and only the fundamentals."

I thought, Cryptobiology is a fundamental?

Students entered the room, quiet as pallbearers. No one chatted or joked. Voluntary, it was clear, was no pep rally.

Dr. Herbert directed me to a high stool in the second row of lab tables, and the students silently took their seats. I recognized some of them from yesterday's Practical Skills class. If I understood Mrs. Velloc correctly, these thirty or so students made up the entire junior class. Which meant there were probably less than 150 students in the whole school. About that many had been in the auditorium during Voluntary.

Two epiphanies: Dunnsmouth Secondary was smaller than I'd thought; and everybody except me was part of their religion.

I felt a chill, as if everyone was staring at me. I was used to being one of the few public atheists in school. But an army of one against the One True Faith of Dunnsmouth? I didn't even know what religion it was. That morning service was like nothing I'd ever heard of.

I kept my face blank and didn't move my head as the students filled the high stools around me.

Lydia sat at the table directly in front of me, in the first row. She didn't look back at me. Two kids took a seat at my table: a short boy with a large nose and fan-like ears, and a girl with blunt bangs and bloodred lipstick. She was the only girl I'd seen in the school who wore makeup. Bat Ears and Goth Girl didn't introduce themselves, however. They barely looked at me—which made me decide that *I* sure wasn't going to say the first word.

Dr. Herbert told us to take out our projects, and my lab mates opened a drawer in the table and withdrew a metal tray much like the one the doctor had been working on. This one, I was relieved to see, contained a normal frog. I'd done frog dissections in my freshman bio class.

Then the girl with the red lipstick took out a large battery, a transformer with a dial, and a bundle of wires. She pushed the battery to me.

"What do we do with this?" I asked.

She opened a three-ring notebook and pointed at a diagram of a frog, decorated with plus and minus signs. "Just hook up the battery to the transformer and the transformer to the subject," she said.

"We keep going till we get a twitch," the big-eared boy said.

"Right . . . ," I said. "And then what? It hops up and dances?"

My lab partners stared at me.

"You know, like the cartoon? Michigan J. Frog. The frog grabs a top hat and cane and starts singing, 'Hello ma baby, hello ma honey, hello ma ragtime . . .'"

The girl with the red lips turned on the transformer.

"'. . . gal,'" I said quietly to myself.

The rest of the period proceeded in silence. Only Dr. Herbert spoke. He visited the tables, murmuring things like "Very nice, very nice" or "More juice!" When he came to my table he put a hand on my shoulder and said, "Don't give up hope, Harrison!"

"But it's dead, right?"

"Of course!" he said.

"For, like, a long time?"

"True! But there's no expiration date on the powers of galvanism!"

Beside me, the girl with the red lips rolled her eyes. It was the first sign of personality I'd seen in the class.

The boy filled out the lab report while I poked the corpse with wires. We never got our frog to quiver, much less dance. My lab partners, however, were doing their own twitching. While we were studying the diagram or waiting for the electricity to have some effect on our frog, they'd tap their fingers. First the girl, then the boy, as if they were playing two ends of an invisible piano. Then I noticed that Lydia was doing the same thing.

This was the problem with a small school in a small town. Not only did the students all look like each other, they'd all developed the same nervous tics. It made me wonder about inbreeding. Take off their shoes, and did they have webbed feet? Was the weird-looking fish boy who'd stolen my book just a relative on the more damaged branch of the family tree?

Only at the end of the class, when I signed the lab report, did I find out that my partners were named Garfield and Flora. "I think we've changed some lives today," I said. That was what my friends and I used to say whenever we'd been forced to do busywork. In San Diego, this was hilarious. Dunnsmouth, however, seemed to be an irony-free zone. Flora rolled her eyes at me. It wasn't quite so liberating to be on the receiving end of that.

As we left the classroom I managed to sidle up next to Lydia. "Mrs. Velloc still says I should follow you."

"That's going to be a problem," she said.

"Why's that?"

She didn't answer. We went downstairs, turned right into a corridor that I may or may not have walked down before, then started down another staircase that I definitely hadn't gone down before.

The stairs went down and down. The lighting became more sporadic, and the stone walls gleamed with moisture. Tufts of gray-green moss furred the seams between the stones. If I hadn't been with Lydia and the rest of the junior class, I would never have guessed that there was a class down here.

The stairs emptied out in a big room. "Cave" may have been more accurate; the ceiling was unfinished stone. Loops of electrical cable connected a few yellow light globes. The steps of my classmates echoed strangely.

Opposite us were two rectangular doorways. Like the word "room," the word "doors" was inaccurate. These were ragged holes, and from them wafted a strange metallic smell.

The girls went into the entrance on the left, the boys on the right. Symbols were carved into the rock above each hole, strange hieroglyphics that didn't look anything like the friendly owls and bulls of ancient Egypt. Just looking at them made me queasy.

"See you on the other side," Lydia said.

4

Under the water it rumbled on,
Still louder and more dread.

L ydia had been right—following her was going to be a
problem. But she couldn't know that following the boys
was also going to be a problem for me. They went silently
into the dark mouth of the other door, and I did *not* want to
go in there.

Garfield passed me, and then looked back. "It's this way,"
he said.

I took a breath and went through. The short passage made
an abrupt turn, and then I entered a long narrow room. A single
stone bench ran down the middle of the space like a spine. Boys
were taking off their clothes and hanging them on hooks drilled
into one rocky wall, and tucking backpacks into cubbyholes
carved into the other wall. As they stripped off, each one seemed
to be more pale than the last.

Oh no, I thought. Physical Education.

And then I realized it was even more horrible than that.
The boys began to pull on swim trunks. This wasn't just PE;
it was *swimming*.

Some of the boys glanced at me. I stood there, holding my
backpack, not moving. I was not about to get naked in front of
these ignorami. I waited until one by one they made their way

out the far exit. When there were just a handful of boys left in the changing room, I went out to the pool.

Again: Wrong word.

I'd stepped into a cavern. The high ceiling bristled with stalactites. The walls were ringed with stone benches, as in a Greek theater. Or a Roman arena. And below—below was an immense black pool.

The back of my neck went cold.

I took a breath, held it, trying to still my rabbity heartbeat. Yellow globes, Dunnsmouth Secondary's sole lighting idea, hung down on cables to hover over the water, making it gleam like oil. The terraces of benches, enough to seat several thousand people, rose up into the dark. The air was cold and damp.

I told myself it was going to be fine. Nothing but a little H_2O, H2. Nothing to fear but millions of cubic gallons of fear itself.

Most of the boys were already down on the wide stone deck that surrounded the pool. The girls were slower to leave their locker room. They came out dressed in dark one-piece suits, some of them in black swim caps. They looked so similar to each other that I couldn't tell which one was Lydia. One of them glared at me, and I realized I'd been staring. Then I realized that glarer was Lydia.

I quickly looked away, and the heat rose in my face. I hoped the lighting was too bad to tell that I was blushing.

I walked down to the water. Goosebumps rose on my arms in the chill, and my leg—the one that wasn't there—ached with the same cold I'd felt this morning. None of the students, however, seemed to be shivering; they stood as still as they had in class. I sat down on one of the benches. No one spoke to me, or asked me why I hadn't changed clothes.

We waited, silently, for two minutes, three. Then a group of boys nearest me stepped back from the edge.

Something moved under the water.

I stood up and stifled a yelp. The pale shape coursed toward the edge of the pool at tremendous speed. At the last moment, the water broke, and the creature threw itself onto the deck. It slid a few feet, then threw out its arms and rose up on its belly like a walrus.

It was a man. A bald man, fat and white as a beluga. He smiled. "Who's ready for laps?"

Lydia and the rest of the students moved down to the end of the pool and formed two lines. They'd done this many times, I guessed. One by one they dove, slipping in with hardly a splash, and torpedoed under the water for dozens of yards. They broke the surface almost gently, pale limbs stroking the surface. They looked like an Olympic swim team. A silent, glum Olympic swim team.

The pale man had gotten to his feet. He saw me and walked heavily over, water dripping from his pale, hairless chest. He wore a tiny black Speedo that seemed to pinch the tops of his thighs. Hanging on a chain around his neck was a silver whistle.

"You're the new boy," he said. His voice was deep, and his vowels warbled as if water had settled into his lungs. He held out a hand. "I'm Coach Shug."

I hesitated, then shook. His hand was cold as raw steak.

"Why aren't you suited up?" he asked.

"I don't swim," I said. I dried my palm on my pants.

His small black eyes narrowed farther. "Everybody swims."

"I have a medical condition," I said.

"Parasites? Heartworm? Shankies?"

"No," I said. "This." I lifted the leg of my pants and tapped the carbon-fiber shin.

"What happened?"

"I got bit by a dog," I said.

"Must have been a hell of a dog."

"I was three," I said. "Snack size."

He grunted. "Well, that's no reason not to get in the water. I know plenty of maimed and limbless people who swim just fine."

Maimed and limbless? I thought. Then: *Plenty?*

"You can't let a peg leg slow you down," Coach Shug continued. "Hell, aquatics may be one of the few sports where a few missing parts is no impediment. You can't be afraid of the water just because you haven't learned to swim with it."

"I'm not *afraid* of the water," I said. I'm pretty sure I kept my voice even. "I'm just not going *in* it."

He blinked at me. "You're serious."

"Yes, sir."

"Huh." He rubbed his belly. "You'll need a note."

"To say that I don't have a leg?"

"To explain why your lack of a few parts should make a lick of difference. Medically speaking. Go to the nurse's office, then hurry back." He turned toward the water and lifted his whistle.

"I don't know where that is," I said.

"Behind the cafeteria," he said without turning around. "Can't miss it." The whistle shrieked, and the sound reverberated in the arena like a silver headache.

Okay, I'd lied to Coach Shug. But "a dog ate my leg" has been my standard answer for so long that it didn't feel like lying.

Besides, the answer was a little more complicated. My lower leg wasn't gone entirely. I had a phantom limb that I carried around with me. Weirdly, it was a lot shorter than my other leg. My doctor back in California told me that there was a part of my brain that still thought there should be a shin and a foot down there, even if it wasn't sure how big they were. Any random signal could be assigned to the missing limb. Some days it felt like I had a meat foot inside my fake one.

But this coldness in the phantom limb—that was new. Yesterday the feeling had died down as the day wore on. This morning it was still going strong, as if my ghost foot was missing the California sun. I know I was.

The main hallway was as empty as it usually was when class was in session. I managed to find the cafeteria in only a couple minutes, a new personal record for locating any room in this place.

The doors were open. No one sat at the tables. What did Coach mean, "Behind the cafeteria"? I walked in, looking for another exit door, but there were only the wide doors that led to the kitchen. I could hear women talking back there.

I walked up to the buffet line—the steam tables were mercifully empty—and called out, "Hello?" No one answered. The big silver table where the woman had been cutting fish was clean and gleaming. I called out again. A voice back there laughed, though the laughter didn't seem to be directed at me.

I walked around the serving line and stood at the entrance to the kitchen. Over in the far corner, three lunch ladies were gathered around a huge metal pot. One of them, the horse-toothed lady who'd tried to serve me yesterday, was pushing a big wooden paddle through the liquid. None of them had noticed me.

I approached slowly. The women were dressed identically in olive green smocks, and differed only in their ages: Old, Older, Oldest. The most senior of them was hunched over the pot, her face hovering over the gray, bubbling liquid. A dense fishy smell kept me back like a force field.

"Excuse me," I said. "I'm looking for the nurse's office?"

The old one—by which I mean the youngest of them—stopped stirring the paddle.

"Who's there?" the oldest said. Her eyes were still closed.

"Give me the glasses," the middle lunch lady said. The one with the paddle handed her a pair of glasses on a chain.

"Oh!" the middle lunch lady said. "It's the new one."

"The one with the weak stomach," the first lunch lady said.

The oldest threw back her head and cackled.

"The nurse?" I asked again.

The old one nodded toward a door at the other end of the

kitchen. "You can go through there. *Once*. Next time, use the outer loop."

"Sorry," I said, and hurried away from them. What was "the outer loop"?

The door opened to a waiting room with four wooden chairs and a small desk with nothing on it but a clipboard and a small metal bell. A hand-drawn placard said DO NOT RING BELL.

The clipboard held a sign-in sheet with columns for IN and OUT. There were only a few names on the list. All had signed in, but no one had signed out.

I signed my name and took a seat with my backpack beside me. I wasn't sure what I was going to tell the nurse. It didn't matter that I didn't have any medical records with me, because there was no medical reason why I couldn't get in the pool. I just didn't feel like explaining myself over and over. At home nobody asked me to go in the ocean anymore; they just accepted that that wasn't my thing.

I looked at my phone. No bars. To torture myself I paged through photos, looking at pictures of my friends. It was three hours earlier in California, and they were probably just getting up. *I* would have been just waking up. For a moment I could picture myself in my old room, lying in bed as the morning sunlight lit up the wall, listening to the seagulls argue outside my window.

A sound made me look up from my phone. Maybe thirty seconds passed, and then I heard it again: a low moan.

I stood and went to the door with the signs on it. The moan came again, louder, and definitely from the other side of the door. I pictured someone lying on the floor, bleeding, waiting for the nurse to come back.

I knocked on the door. "Hello? Are you okay?"

There was no answer. I turned the knob, pushed the door open a few inches. "Hello?"

A woman lay on a padded table. No, not just a woman,

a nurse: She was dressed in a white skirt and white hose.

She turned her head to look at me, and her blond hair fell across her face. She groggily pushed the hair from her eyes and looked at me through half-closed lids. "Do you have . . ." Her voice trailed off.

"What is it?" I asked. "Tell me what you need." The room was only big enough for a desk and chair, the exam table, and a big metal cabinet. The door of the cabinet was ajar, and several of the shelves were filled with orange pill bottles. "Something in there?"

". . . an appointment?" she finished. That word "appointment" seemed to require a great deal of thought. A plastic tube was attached to her left arm. The IV bag dangled above her, half-filled with some yellowish liquid.

"I can come back later," I said. "Maybe Miss Pearl can—"

"No!" The nurse lurched to a sitting position. "I can handle this." She rubbed her hand across her face as if it were numb.

Her gaze swiveled toward me. Her eyes were bloodshot. "You're not from around here," she said.

"I just moved from San Diego," I said. "My name's—"

". . . are you?" she said.

I took a breath. Talking to her was like trying to hit an off-speed pitch.

"No," I said. "I'm not."

But she was no longer listening to me. She slid the needle from her arm and sighed as she let the tube drop. She might have been beautiful if she didn't look like she'd been up for a week straight. There were dark circles under her eyes, and her lipstick was smeared.

She swung her legs over the edge of the table and considered the floor. "Why did you come here . . . ?"

I waited.

She looked up at me and raised a black eyebrow. So, maybe not a natural blonde.

"I need a note," I said. "For—"

". . . to Dunnsmouth?"

"My mom's here doing research," I said.

"For?"

"Herself. She's got a grant and—"

"No, who's the note for?"

"Coach Shug," I said. "Swim class."

"Idiot," she said. She placed a foot on the linoleum, testing the surface as if it were pond ice, then put the other foot down. "Can't stand him."

She made it to the desk and sat heavily. Then she pulled open the center drawer and rummaged through it, picking up pads of paper, putting them down, scrutinizing pens. "I know what you're going through," she said. "It's not easy to live."

"I wouldn't go that far," I said.

". . . here," she said.

She licked the tip of a pencil, then jerked as if she'd gotten a static shock. She stared at the pencil, daring it to shock her again. After a moment she said, "And *what* . . . is this in regard to?" she asked.

"It's because of my leg," I said. "I need a pass out of gym class."

"Pass out," she said. "Can't do that." She began to write on the pad of paper anyway. "They hired me two years ago," she said. "I needed the money. I was straight out of state college."

"Really," I said. She looked at least forty.

". . . Pennsylvania."

She signed the note, and pressed down so hard that the tip of the pencil snapped and went flying. "Give this to good ol' Coach," she said bitterly. "Put it right in his big . . . fat . . ."

Her eyelids drooped. Then she slumped forward in slow motion until her head came to a stop against the desk. Her eyes closed.

I backed out of the room and then pulled the door shut as quietly as I could. In the waiting room I looked at the note. In faint, loopy handwriting she'd written, "I love you. I love you.

I love you. Yours, body and soul, Mandi." She'd drawn a heart over that last "i."

It took me a long time to get back to a part of the school I recognized. I hadn't wanted to go through the kitchen, so I'd taken Door #3, which led to a long, doorless hallway identical to all of Dunnsmouth Secondary's hallways except for an orange stripe painted down the middle. The outer loop, I supposed. I started walking, and ten minutes later the corridor ended with an abrupt turn—and I was in the atrium, standing opposite the cafeteria. Somehow I'd gotten to the other side of the main hallway.

The change gong sounded a moment later. Too late for PE, then. And thank goodness; my note was useless. I stood by the wall as the atrium filled with students, and finally I saw Garfield, the bat-eared boy, then a few other juniors I recognized, and then Lydia, wet hair gleaming in the weird light. I fell into step beside her. For some reason it amused me to keep bothering her.

We turned down a corridor that I was surprised to recognize. "Hey, the library," I said.

"Nobody goes in the library," Lydia said.

"Why not? It's not so bad."

She looked at me. "You really went inside?"

"Yesterday. What's the big deal?"

She harrumphed. I'd never heard anyone under sixty harrumph before.

The next class was taught by the weird little man in the baggy suit that I'd seen next to Montooth during Voluntary. Up close he was even weirder. His eyes were so far apart that they seemed to be looking in two directions at once, like a hammerhead shark. He stood in the corner of the room, hands behind his back, watching the students with a disturbing sense of eagerness as they took their seats. Before I could find a seat he nodded at me, and I had no choice but to walk over to him.

"Welcome to World History," the teacher said. "I'm Mr. Waughm. I am also vice principal of Dunnsmouth Secondary. Go Threshers."

"My name's—"

"Oh," he said. "I *know*." A smile worked its way onto his face like a worm caught aboveground after a rainstorm. "Take a book from the stack by the window, Mr. Harrison. We're taking a test today, so you can use the time to do a little catch-up reading, eh? Hmm? Yes?"

"Uh, yes," I said. "What chapter are you on?"

"The one on Vlad the Third." He pointed at a desk at the back of the room. "That should do for now, yes? Hmm?"

The book was very heavy and bound in what looked like actual leather. The title was *The Subjugation and Domination of Various Peoples and Lands: A Guide to Effective Government*.

Okay then. I took my seat. The test was evidently an essay test; Mr. Waughm handed out question sheets, and the students went to work in their spiral notebooks.

I opened the book and found the chapter about Vlad III, otherwise known as Vlad the Impaler, otherwise known as Dracula's role model. Bram Stoker had based his vampire on this fifteenth-century warlord, who liked to keep the peace by— spoiler alert—impaling his enemies on large wooden stakes.

I glanced over at Lydia. She was reading the first problem but hadn't written anything yet. She clutched the pencil in her left hand, while the fingers of her right hand made a rolling motion, trilling that ol' invisible piano. Then her fingers stopped. She started to write an answer; then her fingers started moving again.

I looked over my shoulder at the rest of the class. At least four other people were also doing the finger-tapping thing. Not constantly. Like Lydia, they started and stopped, like musicians trading off solos.

About twenty minutes into class, the door opened. It was Principal Montooth, and behind him the round form of Miss

Pearl. Mr. Waughm hurried over to them, and then Montooth and Waughm went into the hallway. Miss Pearl waddled over to Waughm's desk, studied the chair, and finally sat down.

Thirty seconds later, Mr. Waughm came back in and announced, "Class, I have something to attend to." He looked at me, then quickly looked away. "Everyone except Mr. Harrison, turn in your tests to Miss Pearl when you're finished. As for homework—" He glanced toward the doorway where Montooth was waiting for him. "Nothing tonight." The door closed.

"Stop gawking and get to work," Miss Pearl said.

No one, however, was gawking. They went back to the essay without a word. Their fingers, however, were fluttering and flicking, like the ghost typists.

The hand-wiggling continued all through World History and continued in Practical Skills class. While Mrs. Velloc sat at her desk, the students seemed to be working hard on their knots—except their fingers were moving way too much.

Finally, it clicked.

When we walked out of class, heading for lunch, I whispered to Lydia, "I know what you guys are doing."

Her eyelids lowered to half-mast.

"The signing," I said. I waggled my fingers.

"I don't know what you're talking about."

"That's what I don't know—what you're talking about. Are you gossiping? Telling jokes? Talking about me?"

"Don't flatter yourself," she said.

"You have to teach me," I said. "Just a few words. What's the sign for 'I'm so bored I could scream'?"

We entered the cafeteria. Lydia looked around to make sure no one was listening. "I'll meet you over there," she said, and gestured toward a lunch table. Then she picked up a tray and joined the serving line.

I walked toward the table, where Garfield and Flora sat with three other kids, one a tall boy with a forehead like an anvil and long black hair that fell to his collar. Flora saw me coming, pursed those red lips, and then set those fingers to moving. Captain Forehead looked my way. Two fingers of one hand tapped the table, twice.

I sat down at an empty spot at the table. They said nothing. "Lydia said I should sit here," I said.

They seemed to accept that, and went back to their own meals, bowls of that gray liquid I'd seen the lunch ladies stirring. I was glad I'd packed my own lunch, and set out the peanut butter and jelly sandwich I'd made this morning, as well as a bag of trail mix. It was the best I could do with the remains of the road supplies. Mom and I really needed to get to a grocery store.

The others at the table looked like they were ignoring me, and I tried to look like I was ignoring them, but I was watching their fingers tap, flick, cross, and uncross. I didn't know what the individual movements meant, but I could follow the flow of conversation. The talk was rippling across the table. All the while, their expressions never changed.

Lydia arrived at the table. She did something with one finger, and the rest of the students picked up their trays and left without a word. She sat down opposite me.

"Wow," I said. "What did you say?"

"You're never going to learn fingercant," Lydia said. "We've been doing it since kindergarten, and you're an outsider."

"Fingercant. Cool. What's being an outsider got to do with it?"

"You'll be leaving Dunnsmouth before you ever learn."

"I'm good with languages," I said. "Give me a try. *Por favor.*"

She rolled her eyes. On Lydia, this was a major muscle movement.

"This is 'be quiet,' " she said. She twitched the pinky of her right hand, twice. "This is 'the teacher's watching.' " She bent the knuckle of her index finger, then pointed it straight.

"Okay, right." I practiced it: pinky twitch, pinky twitch, index bend, point.

Lydia said, "You just said, 'punch me in the back of the head.'"

"I did?"

Lydia blinked, very slowly.

"Oh," I said. "You know, it's very hard to tell when you're joking."

She stared at me.

"You are joking, right?"

"Don't use it in class," Lydia said. "You're too obvious. If you get caught, Montooth will punish you. But more important . . ." She stood and picked up her tray. She hadn't touched the stew. "You'll ruin it for all of us."

"Wait, you have to tell me more!"

I wanted to know what language they were speaking during Voluntary. What those symbols carved above the pool locker rooms meant. And I really wanted to know what everybody was saying literally behind my back.

Lydia walked away carrying her tray. And then I noticed the fingers of her right hand moving: pinky, pinky, index bend . . . point.

I looked around. Mrs. Velloc stood by one gray wall, staring at me.

I walked downhill to the rental place, my backpack ten pounds heavier than it was this morning because of three huge textbooks: one on government from world history class; one from English class called *Catastrophes of New England: 1650 to 1875*; and a much-used book from my last class of the day, Non-Euclidean Geometry. The class was taught by Mr. Gint, a pale, balding man who barely looked at us. The entire class period he sat at his desk with a protractor and pencil, drawing pictures and muttering to himself. The students took worksheets from a stack and did them silently at their desks, and most of them—including Lydia— turned in the sheets before they left. But the questions didn't make any sense to me. At home they still didn't. The first one was:

A fortress of solid granite, two thousand feet square, has four perfectly straight walls rising perpendicular to the level ground. You are alone. The others have abandoned you. The walls are infinitely high. Where do the tops of the walls touch? Show your work.

But walls perpendicular to flat ground would never touch. Certainly not infinite walls—whether you were alone or not. All the questions were like that, involving unlikely shapes and logical inconsistencies. I finally decided to treat the worksheet as a series of trick questions, explaining why each case was impossible. An hour later, I had finished with homework, and Mom still wasn't home.

As night fell I tried not to think about the lurker from last night. I made supper for myself. I rearranged our books on the few shelves in the living room—ignoring the spot where the Newton and Leeb collection would have gone. I stared at my useless phone. No service. My mood started to turn ugly again, but I shook myself out of it. Sometimes you have to just act normal to make the world *be* normal.

So, like a normal person, I turned off some of the lights in the house, and then—like a sane, nonparanoid person—I went to bed. I don't remember if I dreamed. But when I awoke it was morning, and sunlight was streaming through my window, and the police were knocking at the front door.

5

He went like one that hath been stunn'd,
And is of sense forlorn:
A sadder and a wiser man
He rose the morrow morn.

Your mother's been in an accident, they said. Later, I couldn't remember which cop had first broken the news, Detective Lieutenant Hammersmith or Chief Bode of the Dunnsmouth Police. Hammersmith was the squat black man with the glasses who said he'd come down from the Uxton State Police Detective Unit. Whenever he talked, or tried to lead the discussion, Bode, a white, chubby, red-faced man, would try to cut him off.

Their questions overlapped and kept me confused. When was the last time I saw my mother? Had she talked to me during the day? And the topper: Did she know how to swim?

I had only one question of my own. "Is she dead?"

Hammersmith and Bode exchanged a look.

Hammersmith grimaced. "The Coast Guard is running a search pattern with helicopters, and local fishermen are helping out," he said. "The important thing is not to lose faith."

Bode said, "Missing is not dead."

I sat on the couch, folded over like I'd been gut-punched. They tried to tell me what had happened, but I was having trouble processing the information, and I had to ask them to repeat it. Sometime last night, about seven p.m., the owner of the boat Mom had chartered, a fisherman named Hal Jonsson, sent out a distress call and said they were taking on water. He gave their position as about fifteen miles from shore. After that, the radio went silent. By the time the Coast Guard got to the last known location of Jonsson's boat, there was nothing there but flotsam.

"They found some life preservers, a plastic cooler, some equipment," Hammersmith said. "Just the things that would float. Some of it was stenciled with the boat's name."

"I don't understand," I said. "What happened? Was there a storm?"

"No storm," Hammersmith said. "No bad weather, really."

"So what happened? They hit a reef?"

"We don't know, son," Bode said. "But we're working on it." He shouldered his way in front of Hammersmith, and when he squatted in front of me his knees cracked loudly. He was bald except for a narrow fringe of dark hair that gripped the back of his head like a horseshoe. "In the meantime, tell us who we can contact for you. Where's your father?"

"Are you kidding me?" I said. My voice was louder than I intended. I wiped at my nose.

"Is there a reason you don't want us to contact your father?" Hammersmith asked.

They had no idea. Didn't they have records on these kinds of things? "My father died in a boating accident thirteen years ago," I said. "I mean, he *went missing*."

And there it was. My old friend rage. My right leg throbbed.

They waited for me to calm down. *I* waited for me to calm down.

"So . . . ," Bode said eventually. "How about other relatives. Anyone you can stay with?"

My relatives were all distant, either emotionally, geographically, or both. On my mom's side there were thousands of cousins, but they were all in Brazil and I'd never met them. On my dad's side were his father and his sister. Mom never got along with them, especially Selena—Aunt Sel—who was so much the polar opposite of my mother that Mom called her "Antipode." More scientist humor.

I supposed that left only my grandfather. I opened the plastic trunk that contained my mother's research materials. I found the blue spiral notebook that served as her address book and flipped through it until I found Grandpa's entry. "Harrison Harrison the Third," I told them. "He lives in Oregon, but he's not been well. I don't think he can travel."

"We'll give him a call," Hammersmith, holding out his hand.

Bode stepped up and took the address book. "Yes, we will."

They started asking me questions about my mom's schedule, what she was doing out on the water, and then what, exactly, she was researching.

The rage I'd felt gradually slipped away—or I slipped away from it. The longer I talked the farther I moved out of my body. I watched it move, and listened to the strange noises it made, but I was somewhere else, somewhere out over the water.

Detective Hammersmith shook my hand with forced cheer and said he'd let me know as soon as they knew anything. Then Chief Bode drove me in his squad car up the hill, past the school. It seemed crazy that the students inside were going about their business as if nothing had happened.

The Dunnsmouth police station was one of the few brick buildings in town. Bode showed me to a small conference room, looked around, then brought me a stack of old issues of *Rod and Gun Magazine*. I stared at the pile without opening one.

A half hour or so later, Bode returned with a burly, round-faced white woman. "This is Mrs. Llewellyn," Bode said. "She's from the Department of Children and Families, up in Uxton."

"Call me Marjorie," she said in a thick New England accent. Her name came out "MAH-jree"—two syllables. "If you were a year older you'd be on your own, but since you're sixteen—well, that puts you under the 'children' part of my job." As for what, exactly, that job was in my case, she said she was here to answer my questions and generally help out until a parent or guardian could take over.

"Is there anything you need right now?" she asked. "Have you had breakfast yet?"

"I'm not hungry," I said.

"How about something to drink?"

"I'm fine," I said.

"Well I'm starving. Walk me to the vending machine?"

Bode opened the door for us. "I'll leave you two to it."

Marjorie walked me down a hallway. "That's a pissa about your mother. You holdin' up?"

"I'm fine," I said. Then realized how stupid that sounded. Who would be fine in a situation like this? "I'm worried," I said.

"Course you are." She led me into what looked like the cops' break room. There was no one else there. From one machine she purchased a package of little chocolate donuts, and from the other a couple of cans of soda. Perfect components to assemble a sugar bomb. She handed one of the bottles to me without asking me if I wanted it. "My cousin got pulled out of the drink a couple years ago," she said. "Freezing water. Should have been dead. But they found him, resuscitated him, and now he's back to being a pain in the ass."

"You don't have to do that," I said. "Give me false hope."

"This is regular, standard-issue hope," she said. "Your mom's an ocean scientist right? Out on the water a lot? So she's experienced."

We sat at one of the round Formica tables. "She's a marine biologist," I said. "She was putting out research buoys that take sonar pictures and upload them to NOAA satellites whenever they hear something really big."

"Noah?"

"National Oceanic and Atmospheric Administration. She got a grant from them to track squids, especially this one species, the colossal squid."

"That sounds scary." Marjorie popped a donut into her mouth.

"They just look scary," I said, with false bravado. They kinda freaked me out. Not as bad as the fish boy did, though. I hadn't told the cops about him; how could I? *By the way, a were-trout came to my house last night and stole my favorite book.* They'd lock me away. "There's very little evidence that they come this far north, but that's what she was trying to prove."

"Yeah, well . . ." Marjorie bit into a donut, then turned the mouth of the package in my direction. I took one. She said, "There's all kinds of stuff down there we haven't seen yet, right?"

Chief Bode came into the room. He went to the phone on the table, punched a button, then handed it to me. He wore a pained expression. "It's for you."

I took the phone. "Hello?"

"Harry! What the hell happened? What do they mean her boat's *lost*?"

"Grandpa?"

"What in God's name are you doing in Massachusetts?"

"It's complicated. We came here to do research, and—"

"I told you never to go back. Why would you go back?"

My grandfather was yelling into the phone. Maybe he couldn't hear me. Or maybe he'd forgotten that when you asked a question it was traditional to wait for an answer. He was old. Not Regular Grandparent old—Historical Monument old. The last time we'd seen him, three years ago at what Mom and I later started calling the Infamous Last Christmas, he'd been cranky and irritable. The visit had ended in shouting, and we hadn't been back since.

"Is there not enough tragedy in this family?" he said.

"Grandpa, please. Could you settle down? I need your help."

That finally got him to pause. After a moment he said, "Is it the boy?"

"What boy?"

"Your son, of course! Tell me nothing's happened to him."

Oh no. I let the phone drop to my side. My grandfather was still asking questions at high volume. Finally I lifted the receiver and said, "He's fine, Grandpa. Everyone's fine. I'll talk to you later, okay?"

Chief Bode took the phone from me with a questioning expression.

"He thinks he's talking to his dead son," I said.

"How old is he?" the chief asked.

"He's in his nineties." My dad, if he was alive now, would be in his fifties. Everybody on my dad's side of the family puts off babies as long as possible, creating generation gaps as big as the Grand Canyon. The Grandparent Canyon.

"Is there someone else we could call?" Marjorie asked.

I sighed. "Just one."

I was standing at the front window of the rental house when the taxi pulled up. The rear door of the car flew open, and a tall blond woman dressed in red and black marched toward the house, her legs scissoring. The taxi driver stood up, calling after her, but she wasn't listening.

She burst into the house without knocking. Marjorie jumped up from the couch. Aunt Sel looked sharply at her, then saw me.

Mom once said that Selena wasn't a woman but an ad in a women's magazine: glossy, two-dimensional, and smelling like a perfume insert. Even when I was a kid I knew that she was beautiful in a way that threw people off balance. Her clothing was always perfect, and even now, after a day of traveling, she looked like she'd taken time in the taxi to iron her skirt.

She grabbed me by the shoulders and looked fiercely into my eyes. "Harrison."

I didn't know what to say to that. So I said, "Aunt Sel."

She tightened her grip on me as if deciding whether or not to hug me. Aunt Sel had never hugged me in my life. She was an air-kisser.

"Thanks for coming," I said. "And so fast."

When Chief Bode called her, I'd assumed she'd have to fly from Los Angeles, but it turned out that she'd been living in New York for two months.

"The city was becoming unbearable," Aunt Sel said. "I needed a . . . getaway." She turned to Marjorie and said, "You're the child abuse person I spoke to on the phone?"

Marjorie raised an eyebrow. "DCF. You'll be staying here with Harrison?"

Aunt Sel looked around at the house for the first time. Her eyes narrowed. Finally she said, "Of *course*."

The two women exchanged contact info, and Marjorie said she'd be checking in tomorrow. Before she left, however, she walked over to me and said quietly, "You going to be all right?"

"Sure," I said. "Thanks for the food, Marjorie."

She handed me a business card. "You can call me any time, doll. Day or night." She walked out as the taxi driver came in, and they did an awkward dance in the narrow doorway. The driver carried two suitcases, one under each arm. He was a wiry man, bald but for a shadow of stubble covering his skull, with a jaw like a steam shovel. He seemed frazzled. The nearest airport, they'd told me, was an hour and a half away. Not too long a drive, but Aunt Sel could make it seem longer.

"Put them . . ." Aunt Sel surveyed the stacks of cardboard boxes, the cheap couch, the kitchen with the cracked linoleum. "It doesn't matter."

The driver set them down where he stood. "Cash or credit?" he asked.

"Who carries cash?" Aunt Sel asked.

Aunt Selena was unmarried, with no children of her own. Like I said, people on Dad's side put off spawning as long as possible, and I figured she'd probably never swim upstream. When I was little I saw her at a few holidays, up until the Infamous Last Christmas. That morning, while Mom had fought with Grandpa, Aunt Sel had asked me to bring her a glass of wine— it was nine in the morning—and when I'd delivered it she'd handed me a ten dollar bill and said, "I dislike children, but I do appreciate decent service."

I was amazed that she'd shown up here. Yes, she was my closest living, nondemented relative. But Mom had disliked Aunt Sel, and I was pretty sure the feeling was mutual.

"Tell me what happened," Aunt Sel said. "I talked to the police before I got on the plane, but they were almost purposefully vague."

"It's all vague," I said. I told her about Mom heading out on the fishing boat that morning. At some point the boat "took on water" and disappeared.

"What happened?" she asked. "How did it sink?"

"They couldn't tell me."

"That answer is *completely* unsatisfactory."

"I know. She went out, and then . . . didn't come back. I just *sat* here. I fell asleep on the couch." I was surprised at how angry I sounded.

She squinted at me a long moment, as if peering at me through smoke. "You're not going to do that survivor's guilt thing, are you? Blaming yourself for the accident, all that?"

"She was late," I said. "I could have called the police."

"When was she due back?"

"She didn't say. I went off to school, and I thought—"

"So she wasn't actually late. Yet you were going to magically sense that something was wrong." She shook her head. "I'm sorry, Harrison. It just doesn't add up."

I stared at her. Wasn't she supposed to be comforting me? That's what family was supposed to do, right? My mother was missing at sea, for crying out loud.

Aunt Sel said, "So what do you think happened—they hit a rock or something?"

"That's the part that doesn't make any sense. They were in deep water. If there was an island or a reef or something, the guy who took her out would have known about it. He's a local. That's what the detectives should be investigating, but nobody seems to be asking those questions."

Aunt Sel frowned. "So she was looking for that mythical fish thing. She's been obsessed with it ever since your father died."

"What do you mean, mythical?"

Her eyes widened in surprise. "Nothing," she said. Her voice softened. "Stupid word."

I turned away from her, trying to figure out what was happening with my body. *Hey, look at the heart rate. You sure got riled up, didn't you?*

"We'll know soon enough what happened," Aunt Sel said. "Your mother will be able to tell us the whole story."

"How long are you staying?" I asked her.

"Until she comes back, of course." She looked around. "Your mother didn't leave any cabernet in this house, did she?"

I knew she was coddling me. Pretending that everything was going to be all right. Lying to children, I understood, was an adult's first job.

6

Because he didn't know what else to do, he brought it to Mother. Mother always knew what to do.

It was awkward going, though. The package was wrapped in layer after layer of canvas and secured with ropes, and was so big that it overhung the sides of the wheelbarrow. He needed both hands to push, so his right hand had to grip both the wheelbarrow handle and the wire handle of the electric lantern. The stone floor was uneven and deeply furrowed in spots; the wheelbarrow rumbled and bounced and took sudden lurches. The lantern swung about at knee level, throwing light at mad angles against the tunnel walls.

The tunnel had been beautiful once. It had been carved hundreds of years before the pilgrims landed, the walls worshipfully inscribed with symbols and elaborate designs that were now obscured by a black fungus that extruded from every groove and crevice. When he was young, Mother would bring him here for reading lessons. He'd scrub clear a section of wall and try to read the inscriptions. Even after years of study he understood only a small portion of the symbols. Mother couldn't understand his difficulty. She'd scold, and hint, and threaten. She'd punish him for not trying hard enough. But he *did* try. There was just something about the writing that made his brain recoil.

The front of the wheelbarrow dropped into a hole, the wheelbarrow jolted to a stop, and the package slid forward and thumped onto the ground.

It grunted.

He pulled back on the wheelbarrow. The wheel separated from the frame with an ugly crack; the edge of the wheelbarrow clanked against the floor.

He swore aloud then. He tried never to swear, but the occasion seemed to warrant it.

He lifted the lantern to survey the damage. It was clear there was no fixing it, not without a welding kit.

If only the package wasn't so heavy. He thought about throwing it over his shoulder like a sack of rice, but that kind of move would make him throw out his back. Finally he squatted, worked his arms beneath it. One, he thought. *Two . . .*

He grunted and lifted with his knees. He lost his balance for a moment, righted himself. And then he was cradling it in his arms. His lower back trembled with the strain.

The lantern was still on the ground. He swore again.

He breathed deep, readying himself. Then he started walking, carrying the package like a groom crossing the threshold— except that this threshold was hundreds of yards away, across broken rock, in the dark.

His back was going to kill him in the morning.

The cave was lit by a dozen lamps, each one in a different style: a brass floor lamp, a cheap wooden table lamp from a Swedish mail order store, a dining room candelabra, an electric menorah, a turquoise lava lamp. Power cords snaked across the floor. A generator rumbled from a side cavern. The air smelled of . . . Mother.

She was waiting, as usual, in bed. She lay on a huge stone

bench that was twelve feet long and eight wide, filling every inch of it. When he was a boy she had lived aboveground, in a specially constructed barn. When she grew too large and started attracting attention, he had helped her move here. She hadn't left this network of caves in years.

"Ooh," she said. "What have you brought me?" Her voice echoed in the space.

He walked forward, careful not to trip on the power cords or bump into the stainless steel buckets that had held her recent meals. Where were her handmaids? Why was this mess still here this late in the day? True, the women were volunteers, but there was a time when people took pride in their work.

He dumped the package beside the bed. "It's a gift, Mother."

"You shouldn't have," she said. "You know I'm on a diet."

He opened his penknife, knelt slowly to protect his back, and began sawing through one of the ropes.

"I want to be ready for the big day," she said. "I've got the maids making a new dress."

Out of what? he thought, but kept his head down.

"What's taking you so long?" she said. "You really ought to do something about that knife. Your brother—"

"Yes, yes, he has a very big knife." One of the ropes popped free, and he began unwinding it from one end of the bundle. Mother leaned out over the edge, and her hot breath painted his face.

He tugged down the canvas. "Voila."

"I told you," she said. "I'm on a diet."

"You don't recognize her? Think about a dozen years ago."

She blinked at the package, then said, "That one! The brown one and her husband—they ruined everything!"

The woman stared up at Mother in wide-eyed horror. Her face was scraped and bloody. Her mouth was sealed with duct tape.

"What's she doing back here?" Mother asked.

He hesitated. "She nearly did it again," he said.

"What, *ruin* us?" Mother asked. "How?"

"She saw us," he said. "With the First."

"She saw them?!"

"That's why we had to grab her."

"*Grab* her?" Mother rose up, and it was like a volcano thrusting up out of the ocean. "Why didn't you kill her? Why in the world would you bring her here? Especially now, when we're so close!"

He told himself not to wither before her anger. He was a grown man, wasn't he?

"That's why I brought her," he said. "We're so close. And you know what we're going to need for the ceremony, so I thought, rather than use one of the Palwicks—"

"You thought. You *thought*."

"But if we need—"

"Shh! I'm thinking."

What he did not say was that when he had the opportunity to kill the woman, he couldn't do it. He had never murdered anyone—not with his bare hands. The old lobsterman, Jonsson, had gone into the water and never come up. That was an accident, really. But the woman had been floating there, looking up at him. So he'd let her onto the boat, and now she was Mother's problem to solve.

"She's *better* than the Palwicks," Mother said, seemingly talking aloud to herself.

"Do you think so?" he said, keeping all irony out of his voice. All good ideas had to be her ideas.

"Of course! Look at that skin tone! She's so *primitive*."

He glanced down, and cringed. The woman stared up at him with pure hate. He tugged the canvas up over her face again. *Skin tone*. Really, Mother? He wished her attitudes weren't so old-fashioned, but what could he expect from a woman her age?

"We'll have to get your brother working on her right away," Mother said. "The vessel has to be completely empty for the big day!" She clapped her hands. "Oh, your brother will so enjoy a new subject. An artist needs inspiration."

"Like a dog needs meat," he said.

"Better keep the Palwicks on ice, though," she said. "In case your brother doesn't finish. And you, you just carry on coordinating with the First. We can't afford to let anyone interfere again."

"No one will, I promise."

"Yet you're still standing there," she said. "What is it?"

He thought about telling her about the woman's son, that he was in town, and attending the school. But if he brought him up, there was no telling what Mother would ask him to do.

"I was just thinking about the big day," he said.

"Aren't we all, my son." She held out her gigantic paw to him.

He kissed her damp skin. "All blessings to you, Toadmother."

She withdrew her hand. "Now drag her into the corner until your brother comes for her. Lunch is on the way."

7

The Sun's rim dips; the stars rush out:
At one stride comes the dark.

Here's what I learned after Mom disappeared: that your body keeps breathing even when your brain shuts down. That you can talk about trivialities while the world burns down around you.

Aunt Sel slouched into the living room wearing men's silk pajamas and a sleep mask pushed up onto her head like sunglasses. She yawned and said, "Coffee?" This early, and without makeup, she didn't look nearly as magazine perfect as last night. Almost mortal, in fact.

I showed her the coffeemaker and the tin of Folgers. She made a face. "I said *coffee*."

She saw that I wasn't laughing and shrugged. "Any pot in a storm, I guess."

While the coffee brewed she decided that we needed groceries, stat, and began drawing up a list. I had no interest in food, but she made me tell her what cereal I usually ate, what deli meat I liked. Then she tried to make a call on her cell phone. When she couldn't get a signal, she finally used the old-fashioned dial phone that came with the house. It was a monstrosity, heavy enough to bludgeon orcs.

"Oh, to dial with an actual *dial*," she said. "I feel like I'm in a Jane Austen novel."

"Uh, I think Jane Austen died before—"

"Saleem!" she said into the receiver. "I have urgent business." I guessed she was talking to the taxi driver from yesterday. I could hear him arguing on the phone—he was not a personal shopping service, etc.—but Aunt Sel got her way. Of course. She read him the list of items, then said, "And anything else you see that might be fun." He didn't seem to like this, and Selena finally said, "That's what I'm saying, Saleem, I don't *know* what that would be. Surprise us."

Aunt Sel announced she would take a bath while we waited. Not a shower; a bath. She handed me a credit card. "In case he arrives while I'm soaking," she said.

I didn't know what to do with myself. I watched the phone, waiting for word from Detective Hammersmith or Chief Bode that someone had found my mother. I itched to take action. To do *something*, *anything*. If Mom was lost in the forest I could have searched for her. If she'd disappeared down an abandoned mine, I could have roped up and rappelled into the dark. But she was somewhere out at sea, and I was a kid with no boat. It was up to the Coast Guard, Hammersmith had told me yesterday. Just sit tight.

But I could not sit. I paced, and flipped through my mother's books, and dragged her footlocker first to one corner of the room, then another. It didn't fit anywhere. It was a heavy, waterproof hunk of plastic three feet long and almost as tall. It had been with us as long as I could remember, following us from apartment to apartment. She'd kept adding to it all through grad school. There were marine fossils in there, shark teeth, squid beaks. But most of it was paper—articles, printouts from the web, pictures, drafts of her dissertation—even though she could have probably scanned everything and stored it on a single flash drive. Mom's an old-school scientist.

I walked around and around the outside of the house. I think I was daring the pointy-toothed stalker to come back, just so I would have someone to punch.

The taxi pulled up over an hour later, and I went out to help him unload. It was indeed the same driver as last night, the bald man with the jaw too big for his face. He didn't look any happier to be here than the first time. But at least he wasn't pale and hollow-eyed like everyone else I'd met in town.

"You're not from around here, are you?" I asked.

"Thank God," he said. "I live here because it's cheap, but I do most of my driving in Uxton."

"Not for long." Aunt Sel had appeared in the doorway, now wearing a silk kimono. I thought it was possible that 90 percent of her wardrobe was silk loungewear. "He's got an ABD in astrophysics."

ABD stood for All But Dissertation. It was a common condition among grad students. "So almost a doctor," I said.

"Almost is not enough," Aunt Sel said. She opened one of the grocery bags, found a bunch of grapes, and popped one in her mouth. "He's going back to school in the fall."

"I never said that," Saleem said. "*You* said that."

"We'll discuss it later. Did you bring the sorbet?"

"They didn't have any. I brought ice cream."

"That's *completely* different," she said. "But I suppose we must adjust." She took the credit card from me and handed it to him. "Add fifty."

"That's too much," he said.

"It's called a tip, dear," she said. "You may not get them very often out here among the Yankees."

"You got that right."

"Oh, and you're officially on retainer. Don't take any fare further than ten miles."

"You can't be serious," he said.

"As the proverbial, my dear. Go on now. I have to get dressed."

Saleem hesitated at the door. "I'm sorry about your mom," he said to me.

"You know about that?"

"It's all over town," he said. "But don't worry, I'm sure they'll find her."

I really wished people would stop saying that.

As the taxi pulled away, another car rolled toward the rental. The vehicle was long, black, and finned like a shark.

I went inside and told Aunt Sel that company had arrived.

"You don't look happy about it," she said.

"You'll see."

The doorbell rang. I didn't know the rental had a doorbell.

Aunt Sel opened the door to find Principal Montooth, almost as tall as the doorway. Behind him were Mrs. Velloc and Mr. Waughm. What were *they* doing here? Trying to bust me for truancy?

"How do you do?" Montooth said. "I'm Eston Montooth, principal of Dunnsmouth Secondary."

Aunt Sel was now dressed in a red blouse, black flared pants, and a black-and-red bolero jacket. Her hair and makeup were fully in place. Montooth, with his gleaming hair and perfectly pressed suit, was her match in style. When they shook hands it was like two full-page ads reaching across the staples to each other.

"I'm Selena Harrison," Aunt Sel said. "Harrison's aunt."

"This is Mrs. Velloc, one of our senior teachers," Montooth said. "And Mr. Waughm, our vice principal."

"Go Threshers," Waughm said.

He seemed to be ogling Aunt Sel's cleavage. Or maybe the kitchen table. With his walleyed look it was difficult to tell.

We moved into the small living room, then paused for an awkward moment as we took in the single couch and two chairs, assessing the etiquette of the situation. Eventually we all came to the same conclusion, and Montooth, Waughm, and Mrs. Velloc perched together on the couch. Montooth and Velloc were so tall that Waughm, squashed between them, looked like their ugly son.

"I'm so sorry about this accident," Montooth said to me. "How are you holding up?"

Holding up? I was barely up, much less holding.

"He's doing as well as anyone could, under the circumstances," Aunt Sel said, covering for my silence.

"I'm glad to hear it," he said. "Harrison's only been with us a few days, but we consider him a part of the Dunnsmouth family."

"That's so nice of you to say," Aunt Sel said, somehow making it clear that she didn't believe the sentiment, yet appreciated the attempt at a good lie.

"The entire school was shocked at the news," Montooth said.

"Shocked," Mr. Waughm said.

"Though, sadly, this kind of thing has happened before," Montooth said. "We're a fishing village, and lobstering is a dangerous business. The fact that someone inexperienced in boating might—"

"She's not inexperienced," I said. "She's spent more time on the water than most sea captains."

"And she didn't go out alone," Aunt Sel said. "She went out with a local fisherman, didn't she?"

"Hal Jonsson," Mrs. Velloc said, not bothering to hide her disapproval. "An unfortunate choice. He hasn't worked on a boat for years. Spends his days drinking and telling stories."

Silence descended. I couldn't figure out what to do with my hands.

"So," Montooth said. "Is there any word?"

"Nothing yet," Aunt Sel said.

Montooth nodded. "Well I'm sure they'll find her—"

"*Don't*," I said.

Four adult heads swiveled to look at me.

"Don't say it," I said.

Waughm looked up at Montooth in surprise, but Montooth's face softened. "Of course," he said quietly. "Nothing is sure, is it? You're smart enough to know that." He rose from the couch and shook Aunt Sel's hand again. "We don't want to inconvenience you. Just let us know if there's anything we can do. And of course Harrison can take off as much time as he needs. The school will be waiting for him when he's ready."

Aunt Sel thanked them and escorted them the short distance to the door. She said, "With all this talk of lobstering, I'm getting hungry. Is there a good seafood restaurant in town?"

"A *good* restaurant?" Mrs. Velloc asked.

"Try Sophie's," Principal Montooth said. "It's not very sophisticated, but it's right on the water, and the fish is *extremely* fresh."

Mr. Waughm held out his hand to Aunt Sel. "It was such a pleasure to meet you," he said.

She patted his wrist. "I'm sure it was," she said.

When they'd driven off she turned to me. "Well," she said. "I don't think they're creepy at *all*."

Every time the phone rang it was like a fire alarm. The ringer seemed to be actual bells. When a call came in the whole table vibrated.

The first call, just after noon, was from Detective Hammersmith; and the second, a few hours later, was from Chief Bode. The message each time was the same: the Coast Guard and the half dozen volunteer boats hadn't found my mother or Hal Jonsson, but they were checking the open sea, and also looking into each bay and inlet. Both men expressed confidence in the skills of the Coast Guard and offered reassurances.

I was tired of the lies.

The ocean was a killer—I'd learned that when I was three years old. My father was by all accounts a strong swimmer who'd spent many hours on the water. But even the most sea-savvy human couldn't survive long in that environment. We were interlopers there. There was no need to fear imaginary monsters with tentacles, or oil-black creatures with razor teeth who munched on toddler legs. Stinging jellyfish were enough to take us down. Hypothermia and dehydration could sap our strength. Gravity could drag us into the depths.

We were chimps. We had no business out on the water.

"Would you please sit down?" Aunt Sel asked. "You're making me dizzy."

I realized I'd been pacing. "I can't sit down," I said.

"Hmm. We've got to get out of here. Time for dinner." She used the monster phone to call Saleem.

"I'm not going," I told her. "They could call back any time."

"You've got to eat," she said. She called a second number and asked for Chief Bode. "Chief, Selena Harrison. I was wondering if I could ask a favor." She told him they'd be going out to dinner, and unfortunately her cell phone was getting no service. "If you receive any news, could you call us at the restaurant? It's a place called—what's the name—*Sophie's*. Oh, of course you have. Really? You don't say."

She hung up. "He says we've got to have the chowder."

It went against my instincts, but I let her put me in the taxi. Saleem drove us down a narrow, winding road that hugged the coast. The dark came down as we drove, and the ocean gleamed through the trees.

After perhaps twenty minutes we stopped at a little gravel parking lot. Sophie's turned out to be a long shack at the edge of the water.

"I'll come pick you up after you're done," Saleem said.

"I told you, you're on retainer. You can't just leave us here. And I can't let you sit in the car. We're going to come out of there stuffed with food, and you're going to give me that look."

"What look?" he asked.

"Come on now," she said. "Table for three."

"I'm not going to let you buy me dinner," Saleem said.

"What I'm *buying* is a relaxed ride home with a happy, contented driver. Harrison, explain to Saleem that he's not going to win this."

"You're not going to win this," I said.

"Listen to him; he's a smart boy," Aunt Sel said. "Tell you what—let's pretend that we've argued for thirty minutes, and that you only gave in to get me to shut up."

"Oh, I'm already there," Saleem said.

"Perfect!"

The inside of the restaurant was tiny but cheery. The tables were bare wood, no tablecloths, but Mason jar oil candles were set on every table. There were only eight other diners in the place, but they seemed to be in a good mood.

An old white man in overalls brought us baskets of garlic bread dripping with oil and set them down without a word. He started to turn away, and Aunt Sel said, "Could I get some wine?"

"No liquor license," he said.

"Oh sweetie," she said, laughing. "If you don't ask me about my age, I won't ask about your license."

The man did not quite smile. "I'll see what I can do." A while later he came back with a big bottle in a kind of macramé holder and set out two juice glasses. Saleem waved it off, saying he didn't drink.

"More for me then," Aunt Sel said, and filled her glass.

"What'll you have?" the old man said.

"I don't like fish," I said.

Aunt Sel and the old man stared at me.

"I'm sorry," Aunt Sel said. "He doesn't know what he's talking about." She ordered three cups of chowder, then lobster for each of them.

After he'd gone I said quietly, "Really, I don't like fish."

"Lobster is not fish," she said. "It's life."

The only time I'd eaten lobster meat was by accident, when it turned out that the chunks of chicken in my salad weren't. I couldn't remember what it tasted like.

The old man returned a few minutes later with the chowder. It was creamy and chunky, but the consistency reminded me too much of the stuff the lunch ladies were stirring in the school kitchen. I swallowed a few spoonfuls, then set my cup aside.

"You used to love fish when you were little," Aunt Sel said. "Your father would feed you sushi. You were both crazy for it."

"Yeah, well, I'm not my dad. You know Grandpa thought I was him when I called?"

"Your voice is as deep as his now."

"But he's *dead*. Grandpa was all mad at me for coming back to Massachusetts."

"Can you blame him?" Aunt Sel said. "It was a horrible trip. Why your mother would come back here after—ah! The guests of honor."

The old man came toward us, somehow managing to balance three huge platters on two arms. Each dish held a small wooden bowl of drawn butter, a dozen hushpuppies, and a red, armored creature who'd just crawled out of the Jurassic period. Evidently it was steamy back then.

Aunt Sel and Saleem cracked open their victims and dug in. "Oh my God," Aunt Sel said. "This is *amazing*." She pointed a knife at me. "You *will* eat, Harrison."

"Seriously, dude," Saleem said. "I mean—seriously."

My lobster's claws were bound like a prisoner's. A few minutes ago the big guy had been alive. Probably earlier today he'd been swimming in the water somewhere outside this restaurant. What crime had he committed, to be sentenced to death by boiling?

Aunt Sel showed me how to crack open the shell. I poked the tiny lobster fork into the white meat and dipped it into the butter. It took only one bite to lose all sympathy for the prisoner. The meat seemed to melt on my tongue, and it tasted nothing at all like fish.

"I'm sorry," I said to the lobster. "You're guilty of deliciousness."

Aunt Sel was feeling tipsy on the way home. I wasn't sure how she was remaining conscious. She was not a big woman, and she'd drunk an entire bottle of wine on her own. We leaned against each other in the cab, and she kept talking about the amazing food.

"So why was the trip horrible?" I asked her.

"What trip, dear?"

"The one my dad took. When was he here?"

"The last time he was here, well, that was the last time he was anywhere, wasn't he?"

I moved so I could see her face. "My father died *here*? In Massachusetts?" *I met him when he visited the area,* Montooth had said.

"Just miles from here," she said. "Where did you think?"

"I don't know—California?" Mom and I didn't talk about Dad's death too much, but I'd grown up thinking he'd died in the Pacific, off of San Diego. Mom had never corrected that impression. "Are you sure he was here?"

"Not just your father—you all were. Of course, you were too young to remember that shark attack, thank God."

From the front, Saleem said, "Shark attack?"

"It's bad form to listen to the passengers," she said. Then: "Harrison lost his leg when he was three."

"I wasn't attacked by a fish," I said. I remembered tentacles. Tentacles and teeth. But that was a false memory. "A piece of metal from the ship's bulkhead came down. Some part of the boat."

"Hmm," Aunt Sel said. She gazed out the foggy passenger window.

"Aunt Sel?"

"Of course," she said sleepily. "A metal . . . thing."

Her eyes closed, and that was the end of the conversation. I didn't know what to think. Had I really been attacked by a shark? And *here*, in Massachusetts?

If that was true, Mom had been hiding the truth from me for my entire life. And not just when I was little. We'd been planning this trip east for months. And all that time we'd spent in the truck together on the long ride across the country, she still couldn't mention, Hey, this is where it all happened.

Yesterday morning she'd looked at me like she was going to tell me something. *It was a mistake bringing you here.* And she still hadn't said a word.

Saleem helped me guide Aunt Sel into the rental house. She poured out of our arms, into the bed. She pointed at me. "You probably have regular kid things to do before you go to sleep, yes? Brushing teeth and all that?"

"Sure," I said.

"Then let's pretend you've done all that. Now, pay the man." She fell back, instantly unconscious.

I rooted through her handbag until I found her wallet. There was only forty dollars in cash, but a dozen credit cards. I handed him the top one, a MasterCard.

"Not that one," Saleem said. "Try the green Visa."

"What's wrong with this one?"

He looked uncomfortable. "We had a little trouble with that one the other day. Same with the Diners Club."

Saleem took the Visa, went out to the car, and came back with a receipt. I signed it, even though I had no idea what Aunt Sel's handwriting looked like. I locked the door behind him, then went to my bedroom. Once I was in bed, I suddenly wasn't sleepy. Was Mom sleeping now? Was she dreaming of me?

The window was directly across from my bed. Moonlight seeped between the green curtains, gauzy old-fashioned things that had come with the house. I was looking at a gap between the curtains when a shadow passed on the other side of the window.

I didn't move.

A moment later came the creak of wood. The sound came from the back porch, just outside my window.

I slipped out of bed. Fortunately, I'd kept my leg on.

I crouched beneath the window, then slowly raised my head. I could see nothing through the curtains but a glow off to the right. The kitchen light I'd left on, illuminating the backyard.

I couldn't remember if I'd locked the back door.

I tried to convince myself that I'd imagined the shadow, or the sounds. I tried not to think of the fish boy.

After five minutes, I still hadn't heard or seen a thing. I went into the hallway. From my mother's room came Aunt Sel's wheezy half-snore.

The kitchen light shined too bright for my night-accustomed eyes. I went to the back door. And yes, it was unlocked. Because I'm an idiot.

I turned the lock, and couldn't stop myself from looking through the door's little window.

Then I saw it, sitting on the wicker table on the back porch.

I opened the door a few inches. Nothing moved outside. I opened the door more fully, and stepped out. On the table was my book, *The 20th Anniversary Treasury Edition of Newton & Leeb*. A piece of paper rested on top. In blocky handwriting, someone had written:

SHE'S STILL ALIVE. LOOK FOR ALBATROSS.

8

"God save thee, ancient Mariner,
From the fiends that plague thee thus!—
Why look'st thou so?" — "With my crossbow
I shot the Albatross."

Let's say this strange guy comes up to you in the recess yard. He points to his windowless van and says, Hey kid, I really need to find a home for my Labrador puppy, do you want it? And oh yeah, the puppy comes with a new Xbox and a crate of giant-size Snicker bars. All you have to do is hop in the van to get them.

If you're five years old, or an idiot, this is the greatest moment in your life.

My first instinct after reading the note was to look for someone to punch. But the woods outside the porch window were dark, and my book thief was nowhere to be seen. I crumpled the note and jammed it into my pocket.

She's still alive. It was the one thing I wanted most in the world. The thing I needed to believe. But that need was exactly what made me sure that I was being jerked around.

I could have thrown the note away, if it wasn't for that second sentence. *Look for albatross.* What the hell did that mean?

I know I must have slept that night, because I woke with a start. I'd forgotten something, something important, and I needed to find it.

I was in my bed. My phone said it was 4:45 a.m.

As I came awake, I felt cheated. No rest and no dreams, just a fast drop through the trapdoor to morning. How could I sleep and not dream of my mother? I felt her in me, echoing like a doubled heartbeat.

She's still alive.

I remembered then what I'd forgotten. I pulled on my leg, then jeans and a hoodie, and on my way out of the house I peeked into my mother's bedroom. My aunt, in silk men's pajamas, lay sprawled across the bed, one arm thrown over her eyes. Aunt Sel, of course, even *slept* dramatically.

I walked outside into the cold. For a short while I was the only person in the world: the sky black above but purpling to the east; the silent trees beside me; the empty road under my feet snaking down through the mist to the water.

As I walked the sun shouldered its way through the fog. The bay was shaped like a crocodile's mouth, with teeth of jagged outcroppings. Near the base of the jaw, wooden and sheet-metal buildings clustered near the water. Warehouses, maybe, or fish processing plants. A few had boat doors that opened to the bay.

The dock itself looked like the bones of a creature that had died in the crocodile's mouth. Weathered poles stuck up out of the water, the walkways and berths long since rotted away. One pier remained, jutting over the water. Clinging to its tip was a colorless wooden shack. A dozen boats—outboards, fishing boats, a handful of sailboats—were tied up along the pier. Three lobster boats were loading up. Men in baggy pants tossed down metal lobster traps to other men on the decks. They shouted to each other as they stacked the traps, the fog muffling their voices.

Birds wheeled in the air above the boats, keening. They looked and sounded like the seagulls back home. If any of them were albatrosses I wouldn't know—I had no idea what one looked like.

Our pickup was parked in a corner of the gravel lot. It looked lonely with no equipment in the bed of it, like a dog with its chin on the floor. I hoped Edgar and Howard and the other buoys were still out there, still taking sonar pictures, still broadcasting. When Mom came back she'd be anxious to see the data.

I walked over to the truck, tried the door, but it was locked. I cupped my hands against the window. The keys weren't in the ignition—a place Mom had been known to leave them—so I figured she'd brought them with her on the boat. No matter. I went to the rear right fender and felt around until I found the magnetic case. The key was still inside. I'd never told Mom about the spare, because then she'd use it: If you give an AMP a key, she's sure to lose it.

I unlocked the door and climbed in. The cab still smelled like the onion rings we'd eaten somewhere in Pennsylvania. I only had my learner's permit, but I figured I could risk driving the truck back to the house. Then I noticed the crumpled green paper on the floorboard. I remembered the note Mom had found on the hood of the truck.

I picked it up, then smoothed it out. In spidery black cursive, it said, "Stay out of the water."

I stared at it. A note from the neighbors, she'd called it.

The windows of the truck were rolled up, and the parking lot was empty. I felt okay about screaming a few curse words, in a couple different languages.

I thought of Mom yelling into the phone the morning she disappeared. *That, that . . . Viking!* The charter captain's name was Erik Hallgrimsson. Had he left the note? Or was everyone in town trying to get us to leave?

Hallgrimsson was probably out on that pier. All I had to do was go out and find him.

The pier.

It wasn't that I was *afraid* of the ocean—that wasn't it at all. I *hated* it. I wouldn't swim in it or boat across it, and I didn't even like to fly over it. Walking out over it, on some rickety platform that looked like it would fall apart at the first big wave . . . ugh.

But there were questions I needed answers to.

I was relieved that the boards felt solid beneath my feet. I avoided looking out at the water and kept my eyes on the sign above the shack's door: BAIT SHOP. When I reached the shack, I stood with my back against the wall, hands jammed in my pockets.

No one paid me any attention. I watched the men work, and when I thought they weren't looking I studied their faces, wondering, Is he the one?

A slate board was nailed to the bait shop wall. The boats' names were written in chalk. Each boat had been assigned a numbered slip. I wondered which one was the ship Mom had gone out on that first day. The *Bonny*? The *Paste Pot*?

Then I saw the next two names on the list. *Huginn* and *Muninn*. *Huginn* was crossed out.

Huginn and Muninn were the ravens that belonged to Odin, king of the Norse gods. Huginn's name meant "thought." Muninn meant "memory." Good names for boats if you read a lot of Thor comics—or if you were a Viking.

The men still on the pier climbed down ladders to the boats, and my time was running out. I stepped toward one of the men heading for the *Muninn*. He was tall, with thick arms, and blond hair that hung to his shoulders. A black band was fastened around one bicep, and then I knew for sure.

"Erik Hallgrimsson?" I said. "I'd like to talk."

The man looked up at me. "Sorry kid, no work."

"It's not that," I said. "I wanted to know—"

"Try back tomorrow."

The man started down the ladder, and I strode forward. "I want to know why you bailed out on my mother."

The long-haired man paused. Then he said to the man in the boat, "Just a second, Gus." He climbed back onto the pier, put his hands on his hips. He towered over me.

"You her boy?" he asked.

"That's right."

Something changed in his face. He glanced at the entrance of the shack, as if checking for eavesdroppers. "I'm sorry, kid." His voice was quieter. "It's tough to lose a parent."

"I haven't *lost* her," I said. "*I'm* not wearing a black band."

He glanced at his arm as if he'd forgotten he was wearing it. "No. Right. This is for the man who went down."

"Hal Jonsson. He was in the *Huninn*, right?"

"That's right."

"Well. At least he kept his word."

He squinted at me.

"I was in the room when you called my mom," I said. "I want to know why you took her out one day, then canceled the next."

"It's business, kid."

"What does *that* mean?"

"It *means* I had pots to haul. I couldn't afford to take her out again."

"Then you shouldn't have agreed to take her out in the first place."

"You're right about that, kid." He turned back toward the ladder.

"Hey!" I grabbed his arm. I'd been looking for someone to punch since my mother went missing, and he seemed like he could take one pretty well.

Then he looked back at me, one eyebrow raised. I realized that the bicep under my hand had, evidently, been carved out of marble. It made my hand cold.

I dropped my hand.

"I wouldn't hang out on the docks," he said. "A kid could get hurt out here." He didn't say it like a threat. Then he said, "I'm sorry about your mom. I hope they find her."

* * *

93

I drove the truck back to the rental. When I went inside, I was surprised to find Aunt Sel awake, staring at various pieces of the coffeemaker that were laid out on the counter like organs in an autopsy. "I thought you'd gone to school," she said.

"I found the truck. It was down by the dock."

"Could you do something with this? I have a terrible headache."

While I made the coffee she sat in the armchair and rubbed her eyes. "You know, it's fine with me if you never go back. High school is a complete waste of time. The girls have no sense of style, and the boys—don't get me started on the boys."

"I don't care how I dress," I said.

"Clearly. You're like Tom Wolfe, possessed by a single fashion idea. But while he chose an ice cream suit, you've settled on . . . the hoodie."

"I like being comfortable."

"You sound like your father. He went through school looking like an indigent. You can get away with that if you're a genius. Not me, though. My only gifts were clear skin and a dirty mind."

"You're oversharing," I said.

"Your father loved school. Believed in it. Just like your mother. She's so *relentlessly* serious about it. 'My boy never misses a day of school,' blah etcetera blah. She has high hopes for you, you know. Ivy League, top-of-the-class hopes."

"I know what you're doing," I said.

She opened her eyes. "What? You think I *want* you to go to school? Then who would entertain *me*? This place is *stultifying*. True, if there's any news, they can tell you in school just as easily as here, but how much better to spend your time with your most beloved relative? I can teach you how to make a decent Bloody Mary."

"You're not a very good aunt."

"Pardon me, but I'm *fantastic*. The best aunts aren't

substitute parents, they're coconspirators."

I poured her a cup and brought it to her. "I was thinking of going back to school anyway," I said.

"Re-a-lly," she said. She'd loaded the word with half a dozen extra vowels.

"Really."

Her eyes narrowed. "You seem different. Did something happen this morning?"

She's still alive, I thought.

"I'm going to take a shower," I said. "I don't want to be late."

I arrived at school just as the students were being let out of Voluntary. I could feel eyes on me as we climbed the stairs. Of course no one was whispering. But fingers were moving.

I took my seat in Cryptobiology. Flora, the Goth girl in the red lipstick, and Garfield the bat-eared boy said nothing as we wired up our dead toad. But halfway through class I noticed that Flora was giving me a pitying look, and I realized I'd been staring into space.

"Sorry to hear about your mother," Flora said quietly.

"Yeah," Garfield said.

Lydia, sitting a row ahead, glanced back; then she turned away without speaking.

Someone behind us squealed. Everyone in the class turned. On one of the tables, a frog had started to smoke, and the limbs were twitching spasmodically. Dr. Herbert rushed over, clapping his hands. "It's alive!" he cried.

Just as he reached the table, the frog's rear legs jerked in unison, and it leaped off the table. The wire leads snapped free, and the thing fell to the floor with a *fwap*! We gathered around it. The animal was still smoking, but it was inert again.

I was thinking of poor Michigan J. Frog, from the cartoon.

Hello ma baby,
Hello ma honey,
Hello ma ragtime gal.
Send me a kiss by wire,
Baby my heart's on fire.

"Everyone set your transformers to this voltage!" Dr. Herbert said. "We're doing science!"

After class I walked a few paces behind Lydia and followed her into the stone basement that held the pool. Just as we reached the locker rooms she turned and said, "You're looking at me."

"I'm looking at your hands."

The other students passed by us and went inside.

"We're not talking about you," she said.

"Liar."

"Not all the time."

"That's more like it," I said. "What are they saying?"

"We're surprised you're here at all. We all thought you'd have left town by now."

"My mom's missing, not dead. I'm not leaving without her."

"Oh, Harrison," she said. "People around here go missing all the time. There's no use waiting for them to come back."

"All the time? What do you mean, all the time?"

She looked exhausted. "Never mind."

"Wait," I said. "I'm looking for something. An albatross."

She'd been turning away from me, and now she froze. "What are you talking about?"

"I don't know," I said. "I was just . . ." I didn't want to tell her about the note. Or try to explain the Fish Boy. "Someone said something about that bird."

"Go to class, Harrison," she said. "And then go back to where you came from."

Coach Shug came out of the water, shook his head as if clearing his ears, and then lifted his goggles to his forehead. He spotted me in the stone bleachers and lumbered forward. His skin was so white I wondered if he ever left this cave.

"You're back," he said. "And still not dressed."

Or undressed, I thought. "I told you, I can't because—"

"Note," Coach said.

Oh no. All I had was the useless love note from Nurse Mandi. "She wasn't feeling well," I said. "What she gave me I can't really—"

"*Note.*"

I took a breath, then reached into the pouch of my hoodie. I handed him the piece of paper. "She didn't really address my, uh, medical issue."

He unfolded the paper and blinked at it. His wet fingers spotted it gray.

"I can try again if . . . Coach?"

His face had turned bright red. He was flushed from neck to ears.

"Coach?"

He looked down at me, his eyes shining with something other than pool water. "She gave this to you?"

I nodded.

He folded the note, then walked along the pool and entered one of dark archways cut into the bleachers.

The students began to filter out of the locker rooms and took their place by the side of the pool. No one asked me where the coach was. When he didn't appear after several minutes, they silently lined up and began to take their laps.

I sat there, my butt getting colder and colder on the stone bench, and still the coach didn't return. No one was looking at me. Enough of this. There was someone I needed to talk to.

I walked back up to the ground floor. My first day at the school, after I'd fled the cafeteria, I'd found the library by accident. The corridors still all looked the same to me, but after wandering more or less at random, I found the library doors again. They were shut this time, and at first I thought they were locked, but a hard pull got one to open.

Once again the place seemed to be empty of people. There was no one at the front desk, but I couldn't just call out for help—library rules were baked into my DNA. I walked up and down the stacks, past the ancient books, the faint lettering on their spines calling weakly like the voices of elderly hospital patients.

At the end of one of the rows, the room opened up to a space with several wide oak tables. It was very dim, and Professor Freytag leaned over one of the tables, gazing down at a map unrolled to cover most of the table. One hand was tucked behind his back, and the other gripped the side of his head, pulling at his white hair.

"Hello?" I said, keeping my voice low.

He didn't seem to hear me. I walked closer and said, "Professor?"

He whirled to face me. "Look what they've done!" he cried. His eyes were wild.

I held up my hands. "I don't know if you remember me—"

"I've never seen you before in my life. Hah!" He shook his head as if clearing it. "My apologies for shouting. I'm not used to . . . visitors. You frightened me."

"Sorry about that."

" 'Startled' is perhaps the better word. There's no reason for *me* to be frightened, is there? Forget I ever said the word." He turned back to the map. "I get so frustrated sometimes. People come to the library and leave things lying about. Not even refiling them correctly. Just look at this."

It was a nautical map, showing a jagged coastline, and swirls of blue lines to indicate the sea depths. "Is this Dunnsmouth?" I asked.

"Right over here," the librarian said, and waved his hand at the coast. On paper Dunnsmouth bay looked even more like a crocodile mouth.

"My mother left the Dunnsmouth dock in a charter boat," I said. "The police said it went down about fifteen miles out."

"Fifteen miles, eh?" Professor Freytag's finger hovered over the map. His finger drifted slowly from Dunnsmouth, like a boat heading out to sea, and then pointed at a blank spot in the middle of the map. "Perhaps about there, if they went due east."

"I don't see any islands out there," I said.

"No, not a one."

"Are there, I don't know, coral reefs or something?" I thought of the story problem from geometry class. "Big granite rocks? Sand bars?"

"Close in to the bay we have sharp rocks indeed. But not out there, my boy. At least according to this map." He raised his eyebrows. "Why? Is there a mystery afoot?"

"That's why I came here," I said. "You like riddles, right?"

"You've come to the right man!"

I showed him the note I found on the porch last night. The librarian refused to take it. "Open it, please."

I unfolded it. He leaned back, squinting through those grimy glasses.

" 'She's still alive,' " he read. "Ah! And you want to know who this 'she' is."

"I know that. It's my mother. It's the second part. Where do I find an albatross?"

He straightened his glasses. "Why, around the neck of the old sailor, I suppose." He turned and strode down one of the rows of shelves.

"What sailor?" I asked, and hurried after him.

The professor suddenly stopped, turned back, then reversed himself again. He pointed at a shelf at waist height. "Grab that one, my boy. Samuel Taylor Coleridge. 'The Rime of the Ancient Mariner.' "

The book was very thin, almost a pamphlet. I opened it and saw a narrow column of text. "It's a poem."

"A beautiful poem of death and rebirth," the librarian said. He sounded elated.

"I don't think the note is about a poem."

"Don't be silly," he said. "A note can be about anything. A poem, even more so. They're practically equivalent."

"Okay, but—"

"You'll thank me later," Professor Freytag said. "Now, if you'll kindly shut the door on your way out? I have important work to do, and I don't want to be disturbed."

This seemed like a strange attitude for a librarian to take. Then again, it was no stranger than anything else in this school. I did as the professor asked and closed the door behind me, then made my way back to the pool. I'd just reached the staircase when a deep voice stopped me.

"Mr. Harrison. What are you doing here?"

I froze, and turned. Principal Montooth stepped out of the shadow of a doorway.

"Just going back to class," I said.

Montooth said nothing.

"Physical Education," I said. "Swimming. With Coach Shug?"

"I know your course schedule," he said. "I meant, why are you here at all? You know that you're excused from classes during your . . . family emergency."

"I guess I needed to do something," I said. "Just sitting there . . . I was going crazy."

He looked at the book in my hand, and his eyes narrowed. I suddenly realized that I hadn't checked the book out. Professor Freytag had just let me take it.

"I better get back," I said.

"Just a moment," he said. He took a step closer and put a firm hand on my shoulder. "Is there any word on your mother?"

"Nothing yet," I said. I kept "The Rime of the Ancient Mariner" down by my side.

"No updates from the Coast Guard?"

"No sir. We're just . . . waiting."

He squeezed my shoulder. "Waiting is always the most difficult part." He released me and said, "If you need anything, my door is always open."

"Sure," I said. "Of course."

"But let's avoid running around the school unsupervised," he said. His smile seemed forced. "It's easy to get lost here."

"Yes, sir."

I could feel him watching me until I disappeared around the turn in the stairs.

I spent the rest of the day sneaking quick reads of "The Rime of the Ancient Mariner." It was weird stuff. I'm good with language, but there were so many words I'd never heard before. Like right at the beginning of the poem, an old sailor (the ancient mariner himself) grabs a guy before he can go to a wedding:

> *He holds him with his skinny hand,*
> *"There was a ship," quoth he.*
> *"Hold off! Unhand me, grey-beard loon!"*
> *Eftsoons his hand dropped he.*

Who says "eftsoons"?

I started reading the poem again from the beginning on my way home from school. It made more sense on the second try, but I was no closer to figuring out if it had anything to do with the note.

A voice said, "Hey there, Harrison."

I looked up from the book. Saleem sat behind the wheel of his taxi, the window down. He was parked in front of the Standard Grocery.

I walked over to the car. "Delivering food again?" I asked.

"Sort of. I'm waiting for somebody to finish shopping. What are you so engrossed in?"

I showed him the book. "Ever read it?"

"Nope, sorry. Is it any good?"

"It's crazy," I said. "This ship is stranded in Antarctica, surrounded by icebergs. Then they're saved when this albatross leads them through the ice to warmer waters. And the main guy, the ancient mariner, just shoots the albatross with his crossbow."

"Why?"

"I don't know! He just shoots it, for no good reason."

"Maybe he was hungry."

"Maybe. But then he doesn't eat it. As punishment, he wears the bird around his neck for the rest of the voyage. Then they meet Death, or maybe some spirit woman who rides around with Death, and everybody dies."

"That's what you get when you hang out with Death," Saleem said.

"Everybody dies but the mariner. Then the crew turns into zombies and steers the ship home. The mariner then has to spend the rest of his life going around telling everybody his story."

"That's wicked homework, dude."

"It's not homework. I just thought the poem would help me figure something out. Somebody, uh, told me to look for an albatross."

An elderly woman walked out of the grocery story carrying two full paper bags. Saleem hopped out of the car to help her.

"Good luck finding one," he said. "At least you're by the sea."

"Yeah, I was just down at the—" Before I could say "docks" it came to me.

"Albatross" was a name. I began to run.

9

Like one that on a lonesome road
Doth walk in fear and dread . . .
. . . Because he knows a frightful fiend
Doth close behind him tread.

The bay was more deserted than this morning. It was afternoon, and the lobster boats were evidently still out to sea. The buildings near the water seemed empty. At the pier, a few sailboats bobbed in their berths, no crews or passengers in sight.

So. The pier. The wooden structure stretched over the dark water, and I could almost hear it creaking, giving way.

I told myself I was being ridiculous. I'd already walked all the way out to the shack and had made it back unharmed. It wasn't like being out on a boat. It wasn't like being *in* the water at all. A pier was practically an extension of the land, right?

I took a deep breath and started walking. As I mounted the pier I kept my eyes straight ahead like a tightrope walker.

I finally reached the wooden shack. The slate board hung on the wall as before. I ran my finger down the list of boats with berths here. The *Huginn,* Hal Jonsson's boat, was crossed out, but its name was still visible. Other slots were more thoroughly erased. The one name I was looking for wasn't visible.

Where was the *Albatross?*

The entrance to the shack was a heavy metal door plastered with old tobacco ads and flyers for used watercraft. The door complained as I pushed through. Inside, the shack looked like a tree fort nailed together by clumsy children. No line was straight, no timber true. The wooden shelves, crammed with dusty dry goods and fishing tackle, tilted at drunken angles. The warped floorboards buckled and gaped. Even the roof beams seemed out of kilter, like a drawing in which the perspective lines were drawn wrong.

Non-Euclidean geometry, I thought.

The walls swam with dead fish. Stuffed, mounted, sprayed in wax, in all sizes, from tiny gray creatures with spiny backs, to fat glossy beasts with jagged-toothed mouths, to long-tailed sharks trying to twist themselves from their wooden mounts. Threshers. An awful lot of threshers. Each creature seemed surprised, gasping for oxygen in this unmoving sea.

From the back of the room came a snort. I moved in that direction, weaving past a steel rack of propane tanks; an ice cream cooler with a smeared glass top through which I could see Styrofoam containers that I was positive didn't contain ice cream; a pegboard taller than me bristling with rusting fish hooks and drably painted lures; and a huge wooden crate filled with rope, below a sign in black marker that said HAND TIED NETS.

Set into the walls at the far corner of the shack were four small rhomboid windows, too grimy to admit much of the afternoon light. Below the windows was an L-shaped counter and a large, old-fashioned cash register. A man sat slumped against the counter, head on his arms, snoring.

I stood for half a minute, unsure if I should wake him up. He was a large man, or perhaps a small man wearing a great many clothes. At least three layers of shirts were visible, and above those he wore a black cable-knit sweater, a multi-pocketed vest, a thick jacket, and a hooded raincoat. Under the hood he wore at least two wool caps. If the man ever needed medical treatment the doctors would have to hire archeologists.

Finally I said, "Excuse me?"

The man didn't move. If it wasn't for the snoring I would have taken him for dead.

After another thirty seconds I reached out and poked him in the arm.

"*Excuse me*," I said. "I'm looking for a boat."

The man snorted, then coughed. But still he didn't open his eyes.

"I said, I'm looking for—"

His head jerked up. His black-and-gray beard appeared to be leaping from his face like a startled cat. "I heard you the first time!" he said.

He looked left, then right. He rubbed his fingers across his mouth. His hands were covered in fingerless gloves, and the fingers themselves were almost black, insulated by a layer of oil and soot. Finally he said, "*What* are you looking for?"

"A boat," I said.

"Ocean's full of 'em," he said. He reached for a tin can and spit into it.

"The *Albatross*," I said.

He squinted at me, reached out for the tin can again. "Never heard of it."

He was lying; I was sure of it. So I decided to lie myself.

"It was on the slate outside," I said. "But it's been erased."

The man worked his lips as if he were about to say something, then seemed to change his mind.

I said, "What I want to know is, where is it now?"

The man trembled like a diesel engine cranking up, suddenly angry. "Get out of here!"

"Just tell me where it is and I'll leave."

A sharp pain like a dagger of ice cut into my right leg. I almost yelped. "Phantom pain" is an oxymoron.

"That's right, Chilly Bob," said a voice behind me. "Answer the boy's question and he'll leave."

I pivoted on my meat leg. A man leaned against the wall. His head was bowed, and he wore a wide-brimmed hat that hid his face. A coat hung to his knees. The material of the hat and coat gleamed like the skin of a seal. I hadn't heard the door open, but I was sure he hadn't been there when I walked in.

He still hadn't looked up. He was carving something—a hunk of pale stone, or perhaps bone—using a thin, curving knife that tapered to an invisible point. His hands were skinny and claw-like, with yellowing nails.

The man behind the counter—Chilly Bob—seemed to deflate. "I told him," he said. "I told him. Never heard of it."

The man in the broad hat continued to flick at the stone in his hands. *Scritch. Scritch.*

"I swear," Bob said.

"Hmm," the stranger said. His voice seemed to lick at the air. "Then I guess the boy's hit a bit of a wall."

My chest tightened. I turned away from the two men and walked toward the front door, trying to ignore the pain in my leg. At every moment I could feel them behind me. I tensed, waiting for the carver to stop me.

But no. I reached the door, and then I was outside. The sky had dimmed, but there was still an hour of sunlight left. I fastened my eyes on the shore and walked quickly away.

I didn't look back until I reached the gravel parking lot. There was no sign of Chilly Bob, or the man with the knife. The steely cold in my leg had subsided. I started uphill toward town, and then heard the putt-putt of a boat motor. A small orange outboard chugged away from the end of the pier. In it was a bulky figure that could only have been Chilly Bob. The boat crossed the bay, heading for a group of large, box-like buildings huddled near the water.

I jogged along the access road that circled the bay, trying to keep the boat in sight, but it slipped behind one of the buildings . . .

and didn't appear on the other side. On the wall of the building, in big faded letters, it said J. RUCK'S MARINE ENGINEERING.

What would have made that fat man get out from behind the counter as soon as I'd left the shack?

A steep paved driveway ran from the road down to the buildings at the water's edge. I jogged down the slope, and slowed when I reached J. Ruck's. The building's walls were aluminum, the bolts weeping rust. There were no doors or windows on this side.

The driveway ended about five feet from the water, with only a short cement parking block to stop runaway cars. The last of the afternoon light painted the bay with burning orange; the shore on this side of the bay was already in deep shadow. I needed to get home—but not just yet.

Stone stairs led down to my right, to the front of J. Ruck's. I couldn't hear Chilly Bob's engine. The only sounds were the slap of the waves. I walked carefully down the stairs, listening at each step for voices.

At the bottom of the stairs I pressed against the wall of the building, thinking, Maybe this was a mistake. When the sun fell behind the hill, the light would go out like a door slamming closed and I'd be left wandering around in the dark.

I leaned out to get a look at the bay side of the building. It was like an airplane hangar for boats, with a wide doorway almost twenty feet high open to the water. Its corrugated metal door was pulled a quarter of the way down, like a drooping eyelid. I could see only a few feet inside the building, but from the interior came an angry shout that sounded like Bob.

I edged closer to the doorway, then peeked inside. It was a boat mechanic's garage, with an open rectangle of water in the floor. Bob's orange outboard floated there, empty.

On the dry side of the garage, a yacht or fishing boat sat up on lifts. It seemed abnormally large—but then, boats always did seem bigger out of the water. It had to be over sixty feet long, with a big main cabin, and a high bridge above it. Rails curved around the bow. The bottom half of the craft, from the deck rails down, was covered in a gray tarp.

No one was in the room. But in the middle of the back wall was a door, ajar, and a well-lit room behind it. Bob's barking voice came from in there. I couldn't make out the words. I edged around the water bay, then made my way toward the door.

"That's what I'm telling you," Chilly Bob said. "The Scrimshander showed up soon as that boy did."

Whoa. They were talking about *me*.

A voice murmured in reply, and Bob said, "If the boy knows, then who else does? You got to get on that phone and get him to take it *out* of here."

I reached the doorway, then slowly slid my head sideways until one eye was just barely around the frame. Bob stood ten feet away. His back was to the door, and his bulk prevented me from seeing who he was talking to.

The unseen man—J. Ruck, maybe?—said something else that I couldn't catch. Then Bob said, "That's *his* problem, ain't it? If those Uxton cops show up, it's not the Congregation that hangs—we do."

The men kept arguing. I looked at the tarp-covered boat on the other side of the garage.

I had to know.

I made sure Bob was still blocking the door, then slipped across the wedge of open light. I tried to move quietly, and had to step carefully over hoses and electrical cords strewn across the cement. The space was crowded with tool chests on rollers and canisters marked with hazardous material stickers.

Several overlapping tarps covered the ship from the deck to the bottom of the hull. The name of the boat would be on the bow, or at the very back of the ship. Bow first, I decided.

I found a gap between two tarps near the front of the ship and started rolling the canvas back. It was clear where the waterline usually was. Above the line, the hull was painted white, but below it was caked with barnacles and dark grime that could have been old algae. I kept pushing the tarp back, then stopped in surprise.

A large ragged hole had been punched through the hull, just above the waterline. The hole was perhaps three feet long and almost two feet high. Above the hole, in black paint, was the name of the ship: ALBATROSS.

"Now, that's a shame," a voice said behind me.

I spun about, but the spear of icy pain in my leg told me who it was. The man in the wide-brimmed hat. The one Chilly Bob called the Scrimshander.

He wasn't looking at me. He was gazing at the chunk of white bone in his claw-like hand, and scratching at it with the tip of his long knife.

"You know what killed the cat?" the Scrimshander asked.

I couldn't make my throat work. I couldn't move.

The Scrimshander tilted his head. I could see nothing but a narrow chin and thin lips. Then he smiled. The teeth were very white, and sharp.

Then he said, "Me."

You know that phrase, "My knees went weak"? I thought it only happened to people in love songs.

I fell forward, my meat leg as dead as my carbon-fiber one. My hand seized on the canvas, and as I fell the material popped free of whatever held it to the ship. The cloth dropped onto the Scrimshander. He shrugged it aside and moved toward me. I was on all fours, my heart pounding. He reached for me.

The *Albatross* rested on a metal lift. I rolled under the crossbars, then scrambled to a crouch. Too fast, and too high; I bashed my scalp against the keel and stumbled toward the other side of the boat.

The opening to the bay was maybe thirty feet away. I ran, stumbling over hoses and extension cords. I'd almost reached the garage door when I realized I couldn't get out that way; the boat bay, still holding Bob's outboard, blocked me.

The metal door began to descend, the metal wheels shrieking in their tracks. I cut left to circle around the boat bay—

—and the Scrimshander was waiting for me. He'd come around the other side of the *Albatross*. He stalked forward, his head still bowed. The knife dangled at his side, twitching like a fish on the line.

I looked at the water in the boat bay. I knew what I had to do. Jump in, swim under the garage door, then get to the shore and the road.

Now, I thought.

My legs didn't move.

Now!

My body wouldn't obey. My eyes were fixed on the surface of the black water, and I seemed to be hovering above my right shoulder, watching myself. Screaming at myself.

The Scrimshander grabbed me by the throat. "What's the matter? Can't swim?" He squeezed my trachea, choking me. I grabbed at his arm with both hands. The skin of his black coat slid from my grip like something alive.

"Me, I love the water,'" he said. He walked me backward, toward the boat bay. "Practically born to it."

I sucked in air, but his grip was too strong. The garage door rattled down, cutting off the light.

"The thing is, when you're afraid of something, there's only one thing you can do." The Scrimshander shoved me, and I flew backward. The water slapped into my back, and then I was under, into the cold.

I flailed my arms and managed to get my head above water. The Scrimshander dropped to one knee at the edge of the bay and put a hand on the top of my head, almost caressing it. He leaned close and said, "You got to dive right in."

He pushed me down, below the surface of the water, and kept a firm grip on my head, keeping me under. I clawed at his arms, but I couldn't get a grip on the slick material. I couldn't breathe, couldn't see. The water was pitch black.

I wanted to scream, but knew that if I did I would die. Still the man wouldn't let me up. I bucked against his grip, and he pushed me down farther.

I felt my pulse in my ears. My chest burned. I clamped my mouth shut and tried to reach out, to the side of the metal edge of the boat bay, but it was too far away.

Something fastened around my left ankle.

I did scream, then. The air rushed out of me.

The thing around my leg tightened, then pulled down—hard. My skull blazed with pain; it felt like a chunk of hair had been torn out by the roots.

The thing dragged me down, down. My lungs burned, and spots erupted in my vision. I saw my father. He was looking at my face, and he was saying, "Look at the jellyfish." His voice was clear and strong, and for the first time I could remember what he sounded like. I thought, Hi, Dad.

And then I wasn't thinking of anything at all.

10

How long in that same fit I lay,
I have not to declare;
But ere my living life return'd,
I heard, and in my soul discern'd
Two voices in the air.

I woke in the dark, something sharp digging into my back. I moved onto my side to get away from the pain, but then something burned in my chest and I coughed. Water sprayed from my lips. Someone slapped me between my shoulder blades and I coughed again, then again, desperate to clear my lungs.

Finally I stopped convulsing and breathed deep. I became aware that I was wet, and very cold. I opened my eyes.

I lay on my side on a rocky beach. The water was only a dozen feet away, and Dunnsmouth Bay gleamed in the moonlight. I tried to remember where I was. I'd been at the pier, then . . .

I jerked to a sitting position. Someone was squatting next to me, skin glistening like an eel's.

I shouted and scrambled backward. "Get away from me!" My voice was a raw bark.

The figure rose to its feet.

It was the fish boy. His large eyes caught the moonlight. His wide mouth was set in a thin straight line that turned down at each end, and that jaw looked like it could unhinge and swallow a toaster. He raised one hand and spread his fingers. Webbed fingers.

For a long moment we stared at each other.

Finally I said, "You saved me, didn't you?"

He blinked slowly.

"And you can understand me?"

His gills opened on each side of his neck, then flapped shut.

"Just nod if you understand what I'm saying," I said.

"Okay," the fish boy said.

"You can talk!"

"You should keep your voice down," he said. His own voice was low and resonated strangely. His accent, too, was off-kilter, as if all the vowels had taken a step to the left. "We're not that far from the pier."

"You can talk!" I said again.

"Okay, you're in shock," he said. "That's probably hypothermia." I didn't say anything, and the fish boy said, "That's when a human's body—"

"I know what hypothermia is." I was already shivering, and the wet clothes were sucking the warmth from me. My wet hoodie felt heavy as cement.

"We've got to get you dried off," the fish boy said. He stood up, then extended a hand. "My name's Lub."

That hand ended in claws, and reminded me too much of the Scrimshander's. But I shook it. "Thanks, Lub." At least that's what I meant to say. I was shivering so much now that all I managed to get out was a stuttering "Thanks."

"My b-b-book," I said.

"Oh, right," he said. "Newton and Leeb! Sorry about that. But I did give it back. Plus I just saved your life, so that should be worth something."

Lub was naked but for a pair of skater shorts that hung down to his knees, but he didn't seem to feel the cold. I was trembling uncontrollably now, every muscle trying to jump off my bones. I had so many more questions. *Why did you say my mother's alive? What are you? How did you find me?* But my teeth were chattering like a wind-up Halloween skull.

Lub led me up the densely wooded hill, toward a road. He was taller than me but seemed about the same height because of the way he moved, hunched over, arms swinging. He kept pausing to check on me. I was bent almost double, my arms wrapped around my stomach. My feet didn't seem to work properly. My carbon-fiber leg seemed too heavy, and I kept tripping over rocks and tree roots. Because of the shivering I could barely look left or right. I walked in a tunnel.

I bumped into a tree and then leaned against it. My mouth made a hissing sound. I was trying to say *Stop a second,* but my jaw did not want to unlock. I wanted to lie down. Get warm. I thought, Maybe if I take a nap here, just for a little while, I'll feel up to the hike home.

Lub put his arm around me. "Come on, Harrison. You can do it."

He helped me away from the tree, then half carried me up the hill. He was surprisingly strong.

Finally we reached level ground, the edge of the roadway. I tried to remember the number of the highway that ran past town—61? 65?—but my brain wouldn't cooperate. A car's headlights approached from the distance.

Lub said, "Harrison, can you talk? Can you tell them how to get home?"

Tell who? I wondered. But I nodded. "Sh-sh-sure."

"Wait here," he said. He stepped out into the middle of the road and began to wave his arms. The lights grew bright, and the car kept coming.

It's not going to stop, I thought.

Brakes squealed, and the headlights slewed from one side of the road to the other. Lub leaped off to the side. The car shuddered to a stop right where Lub had been standing.

Lub ran to me and crouched. "Terrible driver."

A car door opened, and woman's voice said, "Oh my God! What are you? Get away from him!"

"Got to go," Lub said. "Please don't tell the human about me. I'm serious. They *will* hunt me." He disappeared down the hill, into the trees.

I forced myself to walk out onto the road. A woman in a short white dress gaped at me, openmouthed, like one of the stuffed fish on the bait shop's walls.

It was Nurse Mandi. With a heart to dot the "i."

"Help," I said. I was very proud of myself that I said the word so clearly.

It was a glorious thing to be warm. The next morning, I woke up in my own bed, under half a dozen blankets. I was still drowsy, and my sleep-fuzzed brain decided it would be a good idea to never leave this bed. Mom could make me breakfast in bed, and we could . . .

No. Mom was gone. Missing.

But maybe still alive.

The memories of last night rushed back to me. I'd nearly drowned. The Scrimshander was out there, waiting. But also, Lub was out there. And for some reason that allowed me to think that Mom could really be alive. If the world contained things like a fish boy, anything was possible.

When I'd appeared at the house last night, half carried by Nurse Mandi, Aunt Sel had swung into action like a one-woman NASCAR pit crew. She put me in my bed, then stripped off my clothes. I was too dazed to be embarrassed. She struggled with my leg's snap-lock, then finally got it undone. Water poured out of it.

She found sweatpants and a T-shirt, pushed me into them, then buried me in blankets. At some point Nurse Mandi said, "We should check his . . ."

"Pulse?" Aunt Sel asked. "What?"

". . . temperature." I was surprised the nurse was still there.

Aunt Sel managed to find the thermometer in our bathroom supplies. As I lay there with the thing under my tongue, Nurse Mandi said, "I think he'll be fine."

Aunt Sel said, "Are *you* going to be fine?"

"Why would you ask me that?" Nurse Mandi said.

"Because your mascara is all down your face. Also you seem a little—"

"Heartbroken?"

"I was going to go with a different word, but sure. Man trouble?"

"There are monsters out there."

"You got that right, honey. Now, let me take care of Harrison for a minute, and you just take a seat in the living room and we'll have a nice chat."

"I really should be going."

"Nonsense. Let's have a little girl talk before you get behind the wheel all . . . heartbroken."

I must have drifted off, because the next thing I remembered, Aunt Sel was holding a cup to my lips: hot tea loaded with honey. I'd never liked tea, but I had to admit I liked the sensation of the warm liquid sliding down my throat and into my stomach. I don't remember finishing it.

Now my body ached in strange places: my shoulder, my left ankle, the top of my scalp. I gingerly patted the crown of my head, where the Scrimshander had held onto my hair—held on while Lub yanked me down.

I knew I wouldn't be able to stay in bed all day. I had to get out, and tell someone.

I'd just thrown off the covers when Aunt Sel knocked on the frame of my door. "Back in bed, kid. It's Saturday. Besides, I'm not letting you leave the house."

"We have to call the police," I said.

"Why? What happened?"

"There's a boat. It's called the *Albatross*, and it's in the garage down by the bay. At a place called J. Ruck's Marine Engineering."

"This is where you fell in and banged your head? All you said last night was, 'I fell in the water.'"

"It's got a hole in it, Aunt Sel—right in front. The boat rammed my mom's boat. Or something. I'm not sure how. But I think—"

"Okay, okay," she said. "But breakfast first."

She brooked no disagreement. She sat me at the kitchen table with an afghan around my shoulders and wouldn't allow me to speak until I'd finished a bowl of cereal and a tall glass of orange juice. Nurse Mandi, thankfully, was not still in the house.

Aunt Sel sat beside me. "Okay, who told you this *Albatross* rammed your mother's boat?"

"Nobody told me."

"So you just *decided* the boat had something to do with it?"

I tried to think through how much I could tell her without giving Lub away. "I got a note," I said. "An anonymous note." I told her what it said, and how I'd gone down to the docks to look for a boat with that name, and followed Chilly Bob to the boat garage.

"Chilly Bob," she said skeptically.

"He runs the bait shop," I said. "Maybe he's cold or something."

"Or makes chili."

"It doesn't matter," I said. "The point is, I found the *Albatross*, hiding under a tarp. It had a hole in it. I was going to leave then, but then—"

I couldn't finish.

"Harrison?" Her voice went soft. "What happened?" She must have seen something in my face. "You can tell me."

I took a breath. "There was a man there. He caught me in the building, and he had a knife, and he chased me."

"You were *attacked*? Who was it? What did he—?"

"I don't know his name. Chilly Bob called him the Scrimshander. He pushed me under the water—and then I got away."

I couldn't tell her about Lub. She probably wouldn't believe me if I did.

Aunt Sel was up and pacing the small room. "We've got to call the police."

"That's what I've been saying! This guy, and whoever was on the *Albatross*—they sunk Mom's boat. I'm sure of it. There was no rock or island out there in the middle of the ocean. No storm. This is the only thing that makes sense."

"But why in the world would they do that?"

"I don't know," I said.

Aunt Sel puffed her cheeks, exhaled heavily.

I said, "You believe me, don't you?"

Aunt Sel sat down again, and put her hand on mine. "I want you to hear this. I believe completely that you saw what you say you saw. Whether the hole in the boat means that—well, we'll find out. None of that matters compared to arresting the man who attacked you."

Chief Bode came that afternoon. He perched his chubby body on the edge of the chair and took careful notes while I talked.

I told him the story as I'd told it to Aunt Sel, leaving out nothing—except for Lub. The chief seemed to write every word, asking me to repeat a phrase or slow down. He asked many questions. But as the interview went on it became clear that he was believing my story less and less. And when I said the word "Scrimshander" he looked at me for a long moment, then put down his pencil.

"What?" Aunt Sel asked. "You think he's making this up?"

Chief Bode put up his hands. My aunt's directness could be alarming. "It's not that, ma'am," he said. "But this Scrimshander fella—"

"Ask Chilly Bob," I said. "The Scrimshander was there." I told the chief everything I could remember about him, from hat to knife. I even described his teeth.

"Pointy teeth," Chief Bode said.

"That's right," I said.

Bode looked over my head at Aunt Sel. I hated that look. "You see, ma'am, the Scrimshander's kind of a local myth."

"A myth?" she asked.

"Like Sasquatch," he said. "The boogeyman."

"He was *there*," I said.

"Talk to this Bob person!" Aunt Sel said.

"I will, I will," the chief said. "I'm sure there was *somebody* there. Probably one of the lobstermen who works out there. But as for it being, well . . ." He gave me a tight-lipped smile. "I get it, son. You've been under a lot of pressure, what with your mom going missing."

"Do *not* condescend," Aunt Sel said icily. I made a note to myself: Never piss off Aunt Sel. "You *will* look into this man, and the boat, yes?"

"I'll ask around. You said he had a . . ." He thumbed through his notes. "A hat."

"Yes," I said evenly. "And a knife. A big knife."

"Well, everybody's got a knife around here," he said.

"I'm sure they do," Aunt Sel said. "As for this boat—"

"That's another thing," Bode said. "This ramming theory?"

"What about it?" I asked.

"The *Albatross* has been up on blocks for weeks. Well before your mom went out on the water."

I didn't know how to absorb this information. I felt like an idiot. I'd been so *sure*.

If Aunt Sel doubted me, she didn't let on in front of the chief. She thanked him for his time, walked him to the front door.

"Wait," I said. I went back to my bedroom and fished through the pockets of my jeans. The green paper was nearly destroyed by my dunk in the water, the ink smeared. I took it back to the living room and handed it to the chief.

"Someone put that on our truck," I said. "The morning my mom disappeared."

"I can't make heads or tails of this," he said.

"It says, 'Stay out of the water.' It was a threat. An anonymous threat."

"Right." He wrote in his notebook. "A-nonymous. Got it." He tucked the paper into his shirt pocket. "So how long will you two be staying, now that the search is called off?"

"What?" I looked at Aunt Sel. "You knew this."

"Detective Hammersmith called this morning," she said. "You were sleeping."

"They can't do that!"

"It's been four days," the chief said. "That's well beyond what they usually allow."

I wheeled on him. "Get away from me, you useless piece of—"

"Harrison!" Aunt Sel said.

"Watch yourself, boy," the chief said.

Aunt Sel stepped between us and put a hand on my chest. "Chief Bode, like you said, this is a stressful time."

She gave me the tiniest shove, like a ref directing a boxer to his corner of the ring, and I stalked back to my bedroom.

That afternoon I did nothing but fume, sulk, brood, and seethe. Not very productive activities, but at least I was good at them. I refused to talk to Aunt Sel, and I ate in silence. At nine I went to my bedroom again, sure that I wouldn't be able to sleep—until my body shut down on its own. Evidently I was still recovering from the dunk in the bay.

I woke up Sunday feeling calmer. All that emotion from yesterday seemed like it belonged to someone else. My temper had caused me problems, but punching a cop would have been a new high point in my career as a juvenile delinquent. Mom would have been so disappointed. We'd talked for years about controlling what she called my "dual nature": one side calm and analytical, and one . . . volcanic.

Aunt Sel immediately read my change of mood. "You look like a man who needs waffles."

"That would be great," I said.

"Any idea how to make them?"

She called Saleem. I told her I could drive, but she wasn't hearing it. He arrived in half an hour and drove us to a diner in Uxton. By the time we arrived we were famished, and I plowed through an order of pancakes, bacon, and fried eggs.

"Civilization," Aunt Sel said. "I'll be glad to get out of Dunnsmouth, I'll tell you that." Then: "Did I offend you?"

I realized I'd sat back from the table. "No. It's . . . fine."

She frowned at me. "Out with it."

"I'm not giving up on her," I said. "You can leave if you want to, but I'm staying."

Saleem looked uncomfortable. "I need to call in," he said. "See you outside."

After he left, Aunt Sel said, "I'm not leaving, Harrison. And I won't pressure you to leave, either."

"Really?"

"I can put up with bad food, a lack of culture, and zero cell phone service. I do worry about you, though. Running off like that on your own to find that boat. You have a genetic predisposition for obsession. From both sides. No wonder your grandfather was worried about you coming back here."

"Well, worried about his son coming back here," I said. "He didn't know it was me."

"The details were wrong, but the concern was well-founded."

"Tell me what happened," I said. "I only know what my mom told me, and obviously she left things out."

"Hmm, like that the accident happened near Dunnsmouth?"

"And what my dad was doing there in the first place."

Aunt Sel crossed her legs. "It's so hard to finish a meal without a cigarette in my hand. I do miss them. Whatever you do, don't start."

"Tell me," I said.

She took a breath. "I can't tell you much. I could never keep up with your father's enthusiasms. Do you know what a cultural anthropologist is?"

"Somebody who studies culture," I said.

"Close—it's someone who bores you to death at dinner parties. Oh, I tried to stay conscious as he described the latest cult or superstition he was tracking down, but your mother was the only woman I know who was *actually* interested. Not very successful on dates, your father. He got lucky when he found a geek as beautiful as your mother. No offense."

"None taken. She *is* a beautiful geek. But you don't know why they came out here?"

"Nothing specific. I know he was on sabbatical from Stanford, and couldn't understand why he was going to spend it in the dreariest location possible. You all came along for the trip. You were just a toddler. Why you all ended up on a boat on the Atlantic Ocean in the middle of the night . . . well, your mother never could explain that. And then when you were hurt . . ."

I flashed on an image: a creature with skin like onyx, eyeless, with a round mouth ringed by razor teeth.

"Are you okay?" Aunt Sel asked.

"I'm fine." I didn't know where that memory had come from. "Go on."

"Well," she said. "The Coast Guard had trouble believing that some shark or squid had attacked you. Probably why she changed her story when she told it to you. She was in shock when she called your grandfather. The size of the creature she described . . . well, not exactly credible. If she was confused, or had hallucinated some of it, no one blamed her for it. She nearly died of hypothermia. That's when—"

"I know what hypothermia is."

"Somehow she got you to shore, and you were life-flighted to Boston for emergency surgery. You almost died of blood loss. Then afterward there was some kind of rare infection that kept you in the ICU for weeks." She exhaled, then smiled humorlessly.

"Your mother wasn't the same after that. She did nothing but take care of you for the next two years. And of course she'd lost your father. When she went back to grad school we thought she was finally, well, healing. I had no idea till now that this new focus of hers was still all about what happened to you and your father. I think it's clear now that she always intended to come back here to find . . . whatever it is she thinks she saw."

"Don't make her sound crazy," I said.

"You have to admit, it's all rather Ahab-ish." She paused. "Harrison?"

"Right," I said. I'd had a thought. Several of them, actually. There were at least three things that I needed to be doing right *now*. And most important was to find Lub. He knew something about the *Albatross*. And he knew—somehow—that my mother was alive. But how was I supposed to find him?

"Harrison, look at me."

"Yeah?"

She reached across the table to put a hand on my arm. "Promise me you won't let Dunnsmouth change you. I don't want to come back here in five years and start searching for *you* out in the ocean."

Oh, but she didn't understand: I was already changed. I knew things I didn't know before. I'd met a boy with *gills*. There were monsters out on the water, and on the land.

"No promises," I said.

11

She was surrounded by a sea of pale faces. Their eyes seemed to shift in the flickering light of the oil lamps, so even when her captor was gone, as he was now, Rosa Gabriel Harrison felt as if she was being watched.

Her prison was a cave, but the walls were lined on three sides with shelves made of glossy polished driftwood that held irregularly shaped slabs of white and yellow, some as small as tea saucers, others wide as serving platters, still others long and thin as broom handles. On each surface was a delicately etched portrait: men, women, and children, alone or arranged in family groupings. They stared down at her from shelves that started at chest height and rose into the dark like rows in a coliseum.

She recognized the materials and the method by which the portraits were made. This was scrimshaw, made by scratching with knife or sewing needle at the material of whales—whalebone or baleen, tusk or teeth—until the picture was complete and the lines were filled with black ink. She'd never seen examples so beautiful, or so awful. The faces were mournful, and they seemed to be pitying her.

Her wrists were bound in thick, scratchy rope, and a second length of rope encircled her waist and bound her to a rusty, centuries-old anchor that leaned in the corner. It was eleven feet tall, shaped like a pickax, and weighed somewhere north of a thousand pounds. She could move only a few feet in any direction, and could not reach the shelves, or the belongings of her captor.

He'd assembled furniture worthy of a hermit: a wooden table with a single chair; a chest where he kept his knives and other tools; a collection of nautical bric-a-brac, like the iron trident that hung from a wooden rack in a place of honor. She lusted for that trident. The sharp tips could have cut through her bonds easily.

But the only thing in range of her tether was her "bed," a pile of sailcloth. Some of that cloth had been used like a straitjacket to bind her and drag her from the boat.

She wasn't sure how long she had been in the cave, or even if it was day or night. The light never changed, and her watch and cell phone had been taken from her when they pulled her out of the water. Then she'd been brought to another cave, where she met . . . something. Something gigantic that spoke like a woman but smelled like an abattoir. Rosa had lain in that cave for hours, until she was bundled up again, thrown onto a hard shoulder, and taken here. Wherever that was.

Her body was the only way to measure time. Her captor had fed her eight times—if you could call what he brought her "food"—and judging from her hunger those meals were eight to twelve hours apart. But could her body be trusted? Adrenaline did strange things to one's sense of time, and she was already exhausted from the crash and the unrelenting chill of the cave. She knew only that sometimes she slept, and sometimes her captor sat with her for what seemed like hours, talking in that low, insinuating tone, polishing the plate of white bone in his hands . . . and then he would slip away to retrieve her food and do whatever errands a kidnapper needed to do. He'd left an hour ago, if she was judging time correctly, and she didn't know how much time she had left before he returned. Better make the most of it.

For perhaps the two-hundredth time since that hour began, and an uncountable number of times since she'd woken up here, she gripped the rope that tied her to the anchor. Then she crouched, leaned back to take up the slack, and kicked backward. The rope bit into her spine and she suppressed a grunt.

The anchor did not move.

She crouched, took a breath, and kicked back again. And again.

She thought she felt the anchor shift a millimeter. But she only needed a dozen millimeters to reach her goal. She turned toward the nearest wall, and strained against the rope, her arms outstretched for the nearest portrait.

It was a picture of a couple. A handsome man in his thirties, and his dark-haired wife with wide eyes that seemed both hopeful and deeply sad. They seemed to know what she needed. The edge of the plate was scalloped, and tapered to paper thinness. In the right hands it could be a serrated knife, she thought.

Rosa exhaled, willing herself to be thinner (and she *was* thinner, losing weight every day), and threw herself against the rope.

An inch of air separated her fingers from that portrait.

The couple regarded her with pity. Rosa looked up at the rows and rows of faces. A child with piercing black eyes. A sailor from the last century, staring in terror. A kind-faced man with thick glasses, wearing a cardigan sweater.

What about the rest of you? she thought. You want me to live or die? Or do you just want me to entertain you down here?

The mob remained silent.

"*Vá à merda,*" she said.

She could not give up. Her son was waiting for her. She wasn't about to make him an orphan.

She turned back to the anchor, gripped the rope, and took a breath. Then she heard the clank of a metal bucket striking rock. It sounded impossibly close—but sounds were tricky down here.

Quickly she lay down in the pile of sailcloth. And then, though she hated to make herself more vulnerable, she closed her eyes.

There was no sound for a long time . . . and then he was in the room with her. A thunk as the bucket dropped to the rocky floor. A scrape of chair leg, and then a creak as her captor sat.

"I know you're awake," he said teasingly. "Don't you want your supper?"

She decided to sit up.

She'd grown up in a dangerous town, and had traveled in dangerous places; she'd read all the advice about surviving a kidnapping. Her job in this moment was to make her captor feel at ease. To establish rapport. To make him see her as a human.

If only she was sure that *he* was human.

He slouched in the chair, his wide hat pulled low over his face. Watching her. The bucket had been dropped within range of the tether. "Here's one that didn't get away," he said.

She scooted over to it. The past meals had each been a single can of food—navy beans the first time, then soups, and vegetables, and once, bizarrely and unsatisfyingly, cranberry sauce—rolling about in rusty water that was her ration of drinking water. And when the water was gone, it would become her slop bucket. One bucket for all needs. She tried not to think about that.

She peered inside.

It was a whole fish—an Atlantic cod.

"State fish of Massachusetts," Rosa said.

"Aren't you a smarty girl."

There was water in the bucket, and she hoped it wasn't salt water this time. She lifted out the fish. She could tell by its clear eyes that it was fresh—possibly killed within the hour.

"You don't mind a little of the raw stuff, do you?" the captor asked.

"I love sushi," she said. Thinking: Joke with him. Put him at ease. "I don't suppose you'd cut it open for me, would you?" He'd at least had the courtesy to open the lids of the canned food.

"If you're hungry enough, you'll make do." He smiled. His teeth were bright and sharp.

He opened the wooden chest and brought out a rectangle of sandpaper and the slab of white whale jawbone he'd been working on for days. "You're a lucky one," he said, and ran the sandpaper over the face of the bone. "This is prime canvas. An *honor*."

He'd told her this a dozen times, but again she nodded, showing her appreciation. He'd spent hours polishing that bone. Cooing over it. It was maddening.

She pushed back the cod's operculum, the gill cover, and yanked out the gills. She looked for a place to put the organs. He stopped his polishing and watched her. She realized there was only one place he'd allow her to place them. She dropped them into the bucket.

"Can't rush the polishing," he said. "It's porous, you know, and if you don't sand it down it'll suck all the ink. Look how smooth it is! Like pearl."

"You do beautiful work," she said. She tried to make it sound sincere.

"No one cares about quality these days," he said.

She worked her thumbs into the space where the gills had been. If her hands were untied, she'd simply rip down along the belly now, but she had no leverage. She glanced up at her captor.

"Problem?" he asked.

"Just considering my options," she said. If her captor expected her to be squeamish, he'd picked the wrong woman. She'd eaten and cooked fish her entire life, and for the past twenty years she'd studied and dissected scores of species. She knew her way around a straightforward specimen like the cod. And she understood that if she was going to have the strength to escape, she needed all the protein she could get.

She gripped the head of the fish in her bound hands, getting her thumbs deep inside the gills, then bit into its belly just behind the ventral fin. She tugged down with her hands, and flesh began to rip. She paused to get a firmer bite, tugged once more, and the fish practically unzipped for her. Gore spilled onto her shirt, but she figured it was worth it.

She quickly dug out the intestines and the other internal organs, dropping those into the bucket as well. She hoped there was enough moisture in the meat of the fish that she wouldn't have to drink that water.

"You've done this before," her captor said. He seemed disappointed.

"Not exactly like this," she said. "But I've cleaned a lot of fish."

"You don't say." He leaned forward and snatched the cod from her. She almost yelled, but held her tongue.

He sniffed at the fish, now open for him like a book. "Mmm," he said. Then he bit down and ripped out a long chunk of white, steak-like flesh. It hung from his pointy teeth, and then he flipped it up like a dog and swallowed it whole.

Rosa was too angry to cry. If she could have reached him, she would have strangled him.

He tore into the fish with gusto. A minute later he looked up, smiling. "You know, I almost had your boy for lunch."

Rosa went cold. Her vision blurred, then snapped back into focus.

"What did you do?" she asked softly.

"Nothing," he said. "Missed him by a hair." He tossed the flapping carcass into a far corner, well out of her reach.

"Now," he said, and licked two long, yellow-nailed fingers. "Back to work." He picked up the whalebone. He held it up to the light and said, "I think we're ready."

She could think of nothing but Harrison now.

"Turn to the left," he said. "I said turn!"

She shifted her body.

"No, just your face. That's it. Straight on. Full of grit."

She stared at him. The brim still hid his eyes.

He unsheathed his long knife. Then he pressed the tip to the bone and flicked it lightly.

Rosa felt a whisper of cold along her cheek, as if it had been brushed by the point of an icicle. She gasped, and her captor nodded.

"The first cut's the most important," he said. "Everything depends on it."

12

"Say quick," quoth he, "I bid thee say—
What manner of man art thou?"

By the time I woke up Monday it was no longer morning. Aunt Sel had decided I didn't need to go to school. She was wrong about that, but the reasons I needed to go had nothing to do with my classes.

I showered, ate quickly, and told her that I needed to take a walk—without mentioning that the walk would take me up the hill to school. When I slipped through the doors the atrium was empty. It was just before the end of the school day, eighth period. I wasn't going to world history in Mr. Waughm's room, though. I went straight to the library.

Once again, the place seemed empty. I walked to the back of the room first, and quickly found Professor Freytag in a dark corner. He was sitting on a wooden chair, with a book open on the floor in front of him. He was leaning over his knees, reading with an intense expression.

"Professor?"

He looked up in surprise. "Boy!"

"It's Harrison," I said. I don't think I'd ever told him my name.

"Oh, I wish you hadn't told me that. Names are dangerous. I wouldn't want to spill the beans."

"Right. So is that the book you were looking for?"

"This? No. This is just something someone left lying about. I know it's close, though. I can feel it."

"Well. That's . . . good."

"And what brings you to the library today? It is day, isn't it? I lose track of time. The light's always the same here—so *bright*."

"It's afternoon, sir." I didn't add that this was the most dimly lit library I'd ever been in. "I have a question for you."

"Excellent! Fire away."

"What's a scrimshander?"

The doctor lurched in his chair, a look of fear on his face. "Why do you say such a thing? I can't . . . I can't be heard discussing—"

"Please. I'm just trying to figure this out. A scrimshander does carving, right?"

The professor seemed to regain some of his composure. "Oh. The *craftsman*. You would like to know about a scrimshander in *general*?"

"That's a good start. They carve whalebone, right?"

Professor Freytag removed his glasses, blew into them, and set them back on his face. "Whalebone, yes. Also teeth, and tusks. The artworks they produce on these carvings are called scrimshaw." He hopped up from the chair and strode away. I jogged to catch up.

"It started centuries ago," the professor said as he walked. "Whaling is too dangerous to do at night, so the sailors had time on their hands, not to mention plenty of material to work with. Whalebones, baleens—that's cartilage, looks like an automobile's radiator grill, perfect for filtering out krill. Whales evolved it over fifteen million—"

"Scrimshaw?" I said, trying to steer him back to the topic.

"Ah, yes! Sailors began etching designs upon these materials with sail needles, then special knifes, and the practice soon evolved into quite the art form. I have a book, a diary . . ." He marched down one row, then abruptly turned left. "I know it's here somewhere. Ah!"

He pointed at a high shelf. "Up you go."

"Pardon?"

"Climb! It's that green one that's slightly sticking out from its mates."

I set down my backpack and eyed the shelves. Professor Freytag didn't offer me a hand, so I put a foot on the lip of one of the shelves and stepped up. The bookcase seemed sturdy. Immovable, even. I reached up to another shelf and pulled myself higher. The green book was just out of reach. I stretched on the toes of one foot, got my fingers around the green spine, and in one motion yanked it free and dropped back to the ground.

The professor seemed pleased. "That's it! *Tobias Glück: A Scrimshander's Diary*."

"Uh, thanks," I said.

"There are questions in that book," the professor said. "Important questions, buried in page after page of interminable droning. Isn't that always the way, though?"

"I was kind of hoping for answers," I said.

"You can't have quality answers without quality questions," he said.

The class gong sounded as I left the library. The hallways filled, and I surfed along the crowd, aiming for the front door. I was maybe five yards from a clean escape when Lydia appeared in front of me, scowling.

"What are you doing here?" she asked.

"Are you *mad* at me?"

"Why would I be mad at you?"

"You're always looking at me like that. With your angry face."

She frowned. "I have an angry face?"

"I take it back. That's just your default expression."

This time the scowl was more definite. I pushed past her, and she said, "Why did you go in the bay if you're afraid to even go in the pool?"

Now it was my turn to scowl. "I'm not afraid of going in the pool. And who said I was in the bay?"

"Nurse Mandi." She glanced left. Mrs. Velloc was coursing toward us like the ship of Death in "The Rime of the Ancient Mariner." "This way," Lydia said, and pulled me outside to the front steps. Students moved past us in waves, heading home.

"Some of us heard her telling Coach Shug about finding you in the middle of the road Friday night."

"Mandi was talking to the coach?" I asked.

Lydia looked at me curiously. "You sound happy."

"It's just . . . nice."

"She said you could have died from—"

"Don't say it."

"—exposure."

"I'm fine," I said.

"So what was Chief Bode doing at your house Saturday? Did they have news on your mother?"

"No, that was about—wait, are people watching my house?"

"It's a small town, Harrison."

Mrs. Velloc appeared at the top of the stairs. "Mr. Harrison. I thought that was you."

I put on a smile. "Hi, Mrs. Velloc."

"Your aunt told the office that you were suffering from a cold."

That was *kind of* the truth. "I'm feeling better. I just came to, uh . . ."

"Get his homework," Lydia said.

"Right," I said. I hefted the backpack. "I don't want to fall behind."

"Excellent idea. Lydia, could I speak with you a moment?"

"Of course," Lydia said. She glanced at me, and rubbed her index finger and thumb together. "Talk later," she whispered.

* * *

After "The Rime of the Ancient Mariner" (ROAM as I now thought of it) and now *Tobias Glück: A Scrimshander's Diary* (TGSD? That sounded like a disease), I was becoming a specialist in old-fashioned books. This new one was a historical artifact— Tobias' actual diary, not a copy. The cover was stiff cardboard like a modern book, but inside were the original pages of his journal. The paper was off-color and brittle, the edges ragged and tinged brown. The new cover was probably made after the first one had fallen apart, but it seemed like a disguise, as if someone had been trying to smuggle this old thing into the future—into my hands.

Tobias' handwriting was hard to decipher, and the dark brown ink on the discolored paper was barely legible. You couldn't miss the title, though. Tobias had written it in letters three times larger than his normal script, and had taken time to make extra loops and whorls around the characters.

Tobias Glück, his Book Consisting of Different ports & ships that I have sailed in since the year 1829, Aged 13.

Thirteen! He was just a kid.

I turned the stiff pages slowly, afraid to break them. Tobias wrote a lot about ships, chores, the habits of his crewmates, and especially food. He couldn't stop talking about food. A whole page was about a "pasty," and by the end of the description I still didn't know what it was.

A few pages in I found the first drawing, one Tobias had made himself, of an elaborate ship with two masts, flying dozens of flags from ropes. The caption read, "A poor drawing, but perhaps will make a better etching."

He'd drawn dozens of pictures, almost all of them as practice for his scrimshaw. Some were of seabirds with strange names—petrels, haglets, kittiwakes—but his favorite subjects were ships and whales. I flipped through the diary, and he got better with each passing year. During that time he worked on several different whaling ships, and seemed to visit every port on the Atlantic and a few in the South Seas.

All the things the kid had seen! Tobias had left home when he was thirteen, but he was already doing man's work, and seeing the world. If I hadn't hated the ocean so much I might have been jealous.

"You have the strangest homework," Aunt Sel said. We were having a dinner courtesy of "Chef Mike": frozen Mexican food that had been microwaved into submission. I told her I thought I'd go to bed early tonight.

"Why would anyone do that?" she asked. "Nothing good happens until eleven."

"I'd head out to the Dunnsmouth nightclubs with you, but they're all so crowded."

"Good point."

"I guess I'm still wiped from my dunk in the bay," I said, and felt only slightly bad for lying to her. I lay in bed with the covers up to my chin. The diary rested on my chest, but I wasn't really reading it. After a while I turned out my bedside lamp.

And waited.

Sometime around ten, I heard a tap-tap on my window. I slid out of the bed. I was still wearing my leg—and jeans, shirt, and socks. I pushed up the window. It squeaked, but not too loudly.

Lub smiled up at me. "Ready for another swim?"

"Not so loud," I whispered.

He was dressed as on Friday night, by which I mean he was barely dressed at all: in knee-length shorts and nothing else. His gills were folded back along his neck.

I pushed a paper sack out the window, and Lub caught it. Then I pulled on my shoes and hoodie and climbed out the window.

"Finally you're awake," the fish boy said. "I've been here the past two nights." I kept trying to place his accent—which was silly, considering the place he came from.

"Sorry about that," I said.

Lub was already looking through the bag. In it were three paperbacks: *Newton and Leeb on Patrol*; *Newton and Leeb Can't Fail*; and *Liquid Gunship* 7. He held up the Gunship book questioningly.

"It's manga," I said. "From Japan? You're going to love it."

"Okay. Cool."

"You can keep them if you want."

"Really?" He looked up. "But . . . why?"

"You saved my life."

"If I do it again, will you give me the *Treasury Edition?*"

"That's just crazy talk."

Lub put the books back in the bag. "I'd like to show you something. Can you stay out for a while?"

I looked back at the house. Would Aunt Sel check on me? And if she did, would she mind if I'd skipped out? Hard to say if she'd be angry or proud. "Sure," I said. "Let's go."

Lub led me through the trees, then uphill between two dark houses. It was chilly, and I was happy we were moving. "Tell me about the Scrimshander," I said.

"I'd never seen him before the other day," Lub said. "I'd heard of him, though. He's always been around. The Elders call him—" He made a weird moaning sound.

"That's Voluntary language," I said.

"Nope, that's my language."

"I mean, I've heard kids at school using words like that. Singing them."

"Some people in Dunnsmouth like to copy us," he said.

"Who's 'us'?"

Lub stopped. "*We* call ourselves the First. The lubbers call us the Dwellers, or sometimes the Dwellers of the Deep. But really we don't live all that deep—nine or ten fathoms."

"Lubbers?"

"Landlubbers."

"But your name is—"

"A nickname, okay?" He raised a webbed hand that I could barely see. "My siblings think I'm strange because I spend a lot of time up here."

We arrived at a clearing. We'd climbed the ridge behind Ruck's Engineering and the other bay-side buildings. The sky was clear for once, a deep black full of stars. The half-moon seemed to be admiring its reflection.

Lub pointed northeast. "Can you see that outcropping, out by the nose?"

"Barely." It was a nob at the tip of what would have been the crocodile's upper jaw.

"Just swim straight out from that point and you'll get to the shoals. Then swim for another five minutes after that, and dive. That's where we live."

"You live underwater? That's pretty cool."

"It's b-o-o-o-ring. No books, no TV, no Internet."

"That sounds like Dunnsmouth, actually. Except they have books."

"Well, we have rocks that are kind of like books, except—well, let's just say that they're not exactly Newton and Leeb. And most of us who live there are old. Really old. A lot of them barely do anything but make nets."

"You should totally come to my school."

"I'd love to go to school," Lub said. We walked along the ridge, following some path I couldn't see. "I've been stealing textbooks for years, but it's just not the same. Oh. How's my English? Good, right?"

I stumbled and had to put out a hand to steady myself. Lub never seemed to lose his footing, even though his feet were big and webbed. Maybe he just knew the area better. Or maybe his night vision was better. Those big eyes had to be good for something.

The walk turned into a climb as we moved up into the cliffs of the bay's north side. I was breathing hard, but Lub kept up a steady stream of talk. He seemed very excited to learn I was taking geometry. "I can tutor you," he said. "You wouldn't believe the stuff my people can do with geometry."

Near the top of the cliffs, bushes and trees had taken root between the rocks. Scrawny pines leaned into the air, daring each other to jump. I used their trunks and limbs as handholds to pull myself the last of the way up, to a rocky lip.

We stood on the skull of the crocodile, looking down at the bay and the scattering of lights that indicated the homes of Dunnsmouth. It was so dark. Back home there would have been brightly lit piers, rows of streetlights, gleaming buildings. But this could have been the shore as it looked to starving pilgrims.

"Man, all those *stars*," I said. I'd never seen so many, so close.

"Stars, right," Lub said. "This way."

The forest began a dozen feet from the rocky lip. I followed him into the trees, and we walked for another five minutes. I could hear the ocean—but it was coming from ahead of us instead of from the bay behind us.

We stopped before a pile of rocks. No, a stone structure, about five feet high.

"This used to be a lighthouse," Lub said. "But it fell down."

He led me through a gap in the wall. Inside, it was pitch black. "Hold on," Lub called, and a few seconds later a bright light came on. He'd switched on a big plastic flashlight that hung from a wire. The rafters seemed to be tree limbs.

"My secret hideout," he said.

It was about as big as my bedroom in the rental house. One wooden kitchen chair and one aluminum lawn chair were set up in the middle of the dirt floor. A wooden packing crate served as a table. Along one wall was a tree trunk propped up on two stacks of wall stones. This makeshift shelf was crammed with books held in place at each end by hunks of rusty metal. So many books: textbooks, comics, novels, blue binders that looked like automotive repair manuals. . . .

An orange extension cord draped across one corner, from which was hung a fancy wooden picture frame (empty), a bicycle wheel, and a stop sign. Every recess and niche that wasn't crammed with books seemed to hold some piece of random junk: a rusted trumpet missing a mouthpiece, an elaborate green bottle that looked suitable for housing a genie, a miraculously intact Christmas snow globe.

"Flotsam and jetsam," Lub said.

"Pretty cool for stuff you just found washed up on a beach," I said.

"No—my pets." Lub pointed. Two pairs of tiny eyes stared up at us from a hole under one wall. "The one on the left is Flotsam."

"Whoa!" I said. The eyes disappeared. "Rats?"

"They've got a bad reputation," Lub said. "But they're really quite nice."

Even with the rats, the cave was the coolest place I'd ever been in. Then I thought, No, the rats made it even cooler. "I always wanted a secret hideout," I said. "I never even got a tree fort."

"I kind of need one," Lub said. "My people make your people nervous." He popped his gills and leaped at me, hissing through those sharp teeth. I jumped back, then burst out laughing.

"Right?" he said. "I'm utterly terrifying." He looked around at the cave. "I hang out here a lot. You're the first human I've ever shown this to. First . . . anyone."

"Don't your parents wonder where you are?"

"Uh, 'parents' is kind of a different concept with us. But in general, the Elders don't pay much attention to us youngsters." He sat down in the aluminum chair, which seemed more rickety than the wooden one, and set the books I'd given him on the packing crate. "They spend most of their time in church."

"They go to church?"

Lub paused. "Maybe that's not the right word. I'd guess you call it . . . worship? Ritual? They're all into the God Urgaleth, the Mover Between Worlds. Go on and on about it. We're all supposed to be, uh, missionaries? Preparing for the day Urgaleth returns, and then it's all heaven here on earth, punishment of the wicked, yabba dabba doo."

"I think you mean 'yadda yadda yadda.'"

"Anyway, they're all excited about it again. This happens every so often, when Urgaleth is supposed to be coming. They start having these big meetings out on the water, and that's where . . . well . . ."

"What?"

His gills flapped in agitation.

"You saw her," I guessed. "That's where you saw my mom."

He nodded. "Only the Elders are invited, but I followed them."

"I thought you weren't into religion."

"I was bored. Also, they clearly didn't want us younglings finding out what they were doing. They were practically daring me to spy on them."

"Okay," I said. "Tell me everything."

Every few weeks, Lub said, fifty or sixty of the Elders went out at night to a certain spot far from the bay. They rose to the surface where humans in a white boat—the *Albatross*—would be waiting. The humans would lean out over the rails and call down to the Elders in First language. Lub was never close enough to hear what they were saying.

"That's the way it went, week in, week out, until a few days ago," Lub said. "Shortly after the meeting started, a second boat showed up—a lobster boat, which was strange because they're usually back in port by that time of night. The boat's spotlight hit the Elders and they dove for cover, but they knew they'd been spotted. They *hate* that.

"Anyway, the humans on the *Albatross* —there were two of them I could see—ran back inside the cabin. The lobster boat kept coming, moving that light over the water. The *Albatross* swung about, gunned the engines, then . . . bam."

"They rammed them?"

"Oh yeah. The lobster boat practically split in half. There were two people on board, a man with a white beard, and a man with long black hair. At least, I thought it was a man until I started listening at the docks and heard the story of a woman gone missing."

"Wait, you can't tell the difference between men and women?"

"Not from a distance. Unless they're wearing dresses or a beard—that's the only way I can tell you apart."

"Do you know the word 'racist'?" I asked.

"Oh yeah? I'll test you when you meet some of my people."

"So what happened to my mother?"

"She went into the water with her life vest on. But the old man with the beard, he was on the other side of the boat when it split, and I lost sight of him. Later I swam down to the wreck, but I couldn't find him." He shrugged. "There's a lot of, uh, beasties down there."

"But my mom?"

"Oh, the people on the *Albatross* picked her up. They threw down a rope ladder, and she climbed out herself. The *Albatross* was taking on water by this point, but it could still move, and it headed for shore."

"Why didn't you follow?"

"How was I supposed to know who she was?"

144

"This makes no sense," I said. "Why would they ram her boat, then rescue her?"

Lub had no answer to that. He watched me pace.

"What about the humans on the *Albatross*?" I asked. "Did you see *them*?"

"They weren't wearing dresses," Lub said. "Or beards."

"So you have no idea."

"They *were* all ugly," he said.

"Again, there's this word . . ."

Lub started choking, but he was smiling as he did it. "Is that your *laugh*?" I asked.

"This is the traditional expression of amusement among my people," he said. "You racist."

I snuck back into my room sometime around 1 A.M., thinking that Aunt Sel was right: Everything good did happen after eleven.

But then, after I pulled off my clothes and climbed in bed, thoughts started churning. Chief Bode had lied to me, or someone had lied to him; the *Albatross* had definitely been damaged that night, not weeks before like he said. I kept picturing Mom, swimming away from Hal Jonsson's wrecked lobster boat—and then climbing up into the *Albatross*. Someone was holding her against her will. Either that, or she was now—

I couldn't think about that.

I stared into the dark for a half hour, then an hour, my mind still running like a hamster wheel. Finally I turned on the light and looked for something to distract me. In desperation I opened Tobias' diary.

The kid's drawings kept getting better and better. The later pages of the journal were crammed with drawings that in my opinion could have been in a museum. After about ten minutes I felt my concentration drifting. I kept turning pages, and finally came to the last diary entry. It was dated May, 1832, when

Tobias was 21. It was titled "Out of Dunnsmouth Mass."

I sat up. Tobias Glück had been here? In Dunnsmouth?

12th May, 1832, at sea Out of Dunnsmouth Mass.

I am done with knives. I am done with scrimshaw and ink, with the teeth and bones of whales. Every piece I have made, I have thrown overboard. The crew stared at me like I was mad. Even now I can hear them above decks. They whisper, Murderer.

Something terrible had happened to Tobias' friend George—and to Tobias.

There was no way I was not going to read the rest of the diary that night. I scanned each page, struggling to decipher the words because his handwriting had gotten so erratic. But in an hour I had the story.

I knew where the Scrimshander lived. And I knew who owned the *Albatross*.

13

This seraph-band, each waved his hand,
No voice did they impart—
No voice; but O, the silence sank
Like music on my heart.

I could hear the students singing in the language of the Dwellers. I put my hand against the auditorium door, and before I could change my mind, I walked inside.

The singing stopped. Mr. Montooth, standing at the podium, glanced up from his book. Mr. Waughm's mouth dropped open. The students, almost as one, turned to look at me.

I scanned the rows. So many pale faces under dark hair. And then I saw Lydia.

I walked to her row. The boy sitting on the end, the tall boy with the slab-like forehead, looked sideways at me. Then he realized that I wanted to sit down, and he pulled back his knees. I scooched along sideways, my big backpack bumping against the students.

No one said a word. Not even Principal Montooth.

Lydia stared up at me with those huge eyes—and this time I was sure that she really was surprised. She was sitting next to Flora, the girl with the red lipstick. I gave Flora a significant raise of the eyebrows, and she moved over a seat. I put my pack on the floor and sat down.

"Hi, Lydia," I said.

She glared at me and whispered, "What are you *doing*?"

Mr. Montooth looked around at the students and smiled. "Let's finish with 'Rise, Oh Rise!' Page twenty-eight."

Flora shared her book with me. On the page were bars and staves as in a normal piece of music, but instead of the usual whole-, half-, and quarter-note symbols, the measures were filled with blobs, triangles, stars, and one shape that looked like an eye. And as for the words, they were written in a strange alphabet of jagged lines.

I tried to hum along anyway. Lydia sang without looking at me.

At the end of the song, the students closed their books and set them on their seats. Mr. Montooth said, "We are one day closer. You may go to your classes."

Everyone filed toward the exit. Just as I reached the door, Mr. Waughm called me over. The vice principal swiveled his head, looking at me with one eye, then the other. "So," he said. "What brings you to Voluntary?"

"I was just curious," I said. "I'd heard the singing, and, well . . ."

"That made you *so curious* you had to disturb all the other students by coming late?"

"Sorry about that," I said. "I meant to come early, but I was up so late reading."

"I thought you looked a bit tuckered out," Mr. Montooth said. He'd walked up behind me, and now he put a hand on my shoulder. "Everything all right at home?"

I realized he knew about the swim in the lake, too. Lydia was right: It *was* a small town.

"I'm fine," I said.

"Good, good. Any news about your mother?"

"We're still hopeful," I said.

"We all worry about our mothers," Mr. Waughm said.

Montooth frowned at Waughm and then said, "I'm glad you came this morning, Harrison. But I have to tell you, Voluntary may not be the best fit for you. It won't be easy to pick up the language in the songs. These children have been singing them their whole lives, and even they have trouble." He smiled to show how amusing this was.

"And what language is it, exactly?" I asked.

"You wouldn't have heard of it," Mr. Waughm said. "It's pretty obscure."

I thought: Mr. Waughm, hipster.

"But as I said, it's a little late in the game," Mr. Montooth said.

"I don't know, I'm pretty good with languages," I said. "I speak Portuguese, Spanish, a smattering of Terena, a little French, and I know how to order beer in Gaelic." I plastered a smile on my face. "So see you tomorrow?"

Montooth and Waughm ruined my chances for catching up to Lydia in the hallway. By the time I got to Cryptobiology class, she was at her seat with her back turned firmly toward me. She continued to ignore me for the rest of the day, and I couldn't get close to her: A buffer of kids seemed to surround her at all times.

My little stunt at Voluntary had earned me nothing but stares and possibly some discussion on the fingercant network. In other words, it was pretty much business as usual for me at Dunnsmouth Secondary.

It wasn't until English class that I managed to get next to her. I followed her to her seat. "Lydia Palwick," I said. "We have to talk."

She gave me an exasperated look. "No," she said. "We don't." She opened the textbook for the class, *The Catastrophes of New England*. Evidently we were on chapter seven, "The Great September Gale of 1815." A page showed an engraving of buildings burning and several corpses draped over the limbs of a tree.

I showed her my own my book. "Ever hear of Tobias Glück?"

She ignored me.

"It doesn't matter. He lived almost two hundred years ago. They accused him of murdering his best friend."

"Tragic," Lydia said dryly.

"But he didn't do it. They ran into someone else, someone they called the Dunnsmouth 'Shander."

She glanced at me, then turned back to her book. "You don't say." For a moment I swear she was surprised.

"And you know who else Tobias runs into, Lydia Palwick?"

A sound like a gunshot made me jump. Mrs. Goody-Brown had slapped her cane down across Lydia's desk, nearly smacking my fingers.

Our English teacher was a tiny, ancient woman with a face like a desiccated apple and eyes set so far back in her head she might as well be looking through binoculars. I'd never seen her lean on that cane. She wielded it like an épée.

"*Take your seat*," Goody-Brown hissed. She leaned toward me. Her mouth opened, revealing a set of large, perfectly even, brown teeth. "*And open your notebook*."

"Yes, ma'am," I said, and went to my desk in the third row.

"*Everyone* take out your notebooks," she announced, and pointed the cane at the head of a nearby student. "We are having a *vocabulary quiz*."

Goody-Brown stalked between the rows, calling out words. "Number four," she said. "Squamous. *Squamous*." Her cane whacked the side of a desk. "Five. Rugose. *Rugose*."

After the quiz it was silent reading time—dead silent reading time. Instead of concentrating on the Great Gale of 1815, I snuck out the diary and reread the section that had kept me up last night. Tobias and his pal George are in a tavern in Dunnsmouth when George starts bragging about how good a scrimshander Tobias is. The locals, though, aren't impressed, and one old sailor says his etchings are no match for the "Dunnsmouth 'shander." George demands to see this "great artist." Tobias wants to go back to his ship, but George is having none of it, and so by midnight they're walking down by the shore, "to caves that opened at low tide, full of crabs and eels and creatures I did not recognize."

The old sailor leads them into a certain cave, "a twisty tunnel through the dark," until suddenly the passage opens to reveal a cavern:

Shelves were larded with Ivory and Bone, each piece of purest white. The old sailor bid me to bend close, and cried out, "Behold the handiwork of the Dunnsmouth Scrimshander!"

Oh, and such handiwork! The knifework was so precise, the lines so delicate. This artisan's tools, whatever they were, were an order more fine than my blunt needles. As with all Scrimshaw, the bones had been rubbed with some dark liquid, to make their Designs visible. The old sailor waved his lamp, and the pictures floated into view, like baitfish drawn toward a ship's lantern.

The artist's subject was not ships or whales, as in my own work, or the work of most sailors I had seen: the Dunnsmouth scrimshander drew only human portraits. Here was a beautiful woman, every hair in place, with large eyes that seemed to watch me. Here an old man, every wrinkle rendered distinct. And oh, so many children! A crowd of them pressed to the wall, as if gathered for school. The Art was so detailed, so lifelike, that I could see each of their expressions.

And each expression was the same. Despair.

Drunk George is close to passing out, but Tobias is fascinated. "My art was nothing compared to his. This man was a da Vinci or a Devil."

Then the artist himself shows up, wearing "an oilskin coat, as many whalers do, and a broad hat of the same material." Tobias can't see the man's face, but his voice "seemed to slip through the dark like a water snake."

The Stranger asked me, "What do you think of my work?"

I could not speak. The air had left me, as if I were sitting at the bottom of the sea.

"Be honest," the stranger said.

At last I said, "I have never seen its like."

"You are too kind," he said. I could hear the smile in his voice. He said, "The secret is all in the materials. You have to find the right bones, and prepare them with utmost care. Don't you agree?"

The old sailor who had led us here began to laugh. And George, stupid stupid George, began to laugh with him.

Things go downhill from there.

The Scrimshander takes out his long knife, and Tobias panics. (I certainly understood *that*.) He grabs George and starts leading him through the pitch-black caves. They immediately get lost, but Tobias keeps running, because he can hear the Scrimshander calling to them. At one point Tobias smacks his head against a rock and nearly knocks himself out.

And when he gets up, George is gone.

The class ended, and Lydia was again surrounded by friends: Garfield, Flora, the tall kid with the bulldozer forehead—basically the same crew she ate lunch with. She walked in the center of them, and I could see her fingers moving. Whatever they were saying, Lydia was running the conversation, and her friends were acting like bodyguards keeping the paparazzi away.

Lydia couldn't hide from me in history class, though. She sat directly in front of me, her back straight as the blackboard Mr. Waughm was writing on. I leaned forward and said quietly, "How long have you Palwicks lived in Dunnsmouth?"

She ignored me.

"Forever, right? Probably live in the same family house. I

bet you even give your family boat the same name, generation after generation."

She looked over her shoulder at me. "What is the *matter* with you?"

One of the last passages in Tobias' diary; that was the matter. Tobias stumbles out of the caves, and it's past dawn. He's really late. His ship is out in the bay, getting ready to depart, and all the ship's boats have left. He's stranded.

> *I would have gladly let the Ship go, if I were anywhere but Dunnsmouth. I begged for help. A local fisherman looked at my bloodied face and hands with disgust, taking me for a drunken brawler. But he agreed to row me out to the ship on his skiff, which cut through the water as swift as the sea bird for which it was named.*
>
> *His son, a black-haired boy with the largest eyes I have ever seen, kindly bound my hands with cloth. Something about that boy reminded me of the figure of the beautiful woman I had seen in the cave. "Tell me your name," I demanded. "I will repay you when I can."*
>
> *He told me reluctantly his name, but it was clear he wanted nothing more to do with me.*

In the margins of the diary, Tobias had written a sentence, then underlined it: "*For services—Elias Palwick, The Albatross.*"

"Tell me, Lydia—who was on the *Albatross* the night it crashed into my mom's boat?"

I expected her to pretend confusion or deny everything. I was even braced for a slap to my face. But I wasn't prepared for Lydia's big eyes suddenly filling with tears.

She turned away from me, and I sat back in my seat, feeling guilty—which didn't seem fair at all.

Mr. Waughm finished the diagram he was sketching on the board and turned to us with a pleased smile. With his scrawny neck and baggy suit, he looked like a man who'd lost three hundred pounds in a crash diet but had no money for a new wardrobe.

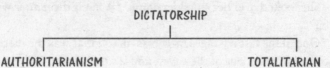

DICTATORSHIP

AUTHORITARIANISM   TOTALITARIAN

He opened his arms. "People throw around these words as if they're interchangeable. But who can tell me what they really mean?"

The room was silent.

"Come now," Waughm said. "Let's start with 'dictatorship.' That's the easy one."

Again, no one said anything.

"A dictatorship," Mr. Waughm said, sounding a little put out, "is rule by one person or a small group. But a dictator is a single, absolute ruler. Like, say, a CEO, or the matriarch of a family, or even"—he smiled at his cleverness—"the teacher in a classroom."

No one spoke.

Waughm's smile faded. "Okay then," he said. He rubbed his hands as if to restore his circulation. "Now the tricky ones. Dictatorships can come in two flavors. What's the difference between authoritarianism and totalitarianism?" He swung his head about, each eye taking in a separate swath of the room. "Someone. Anyone."

No one even looked like they were thinking of an answer. Fingers, however, were moving.

"I need a response," Waughm said. "Yes, both are effective forms of government, but they *are* different." He pointed to the boy with the wide forehead. "Bart. Illuminate us."

"I'd prefer not to," he said. His voice was a cave-like bass.

"What do you mean, prefer?" Waughm said. "I don't care what you *prefer*. Answer the question."

I held up my hand, and Waughm instantly swung an eye in my direction.

I said, "Both are rule without consent of the people."

"Harrison. Yes. Go on."

I hesitated. I knew the definitions—I'd learned all this stuff back in seventh grade, plus the terms were discussed in the opening chapter of the textbook Waughm had given me on the first day—but if the answers were so easy, why wasn't anyone else talking?

"Is that the extent of your knowledge, Mr. Harrison?" Waughm smirked at the other side of the room, as if saying, Can you believe this guy?

"Totalitarian governments," I said, raising my voice, "attempt to rule *everything* about their citizens' lives. Not only what they do publically, but privately too. That's the 'total' part. The system depends on a charismatic leader with some kind of ideology that he gets everyone to buy into."

Waughm nodded, happy to get an answer, even if it was from me. "Yes! Charisma! Every great leader has it. Am I right, people?"

No one spoke.

Waughm coughed and moved toward my side of the room. "Authoritarians are unpopular with their citizens," he said. "They rule for ruling's sake, just to keep control. But a totalitarian is going somewhere. If you want to reduce crime, eliminate terrorism, keep your enemies at bay, and create some *lovely* palaces, there's only one form of government that will do the job." He scanned the room. Everyone seemed to be staring into space.

"Totalitarianism?" I said.

Now Waughm was getting annoyed with me. He turned to address the rest of the room. "You may ask yourself, why is that so, Mr. Waughm? Well, I'll tell you. These governments work because the people are united not only behind a great leader, but a great *idea*. It doesn't matter what the idea is, as long as it appeals emotionally. The citizens can *feel* a sense of purpose that guides everything. 'Everything within the state, nothing outside the state, nothing against the state.' Benito Mussolini said that."

"Didn't we kick his butt in World War Two?" I asked.

All the fingers in the room stopped moving. Mr. Waughm slowly turned to face me.

"That's true . . . ," he said, drawing out the word. "However, that doesn't mean Mussolini was wrong. Human beings *need* a sense of purpose. A hierarchical organization—like say, a church—can provide that. Obedience to the organization relieves stress and provides happiness. Ipso facto, people are happiest when they can stop worrying and learn to love their leader."

"That's bullshit," I said.

Faces turned toward me. I hadn't meant to swear, but come on. Waughm was being ridiculous.

"True power derives from the consent of the governed," I said. "Thomas Jefferson. Declaration of Independence." If I'd been holding a mike, this would be the point at which I dropped it and walked away. Unfortunately, I had no microphone, and the class gong did not ring.

"Language, Mr. Harrison!" Waughm said. "Report yourself to the office, immediately."

"What?"

"You heard me. I will not be disrespected."

"That's another thing," I said. "Totalitarian regimes tend to collapse as soon as people speak up."

"Out! Out this moment!"

I picked up my backpack. Lydia turned in her chair to look up at me. I couldn't read the expression on her face.

I walked straight to the office. Then straight past it. Then straight out of the building.

Aunt Sel was stretched out on the couch when I banged through the front door. "You look like a man who needs a drink," she said. I didn't laugh. "Right, inappropriate," she said. "I'll have yours."

"I'll be in my room," I said. It took some effort not to slam the bedroom door too. I fell into the bed and stared at the ceiling. The brown paint was peeling away like dead skin.

I was prepared for a good long session of fuming and seething—I'm only good because I practice—when those lost hours of sleep rushed me from the blind side and clobbered me.

Seconds later Aunt Sel was shaking me awake. At least it felt like seconds.

"You have a visitor," she said. She was smiling weirdly.

The sky outside the window was black. I wasn't sure what time it was. I sat up groggily and asked, "Who?" Then thought: It better not be Lub.

"You look fine," she said, and walked out.

What did that mean?

I got to my feet, tightened the strap on my non-meat leg, and went out to the living room. Lydia Palwick was standing inside the front door. She wore a heavy black coat with a wide collar, and a black beret. Her hands were tucked into her pockets.

"You two are school friends?" Aunt Sel asked.

"We have all the same classes," Lydia said.

"Do you want to come inside? I have crackers, and the most interesting cheese I found in the market. It's unlike anything I've ever tried."

"I actually came to pick up Harrison for the study group," Lydia said. I opened my mouth, and Lydia quickly said, "Didn't he tell you?"

"He's been asleep since school ended," Aunt Sel said. "I

didn't even wake him up for supper. How about I feed you two before you take off?"

"Oh, don't worry about that," Lydia said. "We have plenty of sandwiches."

"Your mother made sandwiches for your study group?" Aunt Sel said. "That is so lovely."

"I live with my aunt, actually," Lydia said. She nodded at me. "It's how we bonded."

"Yes," I said slowly. "Bonded."

Aunt Sel opened the door for us and said to Lydia, "I have to ask. You have such lovely hair, and it just *shines*. What kind of product do you use?"

Lydia blinked her big eyes. "Soap."

"Ah," Aunt Sel said. "I'll have to try that."

Lydia said to me, "Don't forget the diary. We'll need that for homework."

"Right," I said. I went back to my room and retrieved *Tobias Glück: A Scrimshander's Diary*. Then we walked outside into the cold dark. "I'm guessing there's no actual study group," I said.

"Nope."

"So what's going on here?"

"You said we had to talk," she said. "We're going to talk." She started walking up the road, toward town. "This way."

14

But tell me, tell me! Speak again,
Thy soft response renewing—
What makes that ship drive on so fast?
What is the Ocean doing?

Dunnsmouth was a town too small for streetlamps, but our way was dimly and sporadically lit by the windows of houses tucked behind the trees. Lydia walked fast, thank goodness. The damp had almost instantly worked its way under my hoodie, and I was shivering.

"What's the matter with your leg?" Lydia asked.

"What are you talking about?"

She glanced back at me—I was still having trouble keeping up—and said, "This will go better if you don't lie to us."

Us? I thought.

She said, "I can see the way you walk. You hide it well, but there's obviously something wrong with your right leg."

No one back home noticed my gait. Or if they did, they were too polite to say anything. Lydia, it seemed, occupied a data point on the top right corner of the Observant / Rude chart.

"There's nothing *wrong* with it," I repeated. "It's just made of advanced space-age materials."

"How'd you lose it?"

"Just careless, I guess. Listen, could you just tell me—" To my right, a shadow slipped from tree to tree. I lost a step, and Lydia kept motoring up the hill. I jogged to catch up.

"That's where I live," Lydia said. She pointed at a two-story house to our right. The top windows were dark.

"Do you really live with your aunt?" I asked.

"And uncle." She walked past the house without pausing.

"Okay, now I really don't have any idea where we're going," I said.

"Let me see the book," she said.

I handed her the diary. "I'm not making up the stuff about the Palwicks."

She put the book in her shoulder bag without opening it. "I didn't say you were."

"I do have to return that," I said. "Eventually."

"I'm a fast reader."

At the Standard Grocery she took a hard left into an alley between the store and a tall, narrow house. We cut through a parking lot, then into another alley. I couldn't see a thing. Lydia reached back, seized me by the shirt, and said, "Almost there."

We emerged at a backstreet that was almost as dark as the alley. She walked toward a house with unlit windows. Stairs led down to a basement entrance. Lydia fished out a chain she wore around her neck. More than a dozen keys dangled from it.

"Whoa," I said.

"I collect them." She chose a key and unlocked the door.

"You mean you steal them."

"People are careless." She pushed open the door.

"Is this breaking and entering?" I said.

"Just entering," she said. "It's my house."

"But I thought you lived with—?"

"Get in here." She shut the door behind us. We were in an unfinished basement of cement floors and cinderblock walls, lit by a single bare bulb. Overhead, copper pipes and valves zigzagged through the floor joists. Several pipes dropped to connect to a huge metal tank that could have been a water heater or a fuel oil container. Against one wall, wooden shelves on stacks of cinderblocks were filled with hand tools, jars of nails and screws, and mechanical parts I didn't recognize. One shelf was occupied entirely by a dozen manual typewriters.

I nodded at the ceiling and lowered my voice. "Are we going to wake anybody up, or . . . ?"

"No one lives here anymore."

I followed her across the room, thinking, Does everybody have a secret hideout but me?

She opened a wooden door and gestured; four people were waiting on the other side. I recognized three of them: Flora, with her painted eyebrows and red lipstick; eager-faced, bat-eared Garfield; and the tall, long-haired boy with the Frankenstein forehead. Bart. The boy who preferred not to answer Mr. Waughm.

The fourth person was a short, pinch-faced girl in a dress as long and shapeless as a nightgown. She looked to be a freshman, maybe younger. It didn't help that she held a large porcelain doll in one arm. The doll wore a similar long dress, and her features looked a lot like her owner's. Maybe they'd mail-ordered the doll to match. Girls were weird about this kind of thing.

Both the girl and the doll stared at me coldly. Nobody was looking friendly, except for Flora, who seemed amused.

"Wait," I said. "There *is* a study group?"

This new room was almost as unfinished as the one we'd entered through. The walls were drywalled, though, and the floor was covered by a faded carpet. A collection of beat-up chairs formed a semicircle in the middle of the room.

"It looks like you're set up for Voluntary," I said.

"Just the opposite," Flora said.

Tall Bart frowned. "We've never let an outsider in here." His hands hung at his sides, his fingers fluttering. The others behind him signaled in response. "However . . . ," he said.

"*Extraordinary circumstances*," the girl with the doll said. "*Extraordinary measures*." Her voice was deep yet hollow, like wind through a cave.

"Agreed, Isabel," Bart said. He held out his hand to me. "We've never spoken directly," he said. "I'm Bart."

I shook his hand, and winced. His grip was crushing. "Sorry," he said, and seemed genuinely apologetic.

I held out my hand to the young girl. "We've never met, Isabel. I'm Harrison."

"She's Isabel," the girl said in a whisper. "I'm Ruth."

"Uh . . ."

"*What are you, Indonesian?*" she said in that subterranean voice.

"Isabel!" Ruth exclaimed.

Lydia cut in. "And you know Flora and Gar."

"We're the Involuntaries," Flora said.

"Oh. 'Just the opposite.' Right."

"See? He's quick," Garfield said, grinning. "Kids have no choice about going to Voluntary, but they can decide for themselves to join *us*."

I laughed. "Wait, are you telling me all those kids in Voluntary are faking it?"

"Most of them aren't," Lydia said. "They believe in the Congregation."

"And some are on the fence, but we don't trust them completely," Flora said.

"So you're telling me it's basically you five," I said.

"*Six*," the girl with the doll said. But she'd used that low, spooky voice instead of her whispery one, so maybe it was more accurate to say, "the doll with the girl."

"Who's the leader?" I asked, and looked at Bart. "You?"

"We don't have a leader," he said.

"Come on, there's always a leader. Who decided to bring me here?"

"*Too many questions!*" Isabel said.

"*We* have questions for *you*," Bart said. "Take a seat."

"You sound like a leader to me. What if I prefer not to?"

Garfield laughed. Lydia didn't. She raised her eyebrows as if to say, Are you going to fight me on this?

"Fine," I said. "I'll play along. But it's question for question. Every one I answer, you have to answer one of mine."

Fingers fluttered. Bart nodded. "Deal."

The group parted and directed me to sit in a wide, ratty armchair that had seen better days.

"Tell us how you know about the *Albatross*," Bart said.

"I found it down in J. Ruck's Marine Engineering," I said. "It's got a big hole in it."

"How did you know to—?"

"Uh-uh, my turn. Who owns the boat?"

"That's complicated." Bart exchanged a look with Lydia. "Technically the *Albatross* is owned by Lydia's uncle Micah."

"Okay, but who actually owns it?"

"The Congregation."

That name again. "Who or what is the Congregation?" I asked.

"My turn," Bart said. "Why do you think the *Albatross* had anything to do with your mother going missing?"

I was not about to tell them about Lub. "I got an anonymous note telling me to look for the *Albatross*." I told them about going down to the docks and asking Chilly Bob about the boat, then following him to Ruck's. "I saw the *Albatross* there. And that's when I had my run-in with the Scrimshander."

The Involuntaries—including Isabel the porcelain doll—stared at me.

"Don't try to tell me he's a myth," I said. "Chief Bode called him a boogeyman."

"Where'd you learn about the Scrimshander?" Gar asked.

"He read about him in a book," Lydia said.

"Yes, I did," I said. "But before that he tried to slit my throat."

"You didn't run into the Scrimshander," Bart said. "Because if you did, you'd be dead."

"*Or worse,*" Isabel said.

"How'd you get away?" Flora asked.

"I dove into the water."

Bart looked at Lydia. "And that's how you got away—by *swimming*? That's like outrunning a cheetah."

"Yeah, well, that's what happened," I said. "I guess I got lucky. Now, tell me about this Congregation. Who's in it?"

"That's complicated," Bart said.

"You could stop saying that now," I said.

"Most of the town is technically in the Congregation, so—"

"You can also stop saying 'technically.'"

Garfield laughed again. I was killing it with the bat-eared demographic.

Lydia said, "You have to understand, there are *circles*. Most of the families of Dunnsmouth belong to the Congregation, and they go to the major services. But there's an inner circle of people who run everything."

"Kind of like you guys running the Involuntaries," I said.

"But we think there's an *inner* inner circle of people who *really* run the Congregation," Lydia said.

"*Wheels within wheels*," Isabel intoned.

"Sounds like a university," I said. "My mom's an academic. She said no matter how many committees there are, all the decisions are made by three white guys in a room."

"Sounds about right," Flora said.

"As 'children' we're not supposed to know anything," Bart said. "But the Involuntaries have made it their job to know what the church is up to. We don't trust them. We just can't buy into the religion anymore."

"So you've stopped believing in God," I said.

"*Gods*," Isabel said.

"Of course we still *believe* in the gods," Ruth said in her breathy voice.

"We just don't believe in what the Congregation wants to do for them," Bart said.

"Listen," I said. "I just need to know one thing—who was on the *Albatross* that night? They kidnapped my mother, and I need to know where they're keeping her."

"Back up," Flora said. "Kidnapping?"

"Who told you they had your mother?" Lydia asked.

"Don't say, 'an anonymous note,'" Bart said.

I thought for a moment. "I can't tell you." Bart started to object and I said, "I promised confidentiality, okay? You're going to have to trust me."

"*We do not even know you*," Isabel said.

"She means, not that well," Ruth whispered.

"But we liked the way you stood up to Waughm," Flora said.

"*Oh* yeah," Garfield said. "That was great. It sounded like the kind of thing Bart's saying all the time. This is what the Involuntaries stand for."

"We keep the Congregation in check," Bart said.

"So does that mean you're going to help me?" I asked.

They each took a seat—Ruth put Isabel the doll on a seat by herself—and I told them everything I knew about the night Mom disappeared, except how I knew it. None of the Involuntaries could tell me who'd been on the *Albatross* when it rammed Mom's boat, but Lydia had another part of the story to share.

"My uncle Micah got a call that night," she said. "It was late. He went out, cursing. And when he came back it was nearly dawn. He was soaking wet."

"Who called him?"

"I don't know," she said. "If I'd thought it had anything to do with the Congregation when the call came in I would have listened in on an extension." She said this matter-of-factly. I wondered how many times she'd spied on her family. She said, "It wasn't until later that I realized it might have something to do with your mother. And when you brought up the *Albatross* . . ."

"The boat was damaged, so they called Micah to take care of it," Bart said.

"So is Uncle Micah part of the inner circle?" I asked.

Lydia raised her eyebrows. "I don't think he's that . . . sharp."

"So who is?" I asked. The candidates included several known deacons whose names I didn't recognize, and Principal Montooth.

"Probably Waughm, too," Garfield said. "The whole administration."

"So who do you think is the leader?" I asked. "Not Waughm."

"There may be someone else," Ruth said quietly.

"*The Intercessor*," Isabel intoned.

I blinked in surprise. The doll was in the seat next to me. I could have sworn that a minute ago she'd been sitting on the other side of room.

Bart said, "It's someone we've overheard the adults mention once or twice. We don't know who he is."

"The Intercessor between what and what?" I asked. I already had an idea, though. Lub said the *Albatross* met with the Elder Dwellers every few weeks.

"We don't know that either," Bart said.

"Okay, so Montooth has to report to the Intercessor sometime, right? We've got to put him under surveillance. Find out where this inner circle is meeting."

"Then what?" Garfield asked.

"I don't know. Maybe Montooth will lead us to where my mother's being held."

"This is a pretty flimsy plan," Lydia said.

"What else are we supposed to do?" I said. "I can't go to the cops. Chief Bode already lied to me about the *Albatross*—he said it was up on blocks for weeks. I could go to the detective from Uxton, but what am I supposed to tell him? 'Hey, the principal at my school runs a secret cult, and he's kidnapped my mom, and oh yeah, I have no proof of this at all.'"

"Cult's a strong word," Bart said.

"Doesn't mean it's wrong," Flora said. "I've always thought it was a cult."

Lydia's fingers were moving. "Could you stop with the under-the-table conversations?" I said.

"Sorry," Lydia said. "I need to get back home."

"We'll take shifts to watch Montooth, as best we can," Bart said. "Maybe we'll get lucky."

"Or someone will send you another anonymous note," Flora said.

We turned out the lights in the basement, and then Lydia locked the door behind us. Bart, Garfield, Flora, and Ruth, with Isabel in her arms, hurried up the stairs.

"Hey," I said. They stopped. "Thanks."

"See you tomorrow," Bart said.

I walked with Lydia through the alley, back to Main Street. The cold didn't bother me as much as it had earlier. I think I was so relieved to have someone believe me that I was a little giddy.

"Can you keep listening in to your uncle's calls?" I asked. "If the inner circle calls him, or if he calls them—"

"He's an underling," Lydia said. "There's no telling when they'll need him again, if ever."

"But they need his boat," I said.

"Right," Lydia said. "*His* boat."

"Every couple weeks they take it out. They're going to need it soon."

Lydia stopped walking. "How do you know that?"

"I want to tell you, but I promised confidentiality."

"Confidentiality," she said skeptically.

"Maybe if we keep watch on the *Albatross* we can see who gets on," I said. "I can hang out by Ruck's garage and see who goes in. Of course, the last time I went in . . ."

"Harrison, listen to me. We weren't kidding about the Scrimshander. He can do terrible things. Anybody who crosses the Congregation, crosses the Scrimshander."

"Okay, okay." We resumed walking downhill. Fewer houses had lit windows, and the shadows between the pines seemed deeper. Not quite deep enough, though. Which gave me an idea. "I was thinking, if something happened to the—"

"Oh no," Lydia said quietly.

The door to her uncle and aunt's house was wide open. The silhouette of a large man filled the doorway, his hands on his hips. "Lydia!" he barked. "Where have you been?"

"Later," she said to me under her breath, and hurried toward the house. I turned away, and the man—Uncle Micah, I presumed—yelled, "You! Who's that? Come into the light."

Lydia looked back at me, but the shadows hid her expression. I hesitated, then walked forward. "I'm Harrison Harrison."

"Harry—?" Then: "What are *you* doing with my niece?"

"We had a study group," Lydia said. "For school."

"I wasn't talking to you, girl."

I got close enough to see his face. His black hair was swept back, making a widow's peak, and his beard, while thick, was nothing like the wild shrubbery of Chilly Bob. Behind him was the brightly lit living room of the house. Two hospital beds were set up along the back wall. In them were a man and a woman with gray skin and lank, dark hair. Their jaws hung slack, and they seemed to be unconscious.

"Get in here," Micah said to Lydia. "I think your dad filled his pants."

"You let him *sit* in it?" Lydia said, angry.

"You weren't here to do your job! And you—" He pointed at me. "You stay away from my niece."

Lydia hurried inside. Micah gave me one more dark look, then slammed the door.

Jerk.

I headed downhill, toward the rental. I'd gone a dozen feet when a voice said, "That your girlfriend?"

"I saw you there," I said. "Going to the house and coming back."

Lub stepped out from between the trees. "Because I wanted you to see me," he said. "I guess even ugly girls deserve to be loved."

"She's not ugly," I said. "And she's not my girlfriend."

"I'm not judging," he said. "When are you going to introduce us?"

"You'd give her a heart attack," I said.

"I know, too handsome for human girls. By the way, *Liquid Gunship Seven*? I need more. Now."

"Maybe we can make a deal," I said. "I need a favor."

I was surprised to find Aunt Sel waiting up for me. She sat in the armchair, her legs stretched in front of her, holding a highball glass. "There's my little criminal," she said.

I froze. "What are you talking about?"

"Your clothing, dear. Every day you wear the same thing—T-shirt, hooded sweatshirt, jeans. It's like a school uniform for the Academy of Future Muggers."

"There's nothing wrong with my clothes."

"How about a button-down shirt over a graphic Tee? Or chinos. I'll even allow corduroys, seeing how we're in L. L. Bean territory."

"No," I said. "No no no. I don't need anything. Besides, Mom wears the same thing every day."

"Your mother is not a fashion role model. You dressing like Kurt Cobain is no way to go through life. No wonder your principal wants to suspend you."

"Wait, what?"

"I just got off the phone with Mr. Mandrake."

"Montooth."

She waved a hand. "You've been a bad boy."

"What did he say?"

"You've been using foul language," she said. "I told him I was shocked. Shocked and appalled." She took a sip from her drink. "I'm not sure he understands sarcasm. But as your guardian, I'm now required to attend a meeting at 8 a.m. to discuss our punishment."

"*Our* punishment?"

"A meeting, first thing in the morning? The man's a sadist. But if you do get kicked out of that awful school, I thought we'd have Saleem drive us to Uxton. I understand they have this thing called a *mall*. It's very exciting."

"I told you, I don't need—"

"What if we bought you a different *color* hoodie?"

"We are a family of scientists," I said with mock formality. "We care not for fashion."

She sighed dramatically.

"I would, however, be willing to look at a winter coat."

"You have been running around a lot outdoors," she said. "Speaking of which, how was your 'study group'? Get a lot of work done?"

"It was fine. We—oh."

Her feet were resting on my backpack.

"She's pretty," she said.

"Not everybody thinks so."

Aunt Sel raised her glass. "Haters gotta hate."

15

There was something wrong with her eyesight. Despite the darkness in the cave, she saw everything through a shimmer of white, as if she were encased in ice. She could not focus on anything close to her. Only the portraits—those mournful, pale faces—were sharp and vivid, more real than her own body.

So, she closed her eyes. She found the rope by feel, leaned back until the rope was tight across her back, and threw herself backward.

The anchor did not move. The rusting hulk, resting on its curved arms, had become a fuzzy, dark blob. Sometimes it resembled a squid. Sometimes an immensely tall woman in long skirts. Sometimes both at once.

It was so hard to concentrate.

She found the rope, leaned back, and pulled. And again. And again. The action had become automatic, and her body a machine. Sometimes she forgot why she was pulling at all, and then she would remember her captor. Was that his step coming down the tunnel? How long ago had he left? She couldn't even guess.

Find the rope, Rosa. Brace the legs. Pull.

Her legs slid out from under her and she went down. Her

outflung arm struck something hard, but she stifled her cry. Silence was everything.

She lay on her side on the stone floor, cradling her arm. Listening. Her captor wasn't in the room. What was it she'd hit?

The bucket. Her captor had left the bucket behind. He never did that.

She rolled onto her belly and crawled until her fingers touched the rusting metal. She could no longer smell the contents of the bucket, and for that she was grateful. She got to her knees, then tossed the slop toward a far wall. Oh, he wouldn't like that. Didn't like his nest to be fouled.

She didn't care. She no longer thought it was possible to win him over. The only thing she was certain of was that if she stayed here, she was going to die.

She got to her feet, holding the bucket by its metal handle. She could barely see it in her hands, but she could feel its weight. For the first time, she had a tool. She turned toward the nearest wall and the crowd of faces that had watched her, helpless and mute, as she struggled.

She took a breath, swung the bucket backward like a bowling ball, then forward in a sweeping uppercut. The bucket smashed into the underside of a shelf, and scrimshaw exploded into the air. White on white, like ice shards thrown into a blizzard. She couldn't see where all the pieces went, but she heard some of them clatter to the ground nearby. She crouched and ran her bound hands along the rocky floor. One hand grazed the edge of a plate and she gasped, then jerked back.

Blood welled on two fingers. In this bleached haze, her fingers were pale as snow, and the blood as black as ink.

The pain seemed to slap her awake. She leaned over the plate, trying to get her eyes to focus, and then she laughed. It was her old friends, the dark-haired couple.

Rosa carefully tilted up the bone plate, then held it between her palms. Once more she pushed back to take up the slack between her waist and the anchor. Then she dragged the edge across the rope.

She felt rather than saw the lip of the plate do its work. The rope trembled, and she could almost feel the threads pop one by one. Her hands grew slick—from sweat, and from the blood weeping from her cuts. Twice she dropped the portrait, and was surprised each time that it did not shatter. The surface felt like porcelain, but was so much tougher.

Her captor could come back any moment, and now that she was so close she was frantic to be free. Still she forced herself to slow down, to concentrate on making each cut count. She began to hum to herself, and then the words swam up out of her throat, a melody from deep childhood.

"*Um dia a feiticeira má,*" she sang in her cracked voice. "*Muito má, muito má.*" It was not just the Portuguese that soothed her. Her voice had become that of her grandmother, rocking little Rosa to sleep. "*Adormeceu a Rosa assim, bem assim.*"

One day a bad witch, very bad, very bad, put the rose to sleep this way, this way.

She sawed at the rope for a long time, letting the song carry her—and then there were only a few strands left. She cut through them, and stumbled backward. She was free.

She let the plate slip from her hands. Somewhere far away it struck rock and bounced away, into the white. She thought about finding it again and cutting her wrists free, but she couldn't stand to be here another second.

She could not see the exit through the glare of white, but she knew the tunnel out started somewhere past her captor's makeshift living area. She felt her way to the wooden chair, then leaned on it for a moment. A step more took her to the table, a few more to the wooden trunk.

Her captor had left his latest work sitting on the trunk's lid. The outlines of the figure seemed to shout at her through the haze.

The picture was not yet finished. In the portrait she was crouched, looking up into the eyes of the artist. He'd put much effort into fleshing out the background, making the details of the prison as solid as the cave walls. But her face was only half there: a chin, a partially sketched mouth, a left eye, the merest suggestion of a nose.

She wanted to smash the portrait. Leave no part of her behind for him to leer at. But she couldn't spare the time or strength for gestures. Harrison was waiting for her.

She dropped it to the ground, and walked toward the mouth of the tunnel, an oval of brighter white against the white of the cave, like a photographic negative. She stepped into it, and the glare blinded her, surrounded her. The light had a weight, like an alabaster waterfall.

Her legs were failing. With each step the air grew thicker before her, weighing her down. She dropped to her knees and elbows, her bound hands outstretched like a penitent pilgrim. She thought, What if I've hallucinated this entire escape? What if I am still in the cave, pulling vainly against that half-ton anchor?

Then: What if I'm not here at all?

She could not feel the rock beneath her knees. She could not even tell if she was moving. The weight bore down, until finally it flattened her against the floor.

16

The rock shown bright, the kirk no less,
That stands above the rock:
The moonlight steep'd in silentness
The steady weathercock.

"Perhaps we've gotten off on the wrong foot," Principal Montooth said. Mr. Waughm, Aunt Sel, and I sat in his office, a woodsy affair decorated with brass plaques, framed certificates, and—shades of Chilly Bob's bait shack—a stuffed thresher shark. I wasn't sure how it was good for morale to keep the corpse of your mascot on display.

"Harrison's been here a little over a week," Montooth said to Aunt Sel. "He's had to adjust to a new town, a new school, a new way of doing things—all while undergoing a major life event."

" 'Major life event,' " Aunt Sel said, as if tasting each word. "I do love a—what's the polite word for it? Euphemism."

Montooth smiled and glanced at the papers on the desktop in front of him. "Yes. Well. That is the reason we're here—use of language."

I could barely look at him. I kept picturing him at the wheel of the *Albatross*, smashing into my mother's boat—and Mom plunging into the cold ocean. I had no proof that he was on the boat that night, but I had no proof that he wasn't. Still, I'd promised Aunt Sel that I'd watch my temper. She'd seen how angry I'd gotten with Chief Bode. I'd told her I could handle myself.

Mr. Waughm cleared his throat. He was standing next to

Aunt Sel, hugging himself in his voluminous suit. "I'm sure you understand, Ms. Harrison, there's no call for off-color language, even during, well . . ."

"A major life event?" she said.

"Exactly," Waughm said. "We do things differently in Dunnsmouth. We are a traditional community, with old-school values. *Very* old-school."

"I think what Mr. Waughm is trying to say," Montooth put in, "is that here in Dunnsmouth, we have very high expectations for student behavior. A breakdown in decorum leads to—"

"Chaos!" Waughm said.

"Oh my," Aunt Sel said. "I didn't realize the administration's situation was so precarious."

Montooth seemed annoyed with Waughm. "Perhaps 'chaos' is too strong a word. But we've found that if you fight the small battles, you don't have to fight the big ones."

"Mr. Waughm was trying to make exactly this point in class," I said.

"Is that so?" Montooth said.

"He was explaining how totalitarianism depends on controlling all expression, private and public, to maintain control."

"Yes!" Waughm said.

"So you can't fault Harrison for not paying attention," Aunt Sel said. She gave me a warning look. She could tell I was heating up. "However, this seems to be a lot of fuss over one little word, which you can hear on cable television every day of the week—"

"We don't allow cable in town," Waughm said.

"Be that as it may, we think there's no reason to fight this battle at all," Montooth said. "We're happy to provide study materials for Harrison to take home so he won't fall behind for the short time he'll be in Dunnsmouth."

"Short time?" I asked.

Montooth opened his hands. "We hardly expect you to stay

here very long." He looked to Aunt Sel as if appealing to a fellow adult in the room. "After all, the search has been called off. There's nothing more you can do here."

"I'm not leaving," I said.

"I appreciate that you're remaining hopeful," Montooth said. "That's an excellent attitude. But I'm sure you would find more emotional support back home."

"*Listen*," I said. I leaned forward in my chair. "When she's found, I am not going to be all the way across the country. And she *will* be found."

Waughm snorted.

I'm not sure what happened in the next few seconds. I didn't "black out." I didn't go unconscious. But neither was I in my own head. One moment I was in my chair, across the room from Waughm. The next I was up, one hand gripping his neck, pressing him against the wall.

It was a scrawny neck. One hand was plenty.

"Mr. Harrison!" Montooth said.

Waughm's mouth hung open. He squeaked like a balloon leaking air.

Hands seized my shoulders. I released my grip on Mr. Waughm, and he stumbled sideways into the wall. A glass-framed certificate hit the floor with a crash.

It was Aunt Sel who'd grabbed me. She looked scared, and it was that expression that seemed to suck the rage out of me. "You'd better go outside," she said.

Montooth had stepped around the desk. He was looking at me, but he wasn't upset, or angry. He almost seemed amused. "Ms. Harrison, could I talk to Harrison alone for a moment?"

I stormed toward the exit, moving stiffly. I pushed through the door and nearly knocked over Miss Pearl, who'd obviously been eavesdropping. "What did you *do?*" she asked. She seemed delighted.

I couldn't answer her. What *had* I done? My stomach felt

cold. I'd really thought I could keep control. I walked out into the atrium, and Montooth followed me.

I wheeled on him. "I know, I know, I'm kicked out."

"I really don't have any choice but to suspend you now," Montooth said. "But between you and me, I've wanted to strangle Floyd quite a few times." He gestured toward the bench that sat beside the office door. "Can we talk frankly for a moment? Off the record."

The atrium was empty—class was still in session. Mr. Montooth sat and folded his long legs. After a moment I decided it was all right to sit beside him.

"I grew up in Dunnsmouth," he said. "My father was the pastor of the church, and he ran this school before me. You want to talk about *strict*." He shook his head. "It wasn't easy growing up as the pastor's son."

"I can imagine."

"But I will say this for him—he valued education. So unlike most of the people I grew up with, I left Dunnsmouth. I went to college, then graduate school. I saw the world, traveled, saw how other people lived. And it didn't take me long to figure out how . . . *conservative* Dunnsmouth was."

I would have said "insane," but let it pass. "You came back, though," I said.

He nodded. "When my father died, I felt I had no choice. So, I became a teacher here, and then its principal. I try to do a good job. I try to lead Voluntary like my father did, and do the right things. But I know that some people in town take our traditions seriously. Very seriously."

"Is that a threat?" I said.

"What?" He seemed genuinely shocked. "No, of course not. It's just . . . I want you to be careful, Harrison. For as long as you're here, whether you decide to stay in school or work at home. Because people like, well, Mr. Waughm, they may look odd, even a bit laughable. But they can be dangerous. I'd like you to steer clear of him."

"That's kind of hard," I said. "He's my teacher."

"Yes, well. Perhaps after your suspension is over, if you really want to stay in school, then we'll find you a study hall for that period. Meanwhile . . ." He took a breath and rose to his feet. "Keep your head down, Harrison. Can you try?"

"Head down. Right."

He looked toward the office door. "I suppose now I need to calm down Mr. Waughm." He laughed to himself, then held out his hands and made a choking noise. "Aaagh! Aaagh!" He laughed again, and went inside.

"Harrison."

It was Lydia. She walked toward me from the other side of the atrium, holding her books to her chest. I couldn't imagine how she'd managed to get out of class.

"I heard you were in the office," she said. "Are you all right?"

"I'm fine."

"You're not very convincing," she said.

"I'm also not good at keeping my head down."

"Montooth told you that?"

I thought for a moment. "You should stay home tonight," I said. "Your uncle's going to be getting a call."

"What are you going to do?"

"Shake the tree," I said.

Aunt Sel came out of the office looking exasperated, but then she saw who I was talking to and put on a smile. "So good to see you again, Lydia."

"Hello, Ms. Harrison."

"Please, just Selena. It's been an exciting morning. Mr. Worm's in quite a state, and Principal Manteeth is putting his foot down. So you know what that means, Harrison."

"We're off to the mall?"

"I'll call Saleem."

* * *

179

That night I found myself sitting on a damp log, just inside the tree line on the north end of Dunnsmouth Bay, with a pair of binoculars pressed to my face. I could hear the whisper of surf just thirty feet from me, but looking east I saw nothing but a wall of solid black, ocean and sky slamming together to seal off the town. Somewhere up there, beyond the cloud layer, there had to be the moon and stars, but no light reached the surface. The closest thing to a star was a yellow light to the southeast, bobbing low on the horizon. It was the naked bulb that hung above the door to Chilly Bob's bait shack, out at the end of the pier.

My focus was on the buildings closer to shore, west of me. One building in particular. I stood up, walked to another set of trees to get a different angle. Checked the time on my phone. After thirty seconds I walked back to the log, checked the time again, and raised the binocs. I wasn't really cold, thanks to one of Aunt Sel's credit cards, but I was nervous.

I'd told Aunt Sel that I was going to see a friend, and allowed her to jump to the conclusion that it was Lydia. It wasn't that far of a leap; as far as Aunt Sel knew, Lydia was my only friend in town. Little did she know that I wasn't even sure Lydia liked me. She was so grim, so serious, it was like trying to cozy up to Batman.

Aunt Sel was worried about me, I knew. During the trip up to Uxton she didn't try to pester me, but I could see her watching me, trying to decide what to say. I didn't contribute much. I watched the trees scroll by the car window while she bantered with Saleem. Once we were in the mall it was easier to talk about nothing. Aunt Sel wanted nothing for herself, and so most of our conversations consisted of her holding up some article of clothing and saying, "What about this?" and me shaking my head.

For lunch, Aunt Sel refused to consider the food court ("Because all the food has been found guilty"), and led us to a Mexican restaurant attached to the mall, where she could order a margarita. While we waited for our meals we snacked on tortilla chips and checked our phones. It was a little stunning to have cell coverage again. Alerts and updates from my social apps hit like an avalanche. All that trivia and pocket drama, in-jokes I was now too outside to get, "hilarious" videos and new memes . . . and friend pics. So many pictures of my friends. They were holding on to each other, clowning around, pouting into the camera.

After a few minutes I closed all those apps without responding to anyone's posts. I'd been dying to talk to my friends, but now that I could do it, I didn't know what to say. How could I explain what had happened in the past ten days? I was in a different world now.

I decided to check in on the four friends who'd last seen my mother alive: Howard and Edgar, Steve and Pete. I was able to log in to Mom's NOAA account because Mom, despite my repeated advice, used the same password for everything: "Harrison2." Kind of hard for me to forget.

Howard and Edgar, the buoys she'd deployed on the first day, were still functioning and pinging the servers with their GPS coordinates, every hour. The same with Steve, the first buoy she'd deployed on day two. None of them had uploaded any sonar images of large moving objects, though, so *M. hamiltoni*, AKA the colossal squid, was still going incognito.

Of the fourth buoy, Pete, there were no recent entries. Had she failed to get him in the water? I scrolled back through the logs until I reached the day of the attack, and there it was: a single entry for Pete. On startup, the buoy had sent its GPS location as well as initial status data. By the next hour it had gone silent.

Aunt Sel noticed my expression. "You want to talk about what happened in the principal's office?" Oh. She thought I was still upset about my little Hulk-out. And it's true, it had come as a surprise to me.

"Not really," I said.

"Are you sure?" she asked. "I've had so much therapy I'm sure I'm licensed in something by now. I've recently become an expert in anger issues."

Ah. She was still worried about my outburst. "I'm sorry about that," I said. "I know I'm not making this easier. You dropped everything to come out here, and . . . well, I know it can't go on forever. When you have to go back, just tell me."

"Harrison, you did me a favor. If I was back in the city I'd be facing charges for manslaughter right now, after accidentally knocking my lying boyfriend off the balcony of his Manhattan penthouse."

"Whoa. Did he cheat on you?"

"I found out he was sleeping with his wife."

"Ouch."

"*C'est la vie.* Unfortunately, he was also the owner of my boutique. I held one last fire sale—well, street sale. Kind of a street fire sale."

"You weren't kidding about the anger stuff."

"I've learned to look for silver linings. For example." She opened her purse and placed an onyx credit card on the table. "His parting gift to me."

I picked it up. I didn't know a credit card could be *heavy*. "That was nice of him."

"Harrison, you're adorable."

"You mean he doesn't know that—? Oh."

"I want you to do me a favor, H2. Help me get through this difficult moment in my life, while simultaneously sticking it to the man. A very particular man." She reached across the table and touched my arm. "Will you do that for me?"

I looked down at the table. I was pretty sure this was the most illegal thing I'd ever participated in, if you didn't count assault and battery on a school administrator. Big Day for Me.

"Well," I said. "There *are* a couple of things I could probably pick up while we're here."

Which was how I came to be wearing a rain-resistant parka stuffed with some kind of synthetic material that made geese envious, and watching J. Ruck's Marine Engineering through a pair of Bushnell "H2O" waterproof binoculars. Oh, and breaking the law again.

There was not much light near the Ruck building: a streetlamp over the parking lot, a light over a side door. The only windows, by the front office, were dark. I checked my phone again.

Lub had been inside for fifteen minutes. And for maybe the hundredth time in those fifteen minutes I thought, the Scrimshander is in there.

Lub and I had talked about the possibility. But neither of us thought that the creature could be guarding the *Albatross* twenty-four hours a day. Lub said he'd be in and out of the building in five minutes, tops.

I walked to the other set of trees and raised the binoculars again, this time focusing on the front office. Was that a light flashing inside? Or a reflection on the windows of something outside?

"Hi there," a voice said in my ear. I jumped sideways, then banged into a tree.

Lub made that weird coughing sound that passed for laughter.

"Don't do that!" I said. Then: "Are you okay? What took you so long? Did you do it?"

"It turned out they had the water gate locked," Lub said. His skin was still wet, but he didn't seem to be cold. He was still carrying the plastic bag that we'd packed with a butane grill lighter and the can of lighter fluid. "That slowed me down for a bit. But as for the rest—mission accomplished, Hari-San."

"I don't hear anything," I said.

"Well, the alarms are going crazy in there," he said. "It's sure to be only a matter of time before—here we go."

Headlights plunged down the hill from town. A delivery

van—Ruck's van—jerked to a stop in the parking lot. A man—I assumed J. Ruck himself—ran to the side door and started fiddling with keys.

I lifted the binoculars. "You made sure nobody was in there, right?" I asked. I had visions of the place exploding like a movie set. "No pets either?"

"Don't worry, Hari-San." This was his new hi-larious nickname for me. I really regretted giving him the Japanese manga. "I checked all the rooms; then I set the fire near the *Albatross*. Plenty of oil and rags in that place. It turns out I'm really good at starting fires! Who knew?"

Below, Ruck had gone inside.

"Does Dunnsmouth have a fire department?" I asked. "A volunteer one, maybe?"

"Never seen one," Lub said. We watched the building for several minutes. Then several more.

Lub said, "What'd you call this plan again?"

"Shaking the tree."

"I never really understood that expression."

"Stirring the pot, then."

"That just seems like a good thing to do, cooking-wise," he said.

"Kicking the hornet's nest," I said. "Rattling the cages. Teasing the tiger."

"Now you're just making things up."

"It just means that—wait." Another set of headlights appeared. This time they belonged to a pickup truck that shot down the hill even faster than Ruck's van had. It swung into the parking lot outside the marine garage and squealed to a stop. The man who jumped out of the cab was big and bearded. He ran to the door Ruck had left open and went inside.

"That's him," I said. "Micah Palwick."

"Now I get it—shake the tree until the nuts fall out. What now?"

"Now we wait for Lydia to contact us."

"*Us?*" Lub asked. "Finally!"

"I mean me. I am *not* introducing you." I put away the binoculars. "Besides, you said you had to stay hidden."

We walked back to my house, taking the long way through the trees to avoid being seen on the street by Uncle Micah when he came back—or by anyone else. At my back porch I shook hands with Lub. The skin of his palm was surprisingly soft.

"Thanks for doing this," I said. "Talk to you tomorrow."

"You're going to tell Lydia that you did all this by yourself, aren't you? Even though I'm the one who snuck in and risked everything."

"It wasn't *that* hard."

"I'm practically a superhero! She should know this."

"Superheroes wear masks—they don't try to get credit for everything they do."

"Aquaman doesn't wear a mask."

"Lub, I hate to break this to you, but no one cares about Aquaman."

"Wow. Hurtful. My only human friend, and he's anti-amphibian."

"I'm not—"

"Amphibiphobic," he said. "You're an amphobe."

"Go home, Lub."

The phone call came less than an hour later. "Get here," Lydia said. "Now."

I pulled on my new coat and told Aunt Sel that I was going to Lydia's, and she gave me a knowing smile. "Bundle up, dearie. That's what a proper parental substitute would say, right?"

"You're doing a really good impersonation," I told her.

I practically ran up the hill. Lydia's house was well lit—and quiet. If Uncle Micah was in a panic like I hoped, it hadn't spread to the rest of the household. I knocked at the front door, and after a minute it was opened by a thin woman with a pinched face. Her hair was pulled back, and she grimaced at me as if I'd dropped a dead cat on her doorstep. "*Who* are *you*?"

"My name's Harrison. I go to school with Lydia."

"So?"

Behind her I could see the living room and the pair of hospital beds. The man and woman looked the same as they had before: mouths open, faces pointed at the ceiling. Unconscious.

Lydia suddenly appeared. "It's okay, Aunt Bee. I told you, I have a study group tonight."

"You can't take off! Micah's already run off! Who's going to take care of them?"

"I've already fed them, and they're ready for bed. Just turn out the lights when you go up." She pushed past her aunt.

"Get back here!" Aunt Bee said.

"It's for school," Lydia said. "I won't be long." She marched toward the road, and I followed. When I glanced back, her aunt slammed the door.

"What happened?" I asked. "Did Micah call anyone?"

"He came back here, looking mad," Lydia said. She was holding a flashlight, but she didn't turn it on. "He stomped around for a bit; then he got on the phone."

"I knew it! Who did he call? You were listening, right?"

She gave me a withering look. Of course she had been.

"Who was it?" I asked. "Where are we going?"

"You're so smart—guess."

"Just tell us already," a voice said.

Lydia screamed. A short scream, more like a bark really. But surprisingly loud.

A figure stepped out of the trees and waved a big hand. "Hi there."

Lydia stepped back. "Harrison, run! It's a—"

"*It* is a *he*," Lub said.

"He's a Dweller of the Deep!" she said.

"I can't believe this. Your girlfriend is an amphobe too," Lub said.

"I'm not a—what?"

"She's not my girlfriend," I said.

"Get back," Lydia commanded Lub.

"It's okay," I said. "Lydia, this is Lub. He's a friend."

This took her some time to process. Then she came to a conclusion. "That makes no sense."

"Right?" Lub said. "We come from two different worlds."

"I thought you were extinct," Lydia said.

"I'm just shy," Lub said.

"Do you really live out in the bay?" she asked. Her fear had turned to curiosity. "Do you live for centuries? How long have you—?"

"Don't we need to get going?" I said.

"Where *are* we going?" Lub asked.

"No," Lydia said. "No. He can't just . . . *tag along*."

"We can trust him," I said. "He's been helping me. He saved me from the Scrimshander."

"That's how you got away?" Lydia asked.

"That's right," Lub said. "I'm like Aquaman."

"Who?" Lydia asked.

"Told you," I said to Lub. Then, to Lydia: "Where was Micah going?"

"Waughm told him to come to the church," she said.

"*Waughm*," I said. I was suddenly grateful that I'd taken the opportunity to strangle him. "So where's the church?"

"He means the school," Lydia said. "Same thing, really. It was the only building left standing after the Great September Gale of 1815, so they started using it for everything—church, school, jail, hospital. It still does double duty."

"That explains so much," I said.

We followed the curve of the street, and suddenly the school was looking down at us from its pedestal on the rock. The moon had broken through the clouds, casting a hard light on its walls. It was so clearly a temple. How could I not have seen it before?

We didn't go up the front steps. A long black car with tail fins was parked in front of the school. "I saw Montooth get into that car," I said.

"It's Mr. Waughm's," Lydia said.

She led us around the side of the building. A row of metal garbage cans were set beside a cement loading dock that looked like it had been wedged into the building's stone. The cans reeked of dead fish.

"Something smells delicious," Lub said.

"Shhh," Lydia said. She climbed onto the loading dock and pulled out the necklace of keys. Somehow in the dark she found the one she was looking for and inserted it into the lock of the big metal door. The door opened with a clunk.

"Another key that someone left lying around?" I said.

"Shhh," Lub said.

We were in the kitchen. Lydia flicked on her flashlight and led us through the dark to the nurse's office, then to a long hallway without doors. Her light followed a stripe that ran down the middle of the floor.

"I've been here before," I said. "This is the outer loop."

"What's it outside of?" Lub asked.

"*Quiet*," Lydia whispered.

We stopped talking, but we weren't silent. Lub's big feet slapped the linoleum: *Whap. Whap. Whap.*

Lydia halted. "Would you cut it out?"

"What?" Lub said.

"Clown shoes," she growled.

The corridor took the final turn I remembered—but we weren't in the atrium. We'd somehow gotten to the far end of the school, where the stone steps led down to the pool. "This way," Lydia said, and we went down. The light illuminated only a couple steps at a time, but at least Lub was quieter on stone.

"How do you know they're down here?" I asked Lydia, keeping my voice low.

"Waughm said 'the church.' And this is where the church meets."

"By the *pool*?"

"Baptists have pools," Lydia said defensively.

We went into the girls' locker room. I was braced for a sudden upgrade in the facilities—girls' bathrooms were always nicer than the boys'—but as near as I could tell from the peripheral glow of the flashlight it was the same dismal setup as on the other side.

Lydia clicked off the light. "I'll go check it out," she whispered. "Stay here."

In the dark I couldn't tell if she'd gone. I slowly became aware of a faint patch of light somewhere ahead of me. And were those voices?

Lub said, "How long are we going to wait?"

"Just hold on," I said.

After another thirty seconds, he grabbed my arm and said, "The doorway is right over here. Come on."

He seemed to have no trouble in the dark. He pulled me around another corner and we were in an arched entrance that overlooked the pool amphitheater. Only a couple of the overhead mercury lights were on, casting a yellow glow near the edge of the pool, but most of the space was in shadow.

Someone hissed. It was Lydia, crouched behind a stone row. She gestured for us to get down, and Lub and I crawled over to her.

I could make out figures down by the water. Mr. Waughm, his neck protruding from his suit like a turtle's, paced back and forth at the pool's edge. Sitting in the first row, his back to us, was Micah Palwick. But standing nearby, his arms crossed, was a chubby man whose bald head reflected the light. Chief Bode was part of the Congregation?!

I shouldn't have been surprised. This explained why Bode said that the *Albatross* had been in Ruck's garage for weeks: He was covering for the church. Aunt Sel and I had trusted him because he was a police officer. I wouldn't make that mistake again. Not in Dunnsmouth.

"How damaged is it?" Waughm said. His voice bounced around the big space. It was a terrible place to hold a clandestine meeting. Why wouldn't they do this in Waughm's office?

"It's not good," Micah said. "It weren't so much the fire. Whoever did this, they knocked a new hole right through the patch Ruck had made in the side of the boat."

I looked at Lub. "You did that?" I whispered.

"Aquaman," he said.

Below us, Micah was describing the state of the *Albatross*. "We're back to square one," he said.

"It's *got* to be the boy," Waughm said.

"He did know the boat was there," Bode said.

"But *how* did he know about it?" Waughm said. "That 'anonymous note' story he gave you? Please." He looked out at the surface of the pool, then resumed his pacing.

"Plus he somehow broke into Ruck's," Chief Bode said. "How'd he do that?"

"Ruck said the place was locked tight," Micah said. He sounded nervous. "You all agreed Ruck could be trusted. It wasn't my decision to—"

"Don't try to weasel out of this," Waughm said. He stopped in front of Micah. "Someone is helping him. We have a traitor in the Congregation."

"You can't mean me!" Micah said. "I served the church my whole life."

"Just as your brother did," Mr. Waughm said. "Until he didn't."

Micah jumped up. "I ain't my brother!"

"No," Bode said. "You ain't half the man he was."

"You hold on there, Bode," Micah said. "Badge or no badge, you can't just—"

Something in the water had caught Micah's attention. He tried to take a step back, but the bench was behind him, and he sat down hard.

The surface of the pool was bubbling.

Waughm pointed to Micah. "Now you're in for it."

Something big was surfacing. The water broke, and then a huge creature, big as an orca, burst onto the surface. Waughm jumped aside, and the massive thing threw itself onto the lip of the pool.

It was a woman. A gigantic woman at least ten feet tall and almost as wide. A gigantic woman with a pile of oil black hair, wearing a floral print muumuu the size of a tent.

"This better be important," she said.

17

The very deep did rot: O Christ!
That ever this should be!
Yea, slimy things did crawl with legs
Upon the slimy sea.

I didn't scream. I didn't breathe. Brain and body shut down, almost like my blackout this morning in Montooth's office. But this time it wasn't anger that short-circuited me, but the sheer wrongness of what I was seeing. I couldn't process it. The scale of the woman was impossible.

I think Lub and Lydia were as shocked as I was. None of us moved. None of us made a sound. That probably saved us.

Waughm and Bode had dropped to their knees. "O Toadmother," Waughm said. "Blessed Intercessor, Most High of the Congregation—"

"Yes, yes," the giant said. "Get up, already." Her huge head grew out of the top of her dress like a poisonous mushroom, deathly white splotched with red: scarlet lipstick, pink eye shadow, a smear of blush on each cheek like a rash. My phantom leg ached as if it were in a vise.

"Can I say how lovely you look this evening?" Waughm said.

She (*it?*) pushed at her hair, then swung toward Micah. The man had stayed where he'd fallen between the rows. "You get up, too," she said.

He scrambled to his feet. "I'm sorry, I'm sorry, I'm—"

"Who are you? You look familiar."

"My-my-my—"

"Who is this man, Waughm?"

"Micah Palwick, Toadmother. Elijah Palwick's brother."

"Oh, yes. I see the family resemblance now." She leaned forward until she was towering over him and put a giant paw on his shoulder. Her nails were pink. "Are you a troublemaker, Micah?"

Water from her dripped onto his face. "No ma'am," he said in a small voice. "I mean Intercessor. I mean—"

She released him and eased back. The tail of her muumuu floated on the pool's surface. I realized that she'd never come completely out of the water. Was there more of her down there? How *much* more?

"So what's this I hear about the *Albatross*?" she said.

Waughm told her about the fire at Ruck's, and the damage to the boat, and kept mentioning that it was Micah's responsibility to keep the craft in working order. If the *Albatross* had been a bus, Waughm would be throwing Micah under it.

"We think it's the Harrison boy who did it," Chief Bode said.

Waughm nodded vigorously. "He's a wild one. No self-control. Just today he attacked me!"

"Ooh, attacked by a *teenager*," she said, her voice dripping with mock sympathy. "Thank the stars you survived."

Chief Bode chuckled once, then quickly silenced himself at the Toadmother's glare.

"Micah Palwick," the woman said, turning again to Lydia's uncle. "Do you know what time it is?"

"Uh, ten o'clock?"

"*No!* The time is *nigh*. The First tell us that the Ashen Light will appear soon."

"Uh, Toadmother?" Waughm stepped forward. "Do you think you ought to be telling him about that?"

"The stars are right!" she shouted. Her voice made the air tremble. "The last time we had this chance was over a dozen years ago. We don't know when it will happen again. Urgaleth, the Mover Between Worlds, is returning, bearing its precious cargo, and *you*, Micah Palwick, you have endangered everything!"

Micah looked at Waughm, then Bode. "The scriptures are *real*?"

The Toadmother's great hand smashed into the side of Micah's head. The man flew sideways and crumpled to the ground. Beside me, Lydia gasped, but the sound was masked by the Toadmother's shouting.

"Yes they're *real!*" the Toadmother said, indignant. "Who raised you?"

Chief Bode moved toward Micah's body, hesitated, then crouched beside him. Micah moaned.

The Toadmother turned her attention to Waughm. "Fix that boat by the end of the week," she said. "We will not fail this time. The First are ready. And we have the perfect vessel, primitive yet sturdy."

"Uh, when you say 'vessel,'" Waughm said, "are you talking about the boat, or . . . ?"

"The Harrison woman, you idiot!"

"Oh. Right. So she's still alive?"

"Of course she's alive. We need her breathing, don't we?"

"Yes, but the Scrimshander has a habit of . . . well—"

"He knows his job. Unlike you, Waughm. Now get that Palwick out of here before I eat him. And don't bother me until the *Albatross* is repaired, or the Ashen Light appears in the sky."

"Yes, Toadmother. Thy will be—"

"Can it, Waughm."

She seemed to twist in place. Her head bent toward the water, and her body followed her like a giant Slinky. The splash was surprisingly small.

We hunkered in our hiding spot, waiting for the room to clear.

Waughm stalked out through the doorway that led to Coach Shug's office. Chief Bode looped an arm around Micah and helped him limp out. A few minutes later the lights shut off, and we were sitting in the dark. We waited another minute in silence, and then Lydia clicked on the flashlight.

"I am never going in that pool," I said. My invisible leg still ached, but the pain was receding.

We crept back to the girls' locker room, and from there upstairs to the outer loop, then through the kitchen. We didn't talk, though whether that was from fear of being overheard by Waughm or from, well, fear in general, I couldn't decide. So many thoughts were tumbling in my head, but I kept coming back to this: *Mom was still alive*. The Scrimshander had her, but she was alive.

We finally reached the loading dock outside the school, and Lydia made sure the door locked behind us.

"That was *amazing*," Lub said. He didn't seem frightened at all. "Are there more of them down there?"

"God, I hope not," I said. "I thought maybe she was one of your people. One of the Dwellers."

"Nobody's that fat down there," he said. "Besides. No gills."

We started walking back home. I said, "So this Intercessor isn't a Dweller. Lydia, do you have any idea what she is? Lydia?"

"They're really going to do it," she said. She was holding the flashlight, so I could barely see her face. "They're going to summon Urgaleth."

"And they need my mom to do it," I said. "They called her a vessel."

"A primitive but sturdy vessel," Lub said.

"Yeah, what's that primitive crack about?" I asked. "Is that because she's native Brazilian?"

Lydia hesitated. "Some people in the Congregation are a bit preoccupied with, well, racial purity."

"That woman's half fish!"

"Hey," Lub said.

"Sorry," I said. "But she's half something, right?"

Lub looked at Lydia. I already knew he could see in the dark much better than I could. "What?" I asked.

"Do I have to spell it out?" Lydia said.

"Yeah, I think you do."

Lub flexed his gills. "Years and years ago, the First and the humans living here, they sort of . . ."

"Interbred," Lydia said.

"So you and Lydia are probably cousins?"

"Let's not go that far," Lydia said.

"But yeah, she could be," Lub said happily.

"We're getting off track," Lydia said.

"You're right," I said. "The important thing is to find the Scrimshander before this Ashen Light thing happens. Do either of you know what that is?"

"I never heard it in English," Lub said. "But I think it's the same as the—" He made a warbling noise. "The Elders talk about it all the time."

"It's in our hymns," Lydia said, and sang a string of syllables.

"Your accent's terrible," Lub said.

"The point is, it's happening soon," Lydia said. "Urgaleth will rise."

"Bringing some 'precious cargo,'" I said. "Whatever in the world that is."

"That's the thing," Lydia said. "It's not going to be of our world."

"Too many unanswered questions," I said.

We'd almost reached Lydia's house. The lights were all still on. She said, "I should check on Uncle Micah."

That surprised me. I thought she hated him. I said, "Lub, can you give us a second?"

He ducked into the shadow of a clump of trees, and I walked with Lydia toward the front door. "We need a plan to find my mom," I said. "I was thinking about Tobias Glück's diary."

"Way ahead of you," she said. "We're going to need the Involuntaries. Come to the meeting house tomorrow night."

She reached for the door, and I said, "Wait." I lowered my voice. "Are you ever going to tell me what happened to your parents?"

She regarded me silently. "I told you," she said finally. "Anybody who crosses the Congregation, crosses the Scrimshander."

"I don't understand. The Scrimshander did that to them?"

"My parents were going to leave the church. Move out of Dunnsmouth. They couldn't go along with the Congregation anymore. Then one night, when I was eight years old, they disappeared. They were gone for two weeks. When they found them, lying on the shore, they were like this."

"What did the doctors say?"

"They didn't know what to say. They couldn't do anything for them. Then the insurance ran out and they couldn't stay in the hospital anymore. So, Uncle Micah and Aunt Bee took us in." She took a breath. "Harrison, the Scrimshander works for the Congregation. And if he has your mother . . ."

"I get it," I said. "We just have to find her before that happens."

Lub walked with me down the hill. He kept trying to talk, but I was so distracted I could barely hear him. When we reached the rental house, he pointed and said something about visitors.

Saleem's taxi was parked in front of the house. It wasn't running, and there was no one behind the wheel. "I better go see what that's about," I said. "See you tomorrow?"

"Don't look so worried," he said. "The current will carry us home."

Inside the house, the lights were all on, but there was no one in the kitchen or the living room. Aunt Sel's bedroom door was closed.

"Aunt Sel?" I called out. "Did you call a taxi?"

There was no answer. I went to her door. "Aunt Sel? Are you all right?"

From inside I heard a thunk that sounded like a body hitting the ground. I reached for the doorknob—but then the door opened a few inches.

"Harrison, you're home." Aunt Sel was dressed in her nightgown. "Good study group?"

"It was fine. Did you call Saleem? His car's out front, but—"

She raised an eyebrow.

"Oh," I said.

She smiled brightly. "See you in the morning!"

Morning was . . . interesting.

By the time I woke and hopped out to the kitchen, Aunt Sel was sitting at the table with a cup of coffee, and Saleem was in the kitchen—making breakfast. He noticed me, then did that over-chipper thing people do when they're nervous. "Morning, Harrison!"

Then he noticed my leg. Or rather, my lack of one; I hadn't put on the prosthetic yet. Aunt Sel had told him about it on our way back from the lobster dinner, but the first glimpse of the stump can throw people. Fortunately, we'd pretty much maxed out on awkwardness.

"How do you like your eggs?" he asked.

The same way you like my aunt, I thought; over easy. Instead I said, "Scrambled is fine."

Aunt Sel pushed her coffee over to me. "It looks like you need this more than I do," she said.

I'd had trouble falling asleep, and when I finally did I'd dreamed of walking through downtown San Diego, and everywhere people were sprawled on the sidewalks and streets, unconscious. Coma city. Not too hard to analyze, I know.

"Saleem," I said. "You study stars, right?"

"Astrophysics covers that, yeah." He dropped an egg into the pan. "Mostly I'm trying to figure out what happened in the first couple nanoseconds after the big bang."

"But you've studied astronomy, right? Have you ever heard of the 'Ashen Light'?"

"How'd you hear about that?" Saleem asked.

"So it's real?" I tried to hide my excitement. "I heard somebody talking about it, but I didn't know what it was. Or when it's going to happen again."

"Nobody knows," he said. "It's random—or at least unpredictable with the knowledge we have now. There's a green glow that can be seen around Venus in certain conditions. The earth and the moon have to be in the right position, partially blocking Venus so we can see just the edge of its atmosphere. A crescent moon works best."

I thought of a line from "The Ancient Mariner": "The horned moon, with one bright star within its nether tip." I said, "So that's the Ashen Light, this green glow? I thought from the way they were talking that it had do with the stars, not a planet."

"Well, the ancients thought that the planets *were* stars." He worked the spatula under the egg and turned it. "People still call Venus 'the evening star.' Then again, people used to think the Ashen Light came from Venusians lighting huge fires to burn their crops. That theory's not in favor these days."

"What is it, then?" Aunt Sel asked. She seemed amused by this scientific conversation.

Saleem looked over his shoulder at her and grinned. Oh jeez.

"Lightning," Saleem said. "That's current thinking, anyway. Huge amounts of electricity, lighting up Venus' whole atmosphere. When it's happening, you can see it with the naked eye, if the sky's clear. But like I said, it's random, and almost nobody catches it in action."

"What if it's not random?" I asked. "What if somebody had

figured out the schedule on Venus, and when it would be visible on Earth?"

"If you figure that one out, let me know," Saleem said. "I'll make *that* my dissertation."

I itched to tell Lydia and Lub about what I'd learned from Saleem about the Ashen Light, but Lydia was in school, and Lub—I had no idea on how to reach him. We'd have to work out some system for contacting each other; he couldn't just keep showing up at my bedroom window. What was the Aquaman equivalent of the Bat Signal?

I didn't know what to do with myself. I took a shower and got dressed. I walked around the house, trying not to think of what might be happening to Mom right now. Had she known before we came here how dangerous Dunnsmouth could be? The last morning I saw her, she'd found that note in the truck. *Stay out of the water.* Then she'd tried to send me off to Grandpa. But *she* wasn't going to leave. She'd been determined to get to this town as soon as possible and get the buoys in operation the very next day after we arrived.

Why the rush? I'd chalked it up to AMP mode, but now I thought she was working on another deadline. Did she know about the Ashen Light?

I went to her footlocker, opened it, lifted out all the file folders, and set them in piles in front of me. Where to start?

"Hey, Ahab." Aunt Sel was leaning in the frame of my bedroom door. "Saleem's here. I thought all of us could go up to Uxton, get some lunch, see the sights."

"I'm fine."

"I wouldn't go *that* far," she said. She squatted in front of me. "Seriously, kid. Are you okay?"

"I told you—"

"Yes, you're stupendous, top form, absolutely smashing—

except when you're actually smashing someone."

Waughm. Right.

"What are you looking for?" she asked.

"Nothing. I just thought I'd get Mom's notes in order for when she gets back. She was never that organized."

"Right."

"Go, have fun," I said. "Just don't throw Saleem off a balcony if you find out he has a girlfriend."

"Hmm. Distracting banter. Excellent tactic." She frowned at me, then stood and frowned some more. "You have my cell number, yes? I should be able to have a few bars in Uxton."

"I'll call if I get any news," I said.

I started opening folders. The papers represented every facet of my mother's obsessions: There were articles on every large shark, whale, squid, and octopus, including several on "abyssal gigantism," which described the evolutionary trend of creatures in the deepest depths of the sea to grow huge.

After two hours of reading, I'd found nothing on the Ashen Light, or Venus. Out of desperation I started opening the sample cases. I used to love when Mom let me look through these. I opened up one to find my favorite oddity: a sealed glass jar, filled with formaldehyde, that preserved a section of a colossal squid tentacle. The thick, faintly pink tentacle had a dozen white, tooth-like hooks that were capable of rotating. Sperm whales had been discovered with raking scars in their hides that were probably made by these hooks. The sperm whales usually won the battle, Mom said, but the squids put up a fight.

I started repacking the footlocker. There was one box I didn't recognize; it was metal, with a little padlock on it. None of the other cases were locked.

I stared at it for a long moment. Was Mom trying to hide something from me? Or from other people? It wasn't much of a lock. I'd seen bigger ones on luggage. I could probably bang it open with a hammer.

I decided she'd forgive me.

In the end, it took a pair of pliers and some work with a thick screwdriver. The lock popped off, and I opened the box. Inside was a leather journal. I opened the first page and saw a signature I didn't recognize.

If found, please return to Harrison Harrison, 2824 Hiker Hill, San Diego, CA.

My dad's journal.

I read the first few entries, which were notes about his first trip to Brazil where he met Mom. Then I started flipping pages. I'd learned from Tobias Glück's journal to skip to the end. And I wasn't disappointed.

Folded into one of the late entries was a loose page of onionskin. It was a pencil rubbing of some engraving he'd found. At first I thought it was a drawing of a squid fighting a sperm whale; then I realized that it was a drawing of one creature: a giant thing with the head of a squid and the thick body of a whale. Under it, my father had written: "Inscription: U'glth m'eh rtalgn. Same as Urgaleth?"

Dad had come to Dunnsmouth looking for this. And Mom had come back for it. She wasn't chasing the colossal squid—she was after this thing. She'd been lying to me the entire time.

Well, I thought, I'd lie to me too.

That night I was one of the first to arrive at the basement hideout of the Involuntaries, but Lydia had already been there for some time. She'd taped up maps of Dunnsmouth—mostly of the shoreline—and had marked several areas with red Xs.

"What's this?" I asked.

"I've been going over Glück's diary. It's not too clear where, exactly, he entered the Scrimshander's cave, but these are the likeliest places."

"Wow. Thorough."

The others slipped into the room one by one. When Flora arrived she marched to me and planted a kiss on my lips.

"Oh. Hey. What was—?"

"That was for choking Waughm," she said.

"Too bad you couldn't finish the job!" Garfield said, laughing.

"Well, I didn't mean to . . . uh . . ."

Lydia looked annoyed. Bart solemnly shook my hand. Then Ruth approached, carrying Isabel. For a second I thought she expected me to shake hands with the doll, but then Ruth whispered, "You're famous. Everybody's talking about it."

"*Next time bring a knife,*" Isabel intoned.

"Okay, let's get started," Lydia said. "We have a lot to cover." Everyone took their seats. Ruth again placed Isabel on her own chair. Lydia said, "We now know that Harrison's mother is being held by the Scrimshander."

Garfield's eyes went wide. "That's not good."

"But that means she's still alive," I said. "And we know a few other things as well."

I told them about the fire at Ruck's garage that sent Micah to the church, leaving out the part about how it was set by a Dweller who happened to be a friend of mine. Lydia then told them about Waughm's meeting, and the sudden appearance of the Toadmother.

Bart squinted at me as if he had a headache.

"Minds blown?" I asked.

"Yes," he said. "Some blown-age."

"*Waughm* was running the meeting?" Flora asked.

"Waughm," Lydia said.

"Let me get this straight," Garfield said. He couldn't stay in his seat. "The Intercessor, the secret controller of the inner circle of the Congregation, is a ten-foot-tall woman with super strength?!"

Lydia nodded. "You've gotten it straight."

"Who swims up *inside the school*. In the pool *we* swim in."

"Again, couldn't be more linear," she said.

"I thought it would be Montooth calling the shots," Flora said.

"The Intercessor is working with the Dwellers because she thinks they can summon Urgaleth," Lydia said. "And something Urgaleth is bringing back with it. We don't know what that is, but she called it 'precious cargo.'"

"I know now that my mom was looking for Urgaleth before she disappeared," I said. "Maybe she found out something they didn't like. But they evidently need my mom to do the summoning."

"*They will sacrifice her.*"

"We don't know that, Isabel," Lydia said. "But she's definitely part of the ritual. It's supposed to happen soon, whenever this 'Ashen Light' occurs."

"I have some info about that," I said, and relayed what Saleem had told me.

"If it's random, then how do we know it's so soon?" Bart asked.

"No, it *seems* random to us," I said. "The Dwellers know different. Maybe they're like Mayans or Druids, with their own weirdly accurate calendar system."

"Regardless, the Toadmother thought it would happen very soon," Lydia said. "So that's what we're going to assume too. Now. We have to attack this on four fronts."

I looked at Bart. I was expecting him to take control as the leader—or at least be annoyed that he was being pushed aside—but he was listening to Lydia as attentively as the others.

"Team One has to find the Scrimshander's cave," Lydia said. "We know it's somewhere near here. I've outlined a search strategy. Team Two has to keep eyes on Waughm. We have to know where he goes and who he's meeting. Team Three—"

"I have a question," Gar said.

"No, the teams cannot have names," Lydia said.

"How about colors?"

"I've got a different question," Flora said. "What are we

supposed to do if we *find* the Scrimshander?"

Ruth looked stricken.

"*Bring knives*," Isabel said.

"I'll lead the search team," Bart said.

"Nobody's bringing knives," Lydia said. "When we find the cave, we call in the authorities. Not Chief Bode, obviously."

"I have the number for a police detective in Uxton," I said. "We can trust him."

"How do you know?" Garfield asked.

"Because he's not from around here."

"What's Team Three do?" Flora asked.

"We have to keep watch on the *Albatross*. As soon as it even looks like it's leaving Ruck's garage, we have to know about it. I'll be spying on my uncle as much as possible, but I can't be at home all the time. That means we're going to have to trade off sick days."

" 'Truancy is a crime,' " I said. "Someone told me that."

Lydia shot me a look.

"*Extraordinary circumstances*," Isabel said.

"Harrison's the only one who's got all the free time," Garfield said.

"Maybe we should all get expelled," Flora said. "I've got some ideas about that."

Ruth said something I didn't catch. "What was that?" I asked.

"I can stay home as much as I want," she said a bit more loudly.

Flora and Gar exchanged a look I couldn't interpret. I waited for a waggle of fingers, but then realized that wouldn't work to talk about other Involuntaries—everyone here spoke fingercant. Everyone except me, but I was picking up a few phrases.

Bart had been staring at the floor, and looked up. "You said four fronts."

"That's right," Lydia said. "Team Four is secret."

"The team's secret, or what it's doing is?"

"Both."

Bart thought about this. "Okay, then."

I raised a hand. "Guys? We have a problem here. There's only six of us."

"*Seven*," Isabel said.

"Right. But that isn't nearly enough to do all this surveillance, much less search all the cliffs in Dunnsmouth Bay."

There was a moment of silence—but now the fingers were moving overtime.

"We thought you understood," Lydia said. "This is just the inner circle. There are many more Involuntaries."

"Oh," I said. "In that case, team away."

"Dibs on Team Black," Garfield said.

The others left, and I stayed behind in the basement with Lydia. "So," I said. "That went well."

Lydia looked up at the ceiling. "You can come out now."

From above us came a clunk, and then the door at the top of the stairs opened. Lub bounded down the stairs. "O great leader, please tell me my assignment!"

"The Involuntaries don't have a leader," she said.

"Right. Just tell me I'm on Secret Team Four."

"You *are* Secret Team Four," she said.

"Could you hear everything?" I asked.

"Mostly. The vent worked great."

"Just remember it goes both ways," Lydia said.

"Hey, did they suspect a Dweller *above*? I think not." Lub plopped down in one of the chairs. "So. What's my assignment? Raid a munitions dump? Smuggle arms across the border? Fight a giant robot?"

"What are you talking about?" Lydia said.

"Too much manga," I said.

Lydia said, "We need you to watch your people."

"The Elders? Ugh. I already do that. They're boring. There's a reason I spend all the time I can on land."

"It's still spying," I said. "You need to find out if the Ashen Light is coming. And if they start gathering together for the ritual, then you have to tell us. Besides, you're the only one who can do this."

His gills flapped open, and a fine spray shot out. "Okay. Fine. But you have to call me Team Aquaman."

18

I moved, and could not feel my limbs:
I was so light—almost
I thought that I had died in sleep,
And was a blessed ghost.

That Sunday afternoon, I found myself climbing the cliffs on the north side of Dunnsmouth Bay. It was the third day of the search, and Lydia and I were working our way up a long chimney between the rocks. Below us, over twenty students, most of them kids I'd never met, clambered over boulders. It knocked me out that so many of them were willing to spend their weekend searching for caves, even though we couldn't explain exactly why we needed them to do this. Lydia had said not to worry about it. The Involuntaries, especially the newest or most auxiliary members, were used to secrets within secrets, and we'd promised them we'd tell them someday. All they needed to know now was that it was for a good cause.

I'd been so wrong about Dunnsmouth Secondary—the students of the school, anyway. On my first day I'd seen nothing but zombies, brainwashed cult kids. I'd been taken in just like the teachers. All that time, these high-schoolers were sending secret messages to each other, right under the noses of the teachers. And they'd come together, to help an outsider.

Bart and several other students were wading in the water at the base of the cliffs. Every time someone found a hole, Bart was the first to go in. So far they'd found no actual caves, but if the

Scrimshander's hideout was here, that's probably where it would be. In Tobias' diary, the entrance to the Scrimshander's cave sat down near the shoreline. Then again, that was a hundred and fifty years ago, and we didn't have a clear idea of how high or low the waterline was then. Maybe the cave entrance had collapsed long ago. Maybe the Scrimshander moved from hole to hole, like an eel. Maybe he'd found himself a nice condo.

It was nearly 5:30 p.m., high tide. Even if the Scrimshander had kept his home in the same place, the entrance might be underwater right now. We could be walking right past it. I felt a little guilty that I wasn't down there in the water. At the beginning of the search, when we split up to cover more ground, I chose the high ground. The dry ground.

From up here, though, I could see the whole bay. The sun was going down, lighting up a bank of storm clouds. Two lobster boats where chugging into the bay. I was happy to see the clouds moving in. With no Ashen Light visible, we'd get another day to keep searching.

"Wait up," I said to Lydia. She looked down at me. For these climbs she wore dark pants and sturdy boots—the only time I'd seen her not in a long black dress. This was Action Lydia. "We shouldn't go any higher," I said.

"Why not?" she asked.

"Lub," I said. "His place is at the top of this cliff. In an old lighthouse."

"*Really*," she said. She sounded peeved that Lub hadn't told her this.

"We don't want to lead the rest of them up there," I said. "Besides, the cave entrance is supposed to be near the water."

"Fine." She began to climb down past me, and in the narrows we were face-to-face, our hips touching. I put out an arm.

"I know you're the leader of the Involuntaries. You may be trying to keep it a secret, but you're really bad at *not* being the leader."

"That is completely untrue," she said.

"I'm just trying to say thanks."

"Then you're really bad at *that*."

"I'm serious. I don't know what I'd do if you weren't . . . you. Commanding this secret army."

"This 'army' isn't doing much good, is it? Three days and nothing to show for it." She dropped past me and started down. "All right, people!" she shouted. "Head home. We'll use the phone tree for any news—standard homework code."

She glanced up at me.

"Yep," I said. "You're just one of the troops."

She almost smiled.

The inner circle of the Involuntaries met every night, sometimes only for ten minutes. After three days, everyone was getting frustrated with the lack of progress.

"Waughm's all over the place," Flora said. She was in charge of following him, and had recruited a team of people to keep him in sight wherever he went in the school. She kept all the surveillance notes in a spiral notebook. "He's up and down the hallways, barely sitting down."

"He's nervous," I said.

"Seems like it," she said. "He also runs errands outside of school, though we keep losing him every time he gets in the car."

"We know he's visited Bode at least twice," Garfield said. He had another team following the police chief, but that was mostly accomplished by tracking where his squad car went in town. And all the reports ended more or less at 10 P.M., which was the start of curfew.

"Any news about the *Albatross*?" Lydia asked.

"Not much," Ruth whispered. The girl had practically dropped out of school to watch Ruck's garage. She hung out in the woods by the docks, talking to Isabel. "Micah was there last night for fifteen minutes, but he's been the only visitor. No Scrimshander."

"And no Waughm or Bode?" Lydia asked.

"*Do not doubt us*," Isabel said. The doll was sitting two chairs away from Ruth, but I swear her voice came straight out of Isabel's porcelain mouth.

"Nobody's doubting you," Lydia said to the doll.

"Ruth, have you ever read Newton and Leeb?" I asked. Ruth looked at me blankly. "I think you'd like it. It's a comic strip, about this boy whose best friend is a robot that he thinks is real."

"*Sounds stupid*," Isabel said.

"Okay then . . . ," Garfield said. "Any news from the 'secret' team?"

"Sorry," Lydia said. "No leads there." Lub had told us none of his people had headed out to open water for their regular meeting with the humans—which made sense, considering the *Albatross* hadn't left the garage. He'd tried listening in on the Elders, but he hadn't heard anyone talking about Urgaleth or the Ashen Light.

"We have some good news, though," I said. "I think we know where this summoning of Urgaleth is supposed to take place. A few days ago I was in Uxton, and I was finally able to get on the Internet and confirm it."

"You found this on the *Internet*?" Bart said skeptically.

"Not exactly. I used my mom's account to log in to the NOAA servers. See, my mom set out radio buoys that send positioning signals to satellites. Three of them are still working. But one of them only pinged its location once, and then went offline—on the day my mom was attacked."

"Someone knocked it out?" Garfield said, excited. "It had to be Waughm!"

"I don't know who," I said. Actually, I had a pretty good idea who'd destroyed the buoy. The Elders probably took it out soon after the *Albatross* crashed my mom's boat. "But this turns out to be a good thing. Disabling the buoy is more suspicious than leaving it in place."

"You seem pretty confident about a single data point," Bart said.

"I like a confident man," Flora said.

"Yeah, well . . ." I couldn't tell them that I'd confirmed the location with Lub. When I showed him the map of the buoy's former location, he said that it seemed like the place where the Elders were meeting. Then again, Lub thought human maps of the sea were laughably inaccurate. "We still need to find my mom before they take her there."

"We can't find the Scrimshander's cave," Bart said. "Dozens and dozens of little cracks in the rock, sure. Lots of tunnels that go nowhere. But no secret lair."

"We need to narrow down the search area," I said. "What do we know about him? We should be thinking like my mom. Tracking the subject according to his known habits and habitats."

"If you run into a Scrimshander expert, let us know," Bart said.

"Oh," I said. Then: "*Oh.*"

"What is it?" Lydia asked.

"I need to visit the library."

"Nobody goes in the library," she said.

"Yeah, you keep saying that. I'd sneak in at night, but it has to be during the daytime." I needed to catch Professor Freytag before he went home.

"But you're suspended," Bart said. "And Waughm's patrolling the hallways like crazy. You'll never get in."

"Leave it to me," Flora said.

At 9:52 A.M., just as third period was starting, the big double doors of Dunnsmouth Secondary burst open, and the entire population of the school began pouring out, pushed out by the insistent *blat* of the fire alarms.

I strolled across the street toward the crowd. I'd ditched my down jacket and had put on a heavy black wool coat that Bart had lent me. Gar had given me a toboggan hat, which I pulled down to my eyebrows.

Mrs. Velloc appeared at the top of the steps. She stood in the middle of the flow of students, scanning the crowd—for anyone laughing, smiling, or otherwise indicating that they had pulled the fire alarm. I ducked behind a tall student. Then Flora sidled up and looped an arm through mine.

"Nice costume," she said. "Are you wearing makeup?"

"What? No."

"Pity."

Advance word must have gotten out to the students, because almost everyone was wearing a coat and hat. We milled about in the chilly air. I saw tall Bart on the fringes of the crowd, but I couldn't find Lydia or the other Involuntaries. The alarm went on and on.

"Where's the fire department?" I said.

"Oh, they're in Uxton," Flora said. "They never come for us unless we call and say it's a real fire."

"I can't believe this whole town hasn't burned down," I said.

"Again," she said.

A few minutes later the alarm went silent, and then Principal Montooth and Mr. Waughm came out to wave us back in.

The students began walking up the steps. Montooth and Waughm went back inside, but Mrs. Velloc remained planted by the front door, studying each face that passed. Flora must have sensed me tensing up, because she whispered, "Act two."

Someone shouted. A boy with black spiky hair stumbled backward and hit the ground. Another boy jumped on top of him, yelling, "She's *my* girlfriend! Mine!"

Mrs. Velloc ran to pull them off each other. Flora and I

strolled inside, arm in arm.

"What was that about?" I asked.

"Classic love triangle," Flora said.

Waughm and Miss Pearl stood by the office door, talking to each other. I dropped my head, and Flora steered me to the right, away from them. In a minute we turned a corner, and we were out of sight of the teachers.

"What would have happened if they were stopping people inside the atrium?" I asked.

"Act three. I really wish we could have used it." She handed me a key. "This is from Lydia, in case the library's locked."

They'd thought of everything. "Great show," I told Flora. "Four stars."

"I think we changed some lives here today," she said. "Ta!"

I jogged down the hallway ahead of the wave of returning students. The corridor in front of the library was empty when I reached it. The doors were closed, but unlocked.

"Professor Freytag?" I called. The library was dimly lit, as usual. I pulled off the borrowed coat and hat and left them by the front desk. Then I began to walk up and down the aisles, calling the professor's name.

The big table in the back of the room was still covered by the nautical map I'd seen on my second visit, but now there was a newspaper there. *The Uxton Beacon*, from several days ago. The second story on the front page said, SEARCH FOR SCIENTIST AND AREA MAN CALLED OFF.

Police say that the search for a man and woman missing at sea since last week has been discontinued. Rosa Harrison, of San Diego, California, and Hallgrim Jonsson, of Dunnsmouth, were in Jonsson's boat somewhere east and north of Dunnsmouth Bay when they lost radio contact. The boat has not been found.

Hal Jonsson's first name was really Hallgrim? That explained something I'd been wondering about.

I went back to the front desk. The surface was dusty, but the big ledger for signing out books was open, with an old-fashioned pencil still in the crease. The last entry was for *Ohio on Two Dollars a Day*, lent to Ishmael Shemp on October 11, 1972. I found a scrap of paper in the pocket of Bart's coat and wrote, "Prof. F, I must see you right away. Please call." I wrote the phone number of the rental house, then placed the paper in the middle of the desk. I turned toward the door—and there was Professor Freytag.

The man was studying the spines of the books on the shelf nearest the desk, muttering to himself. "No no no," he said. "Not that one, not that one . . ."

"Professor!" I said. "I've been looking all over for you!"

He wheeled about, startled. "Who are you?" He blinked at me through those thick glasses. "Wait. You're the science boy. Don't tell me your name."

"I know, I know, there's power in names," I said. "But I don't care. It's Harrison Harrison."

"I really wish you hadn't told me that."

"You owe me an explanation, Professor."

"I do?" He seemed upset by the news.

"You gave me the diary of Tobias Glück. You knew what was in there, didn't you? You knew it would tell me about the Scrimshander—*the* Scrimshander."

The professor raised his hands to his ears. "Please! I'm not permitted to talk about . . . certain subjects."

I stalked toward him. "You're going to have to. You have to tell me everything you know about him—starting with where his cave is located."

The professor strode away from me. "I'm sorry, I really can't help you. I told you, I'm not permitted—"

I reached for his arm—and my hand passed through his body.

I looked at the professor, then at my hand, then back to the professor.

He turned to face me, looking sheepish. "Ah. About that."

I couldn't speak.

"I should have been prepared for this eventuality," the professor said. "It's been obvious since you first saw me that you're a sensitive. Tainted by some exposure to the Other Side. The fact that you managed to *see* me as well as hear me shuffling about—well, that hasn't occurred since little Claudia, back in—"

"You're a ghost," I said.

"Let's not be vulgar. We are men of science. Let us say, rather, that I fit all the criteria for a Sturgean Standing Wave, which is to say, a coherent sympathetic oscillation in the luminiferous aether, although with certain atypical properties."

"So, a ghost."

The professor sighed. "Yes."

This made no sense, but it also made a lot of sense. I'd never seen him touch a physical object. I'd never heard of anyone who'd even seen him. "No wonder nobody goes in the library," I said.

"It's a sad commentary on the state of modern education," he said.

"I mean, because it's haunted."

"Oh, yes! That."

"Are you trapped here?" I asked.

The professor brightened. "Interesting question! I *am* strangely attracted to this place. I feel that what I'm looking for is close—very close. Furthermore, I don't seem to *want* to leave, which raises the thorny issue of free will. Do I not want to leave because I do not want to, or because I am not capable of *not* wanting to, do you follow?"

"Uh . . ."

"Let's just agree that I never seem to go anywhere else."

"Fine," I said. "I have a real problem. The Scrimshander's kidnapped my mom. I need to know where he's taken her, or where he's going to take her."

Professor Freytag frowned. "I wish I could help, my boy, but as I mentioned, I'm not permitted to discuss it."

"*Who* doesn't permit you?"

He pursed his lips. "I'm afraid I can't say. I mean this literally: I cannot say who, or what, has done this. I can only say there are certain restrictions on my waveform: a set of boundary conditions that—"

"*Stop!*"

The professor recoiled. "There's no call for anger."

And I was angry. Something churned in my head—a wild animal bashing against a cage. My right leg burned.

I took a step back, trying to calm myself. "Okay, you're saying there are rules you can't break. But you don't know why."

"As I said, free will is a tricky—"

"Are you a man of science, or not?"

The professor looked affronted. "Of course I am. Even though I'm immaterial, that doesn't mean I lack substance."

"*Then tell me where my mother is!*"

Professor Freytag opened his mouth. His form abruptly blurred, and he began to sink into the floor, shuddering like a heat wave on a desert highway. His arms flew out to his sides, and he began to vibrate, faster and faster. His body began twist into the ground. His shins vanished, then his knees.

They're reeling him in, I thought. Keeping him from me.

I didn't know who "they" were. I wasn't thinking at all. I jumped forward, arms wide, to stop him before he disappeared.

Then the entire room began to vibrate—or else I was vibrating with the professor, falling into his frequency. My arms were wrapped around his chest, heaving him up. I could feel his scratchy wool sweater, smell the years of tobacco smoke in its fibers.

Then, just as suddenly, he turned to vapor again. I fell through him, onto the floor. When I looked up, he was standing above me, both feet on the ground.

"Well, *that* was interesting," he said, sounding stunned. "What did you do?"

"It wasn't me," I said.

"Oh my boy, it most certainly was. You commanded me to speak, and now . . . I'm speaking, aren't I? I can even say . . ." His eyes widened in delight. "*Scrimshander*. There. I've named the beast himself."

I got to my feet. The professor said, "Quick, Harrison. Before it wears off. What do you want to know?"

"The Scrimshander is an ancient creature," the professor told me. "According to oral histories I was able to record when I . . . when I resided in a body, it was a simple messenger, ferrying messages between the human Intercessor and the Dwellers. But over time he became something else. A weapon."

"I've seen his knife," I said.

"More than that, my boy. What this creature does is prevent his victims' waveforms from dissipating. By some process I do not understand, their essences are frozen, as definitively as the portraits in his scrimshaw."

"What are you saying—he traps their souls?"

"Speaking unscientifically, yes. They become his possessions. They cannot act against him, forevermore. The most they can do is talk in the abstract about him—or perhaps point out a book or two that might be of interest."

"I'm so sorry, Professor. When did he—" I was going to say "murder you," but that seemed harsh. "How long ago did you run into him?"

"What time is it now?"

"About eleven-thirty in the morning."

"Then it was about ten hours ago," he said.

"Uh . . ."

"Why are you looking at me like that? Oh. It's not September seventh, is it?"

"No."

"Or 1932."

"Not even close."

"Hmm." He looked glum. Then he straightened his shoulders. "Let's consider that a benefit, shall we? In a way, this is a kind of time travel." His eyes widened. "Have we put a man on Mars?"

"Not yet. Professor, I need you to concentrate. Any day now, the Scrimshander's going to take my mother out to meet the Dwellers. For some reason they need her to raise Urgaleth—"

"The Mover Between Worlds!"

"That's the one."

"My mentor, Professor Armitage, first ran across mentions of this Urgaleth, but the texts were always incomplete. It was the rumor of a complete set of scriptures that first brought me to Dunnsmouth. I heard of the town from—"

"Professor. My mom. I need to find the Scrimshander's cave before they sacrifice her to Urgaleth."

"My boy, they aren't going to sacrifice her," he said. "The Mover comes whenever the stars are right, regardless of whatever human they toss on to the water. No, they probably need her to be the host, though why they're using a grown woman—"

"The host of what?"

"Oh! Is she pregnant?"

"No, of course she's not pregnant."

"Because the scriptures refer to choosing a child, as young as possible. Someone without much of a defined personality, you know, and what's more undefined than a fetus, eh? My theory, which I'd once hoped to publish before I perished, is that every

220

visitor from the Other Side needs to take on earthly form in order to persist on this plane—an empty vessel to act as a kind of, say, *diving suit* to allow it to walk around here."

"Professor, *what* visitor?"

"Hmm, what would be the phrase in English . . . ?" He held up a finger. "In Armitage's notes he used the Latin phrase '*sanguinem gubernator*,' which I thought a trifle dramatic, but that's Armitage for you."

"Blood pilot," I said.

"Ooh, you speak Latin?"

"Enough languages that are close to it," I said. "Okay. Do they need my mother at the same time as they're summoning Urgaleth?"

"Most likely," he said. "The Scrim—" He cleared his throat. "The Scrim—"

"What is it?" I asked. What could a ghost choke on—ectoplasmic phlegm?

"The, uh, *folk artist*," the professor said.

And then I understood. The rules were kicking in again. "What about him, Professor?"

"He will want the host to be very close by when Urgaleth comes," the professor said. "You'd better hurry, my boy. I seem to be losing my ability to—" He opened his mouth, then shut it.

"Quick then," I said. "Do you know where the Scrimshander's cave is?"

He shook his head.

I said, "Do you mean you don't know, or you can't tell me?"

He looked at me with a pained expression.

"Okay," I said. "Just talk in the abstract. Where might the home of such a creature be, in theory?"

A grin appeared on his face. Then he cleared his throat again. "In *theory* he would stay close to his possessions." He looked me in the eye. "And vice versa."

"Thank you, Professor Freytag." I started for the door, then turned. "Someday, I don't know how, I'll make this up to you."

That afternoon, I was waiting outside the school when Lydia walked out.

She saw something in my face. Raised an eyebrow.

"I know where the Scrimshander's cave is," I said.

"Under the *library*?" Lub said.

"You can quit saying that now," I said. We were in the alley outside the school. Lydia unlocked the kitchen door, and we slipped inside. We were getting to be old pros at this.

"But why would they do that?" Lub said. "Go to all that trouble to hide in a school, right under the biggest number of people in Dunnsmouth?"

"You're thinking about this backward," Lydia said. She clicked on her flashlight. "The caves are older than the school— and it was a temple before it was a school. They chose the site *because* of the caves—especially the main cavern."

"And it's worked till now," I said. "He's been hiding down here for over a hundred years."

In the Involuntary meeting room in Lydia's house, we'd gone over the maps of the school. There were no official floor plans to the building, but the students had made their own. As far as they knew, there were no rooms of any kind below the library. The only basement rooms at all were the locker rooms, Coach Shug's office, and the pool cavern.

Lydia led us down a hallway that I hadn't noticed on the Involuntary maps. From the inside it looked awfully similar to the outer loop I'd been in twice before, but this was obviously a different hallway, because it ended in a big oak door painted red. The door was unlocked, and opened onto the staircase that led down to the pool.

"That's odd," Lydia said. "All the hall lights are on."

"Is someone here?" I whispered.

We stood for a moment, listening. The only sound was the

faint hoot of air rising up the staircase. Lydia shrugged. "Might as well keep going."

We went down the stairs. The lights were on here, too. We went through the girls' locker room (dark, thankfully), but didn't step out to the arena because a) the entire place was lit up, and b) someone, maybe a few someones, was splashing and laughing like it was a pool party. A deep male voice and a higher female voice echoed in the large space, but we couldn't make out their words.

We hid in the locker room for another minute, but the sounds never died down. Finally I said, "I'll go look." So of course both of them decided to follow me. We got down on all fours and crawled out of the locker room. As quickly as we could we ducked behind the stone rows. I took a breath, then slowly lifted my head above the bench.

Down in the pool, Coach Shug and Nurse Mandi were . . . frolicking? Mandi pushed down on the coach's big white shoulders, and he allowed himself to be dunked. Her laughter ricocheted off the walls.

"Do they know that a giant toad woman lives in there?" Lub asked.

"Or the Scrimshander," I said.

"He must not," Lydia said. "Or else he knows that they never come unannounced."

We ducked down and crawled back to the locker room. Lydia kept her flashlight off. Our only light was the glow from pool lamps coming through the open doorway.

"Were they naked?" I asked, keeping my voice low.

"I don't want to know," Lydia said.

"*I* don't see what the big deal is," Lub said.

"Of course you don't," she said.

"So how long do we wait here?" I said.

"I say we take our time," Lub said. "I never liked this plan in the first place. I'm supposed to go into that water, alone, and look for a tunnel that might lead to either a sea troll or a knife-wielding mass murderer."

"Or both," Lydia said.

"I don't see how we have any choice," I said seriously. "My mom could be somewhere down there."

"And you are the only one with gills," Lydia said.

I said, "With great power—"

"Comes great gullibility," Lub said.

Out in the pool, the laughter had stopped. I couldn't hear either of their voices. Then the glow through the open doorway dimmed, then dimmed again; the mercury lights in the arena were being shut off, one by one. Then we were in the dark.

"Should I check out there?" I asked. "I don't want to . . . interrupt anything."

"Don't rush it," Lydia said.

We sat in the dark for another minute, and then we felt our way out to the arena. We couldn't hear Coach Shug or Nurse Mandi. Lydia turned on her flashlight—and I held my breath. No one yelled at us. Finally we walked down to the pool.

Lub stood at the edge with his big webbed feet hanging off the side.

Lydia touched his shoulder and pointed back the way we'd come. "The library is in that direction."

"Right," he said. His gills opened, closed. "No problem."

"You don't have to do this," I said.

"It's okay," he said. "I can always swim away, right? Nobody's faster than me in the water."

"Good luck," Lydia whispered.

Lub slipped into the water, feet first. Then a moment later he bobbed to the surface. "If I don't come back, donate my books to the library."

I started to answer, and then a row of lights lit up above us.

"Hey!" a deep voice shouted. "Who's down there!"

"Go!" I said.

Lub saluted, then vanished.

19

The creature's face loomed out of the haze of white and hovered within inches of her. His eyes narrowed, studying her. His lips parted. He looked like a man in love.

"Yes," he whispered. "Almost finished." And then, at the periphery of her vision, his hand appeared out of the ice-white mist, and the tip of the knife caressed her again.

She felt no pain. She felt almost nothing now but the cold of the rock floor against her back. She longed to close her eyes, but she feared that her eyes were already closed. There was only the white, and the creature, and the knife.

The creature talked to her as he worked. " 'Hurry,' she said. 'We need that body.' But does she understand me? Does she understand my work?" He touched her with the knife. "Art cannot be rushed."

Sometime later he sat back. His eyes roved her face. Then he nodded, and his eyes glistened with some emotion. "There," he said. "Yes."

The world tilted, and suddenly she was looking down at the creature. He smiled up at her with his sharp teeth. Regarding her with approval. Was she floating? No. He seemed to be holding her in the air with one hand. And at his feet lay something impossible:

Her own body, sprawled on the cave floor.

She could feel the rocky floor against her spine, the heat-leaching cold of that surface. But she was also above it, in his hands, feeling nothing.

"One last step," the creature said.

He set her on the floor, beside her body. Now she was staring up at the roof of the cave, and at the cave walls with their rows of shelves. The gallery of faces stared down at her. The man with the thick glasses. The dark-haired couple with wide eyes. The sailors and children and families. All of them vivid, almost moving but not quite. All of them so sad. She could hear them whispering to her.

She felt a stab of pain. Her palm. He'd cut into her palm.

It was almost a relief to feel something besides the cold floor. She held onto that pain, concentrating on it. The bright sensation was connected to her hand, and arm, and body. All she had to do was move that arm. . . .

"Shhh," the creature said. "You're about to become immortal."

She saw her own hand. The creature was holding it before her. There was no color in her vision. The thin wound in her palm welled with blood that seemed as glossy and black as ink. A dollop of blood detached, and dropped onto her. Into her.

It was so warm.

Another drop fell, and another. The blood slid eagerly along her cheek, along the lines that made her lips and eyes and nose. It filled her. Defined her.

"From blood and bone, to blood and bone," the creature said. "A new body, incorruptible. Do you know how beautiful you are?"

He lifted her from the floor and carried her across the cave. "You belong to the ages now," he said, and set her on the shelf.

20

With sloping masts and dipping prow,
As who pursued with yell and blow
Still treads the shadow of his foe.

"You want to explain what you're doing here?" the coach shouted. He marched toward us, still wearing nothing but his swim trunks. His body was huge and pale.

I nearly jumped into the water after Lub. But Lydia turned to face him and said, "I could ask you the same question." This was, hands down, the coolest response under fire I'd ever seen.

He stopped. "What did you say?"

Lydia nodded to a spot behind him, and he glanced back. Nurse Mandi stood in the doorway that led to the coach's office. A towel was wrapped around her body, and her hair was still wet and curly.

So much pale flesh turned red so quickly.

"We were thinking of a midnight swim," Lydia said. "We didn't realize how popular the idea would be."

"How did you get in here?" he said.

Lydia ignored the question. "I'm willing to make a deal," she said.

Nurse Mandi came forward. "Wilbur? Is that the Harrison boy?"

"It is," he said, and glared at me. "I thought you couldn't go in the water."

I had no good answer for that.

"Are you all right?" Mandi asked me. "No aftereffects from the accident?"

"I'm fine," I said.

"I'm glad," she said. "Tell your aunt that I also appreciate her not . . . well, calling anyone about me."

I had no idea what she was talking about. "No problem," I said.

"What accident?" Coach asked.

"When he fell in the bay," Mandi said.

"So," Lydia said. "Why don't we just go, and everybody forgets that they saw anyone down here. Deal?"

Go? I thought. What about Lub? He was still down there. Then Lydia caught my eye and silenced me.

The coach looked uncomfortable. "Don't do this again," he said finally. "It's dangerous to come down here at night."

I bet it is, I thought.

"Have a good night," I said, and then Lydia yanked me up the steps.

"We can't just leave him there," I said. We were striding down Main Street. The wind had picked up, and cold gusts were blowing off the sea. Storm clouds hid the stars.

"No choice," Lydia said. "Later, after the coach and Nurse Mandi leave, we can maybe sneak back in—but not now."

"But he's going to come back up and think we ditched him!"

"Harrison, you've got to stop panicking about things we can't change. Lub knows we were almost caught, and he knows where we live. It's not like he can't get out of the school without us."

"I guess. It's just . . . I hope he's okay."

Icy rain began to fall. The wind was fierce, and Lydia's hair whipped away from her face. I was happy to have the coat Aunt Sel had bought me.

We'd almost reached Lydia's house when we saw the light of a bicycle coming up the hill. It was Garfield, pedaling hard to move what looked like a hundred-pound relic from the 1950s. He practically fell off the bike when he reached us. "They're at Ruck's!"

"Who is?" Lydia asked.

He gulped to get his breath. "Waughm and your uncle! They're getting on the boat!"

I looked up at the sky. Where was Venus, and the green glow the Congregation had been waiting for? The storm clouds now cloaked everything, even the moon.

Gar turned and zipped down the hill. We ran after him, and suddenly it was as if all of New England had decided to stop us. The wind kicked up leaves and grit into our faces. Thunder boomed overhead, and the rain came down. It struck us in sheets, dousing us. We pushed the water from our faces and kept running. In the distance, lightning spiked between low clouds and the black sea.

Ruth and Isabel were waiting in the gravel parking lot of the pier. Ruth pointed at Ruck's garage. The *Albatross*, outlined by its red and white running lights, slowly backed out of the big open doors.

"Did they bring my mother onboard?" I asked her.

Ruth said something I didn't catch in the roar of the wind.

"What?" I yelled.

"*Slay them all,*" Isabel said.

"I don't think Ruth said that."

"I didn't see your mother!" Ruth said, shouting now.

The boat swung about, and I could see the main cabin, and the bridge above it. Several figures were silhouetted in its lights, but we were too far away to see who they were.

"It's going to cross in front of the bait shop!" Lydia shouted. She ran out onto the pier. I hesitated for a second, then chased after her.

The lights along the pier swayed in the wind. The entire structure seemed to shudder as the waves struck the pilings. At the end of the pier, the lights of the bait shop shimmered through the rain. I wouldn't have been surprised if everything suddenly went dark, the pier broke free from the shore, and the shack dropped into the bay. The lobster boats bobbed heavily in their berths. Lights shined from a few pilothouse windows. No doubt the crews were trying to tie everything down before the storm hit in full. Battening down the hatches.

Lydia was twenty feet ahead of me. A bulky figure appeared in front of her—Chilly Bob. He raised his hand to shield his eyes from the rain and yelled, "What the heck are—".

Lydia dodged to his right, barely breaking stride. He twisted to reach for her, and I went around to his left. Out on the water, the *Albatross* was aiming for the mouth of the bay, and seemed to be moving slowly in the choppy seas.

Lydia stopped, pointed over the side of the pier. "Bob's outboard," she shouted.

I looked over the side. Below, Bob's orange boat was tied to the pier, bucking in the waves. The boat rose up, then slammed into the pilings. No *way*, I thought. We'd die in that thing.

Someone grabbed my arm. "What you up to, little man?" Chilly Bob bellowed. His salt-and-pepper beard was strangely matted by the rain, becoming five separate beards fighting for control of his face. He'd added another layer of clothing, a green plastic poncho with a peaked hood, and rain coursed down the creases in streams and rivulets. He looked like a mountain in the rainforest: not just his own landscape, but his own ecosystem.

I tried to yank my arm free, but his grip was fierce.

"No more messin' about on my pier!" Chilly Bob said, and pulled me toward him. He shouted something else, but I was beyond hearing him now. The only thing in my head was the roar of static.

Instead of pulling away, I grabbed the front of his poncho

and yanked him toward me. His eyes went wide in surprise.

Pictures flashed behind my eyes: a dozen violent things I wanted to do to this man. "*Get out of my way,*" I said.

Chilly Bob released his grip. He backed away from me, then stumbled. He caught himself, then turned and ran down the pier, poncho flapping.

Lydia stepped up to me. "What did you say to him? Harrison?"

I turned to face her, and Lydia stepped back in alarm.

I took a breath, trying to calm myself down.

"Are you okay?" she asked. Rain had plastered her hair to the sides of her face.

"We've got to catch them," I said. The *Albatross* had passed the pier and was heading out to sea, picking up speed. "This way."

I ran toward a berth closer to the shack. Below was the lobster boat *Muninn*, parked nose-first against the pier. The rear of the boat was stacked high with lobster pots. No one was on deck, but the cabin lights still glowed.

I took a breath, then climbed down the ladder to the platform below, and then jumped onto the rocking deck of the boat. A man in a yellow rain slicker came around the side of the cabin, a length of rope wrapped around his shoulder. He saw me and stopped.

I shouted, "Mr. Hallgrimsson! We need your help!"

"Get off my boat!" Erik Hallgrimsson yelled above the wind. He looked up to see Lydia climbing down after me. "*All* you kids."

I pointed toward the back of the *Albatross*. "They're taking my mom. Trying to finish the job."

He glanced toward the departing ship, then turned back. "I can't help you. You're the worst kind of bad luck, kid."

"That's the boat that rammed the *Huginn*!" I yelled. "Those are the people who killed your father!"

He stared at me.

"Hal Jonsson *was* your father, wasn't he?" I hadn't figured this out until I'd seen Hal's true name in the newspaper in the library. Icelandic names are patronymic—so the son of Hallgrim Jonsson would have the last name of Hallgrimsson—and Erik's son, if he had one, would be named Eriksson. I stepped closer to him. "Are you telling me you're going to let them get away with it?"

He looked again at the *Albatross*. Its lights were barely visible through the rain. The ship looked like it had almost reached the mouth of the bay.

"You know this?" he said. "For a fact?"

"Guaranteed."

By the time Hallgrimsson cast off and we'd turned the *Muninn* toward the mouth of the bay, the *Albatross* had disappeared into the rain and fog.

"She could be two hundred yards in front of us," the lobsterman said. "Can't see a thing."

"You've got to go faster," Lydia said.

"If she gets to open water, we're not going to catch her," he said. "She's bigger and faster than us."

"Then go faster *now*," Lydia said.

As far as I could tell, most of our motion was vertical. The waves threw the nose of the boat up and slammed it down. The pilothouse was a small space, and smelled of lobster and diesel. I could barely stand to look out the small rectangular windows, preferring to concentrate on a patch of wall that wasn't moving, relatively speaking.

"Don't you hurl on my deck," Hallgrimsson said to me. With his foot he nudged a plastic bucket toward me. "Or on my life jacket." He'd insisted that Lydia and I both put on life preservers.

"I didn't think it would be like this," I said.

"This ain't nothing," Hallgrimsson said. "Wait till we get out of the bay."

Perhaps I moaned. He definitely laughed.

"Do you know where they're heading?" he asked.

I took a breath. "Back to where my mom was setting out the buoys on the second day."

"That's a pretty wide area."

"I can give you coordinates."

"Oh," he said. "Then punch 'em into the machine." He nodded at the GPS to the left of the wheel. It looked just like the car models, though the screen was bigger than usual. I detached myself from the wall and managed to make it the two steps to the machine without losing my dinner.

"Lights!" Lydia said. She pointed out the window. I could see nothing but the smear of rain across the glass.

From a rack above his head, Hallgrimsson took down a gigantic pair of binoculars—much bigger than the pair I'd bought in the mall. "They've stopped just outside the mouth of the bay, near the shore." He lowered the glasses. "I thought you said they were heading out to sea."

On the GPS screen, the crocodile mouth of Dunnsmouth Bay was easy to see. The *Albatross* was right up against the lower jaw. I zoomed out the map another level. "Lydia, the school's right about there, right?"

She came over to the GPS. Five or six hundred yards of rock separated the *Albatross* from the school.

"Okay, but—" Then she got it. "The Scrimshander's cave."

"We never searched out that far, because there's no beach," I said. "Now." A hundred and fifty years ago, Tobias Glück had walked to the cave from the docks. We'd assumed he'd gone to the north-side cliffs, because those were the only caves we could get to. But who knows how much the coastline had been reshaped by surf and storms and rising water levels?

"Global warming," I said.

Lydia said, "The tunnels could run right to the school."

I was such an idiot. Lub had told me that his people lived a ten-minute swim from the tip of the bay. It would make sense for the Scrimshander and the Toadmother to have made their tunnels there.

"What are you two talking about?" Hallgrimsson said.

"I may have lied to you," I said. "My mom's not on that boat—yet. I think they're stopping to load her onboard."

"That means we can still catch them," Lydia said.

"And what do we do when we do that?" he asked. "Board them like pirates?"

"As soon as we know she's on their ship, that's kidnapping," Lydia said. "We radio the authorities."

"Do you have an answer for everything?" Hallgrimsson said.

"For questions that dumb, I do," she said.

Hallgrimsson steered so that we'd skirt the cliffs. Finally I could see the lights of the *Albatross* and little else but a shadow that suggested the bulk of the ship. Hallgrimsson could see more with the binoculars. "There's a dinghy tied up to the back of the *Albatross*," he said. "And they've got something . . . What in the world are they doing?"

"What?" I asked.

"It looks like they've captured a whale or something. It's a big one. They've got a net over the side, and they're hoisting it up onto the deck."

Lydia and I exchanged a look. That was no whale.

"Just try to get close," I said.

The *Albatross* was hugging the shore, so Hallgrimsson aimed for the bay side of the ship. That way, he said, we wouldn't risk being pushed into the rocks, and if we got in front of them we might be able to stop them from getting to the sea.

We'd pulled within perhaps a hundred yards, and finally I could see the ship through the rain. "They've got her onboard," I said.

"Who, your mother?" Hallgrimsson asked.

"He means the whale," Lydia said. "The net's empty."

"I can see that," he said, looking through the glasses. "Must be heavy too; they're listing to one side."

"Pull up alongside," Lydia commanded.

"What do you think I'm trying to do?" He jammed the throttle forward, and the lobster boat roared up the next wave. When we came down, my stomach was a dozen yards back. But suddenly the *Albatross* seemed much closer. I could see the lights of the cabin windows now.

"What now?" Hallgrimsson said. "Some idiot is climbing up the back of the ship."

The nose of the *Muninn* rose up, blocking my sight. When it came down I could make out a dark shape pulling itself up the rope that connected the dinghy to the *Albatross*. There was something long and pointy strapped to its back.

"Is that a *trident*?" Hallgrimsson said.

I thought it was the Scrimshander, now outfitted with a longer weapon. Then I realized that the climber was naked except for some kind of satchel—and a pair of skater shorts.

"It's Lub!" I said.

"You know this guy?" Hallgrimsson said. We were within fifty feet of the rear deck now, and Hallgrimsson was trying to aim us to the left of the ship. Then the *Albatross* surged forward, and Lub slid down the rope.

"They're moving," Hallgrimsson said.

The ship's props churned the water beneath Lub's big webbed feet. He heaved on the rope, and regained some of the distance he'd lost. A moment later he lunged, and his hand fastened on the lower railing.

"Yes!" I shouted.

"No," Lydia said.

Another person had appeared on the rear deck. A tall man, dressed in black.

I looked at Lydia. "What's Montooth doing on there?"

The principal had seen Lub. He seemed shocked for a

moment. Then he crouched, and when he rose again he was holding a wooden oar. He extended it toward the fish boy. Lub kept one hand on the railing, released the rope, and reached for the oar.

Then Montooth jerked the oar back, and slammed it into Lub's face. Lub tumbled back into the water.

"Stop the boat!" I yelled. I may have yelled that several times.

"We'll lose the *Albatross*," Hallgrimsson said.

I froze for a moment. My mother was on that boat, only fifty feet away.

"We know where they're going," I said. "Save Lub."

The lobsterman swore, but he cut the throttle and started yelling directions: "Outside to the side deck. Unfasten the life preserver from the rail. Don't throw until you see him!"

The rain hit us full on, and I had to hold on to the rail myself to avoid being thrown off. Lydia said something, but the roar of the wind tore her words away. "Do you see him?" she shouted, louder.

Hallgrimsson switched on a bank of lights that lit up the water around us. Whitecaps intersected in crazy patterns; this close to the cliffs the waves were crossing each other. I leaned over the rail, feeling a sick fear in my stomach. I was going to fall in, and I was going to die.

"I can't see him!" Lydia yelled.

"Me neither!"

I moved to the back of the boat, between the stacks of metal lobster cages. Had we already passed him? He'd been hit in the face. Was he unconscious? Cut by the props of the *Albatross*? The water behind the boat was a white froth.

Someone grabbed my shoulder and I spun around. Lub grinned at me.

"Did you see me?" he said. He wore a canvas satchel like a

newspaper delivery boy, one strap over his neck. He was holding the trident in one hand; or rather, the trident was holding him. He was leaning on it hard. A gash was open on his forehead. "Total Aqua—"

His knees buckled, and I jumped forward and caught him before he fell. The trident clattered to the deck. Lydia appeared a moment later.

"I don't feel so good," Lub said.

I picked up the trident, and then Lydia and I got our arms under his and dragged him toward the pilothouse. Hallgrimsson, keeping one hand on the wheel, reached over and yanked open the door for us. We pulled Lub inside, and Hallgrimsson swore in surprise.

"Yeah," I said. "He's a Dweller."

Lub lifted a webbed hand. "Be ye not afraid," he said weakly. His eyes were drooping.

Lydia bent over him and touched the edge of the wound on his forehead. Now that we were out of the rain, I could see that he was bleeding. Bleeding a lot. Lydia said to Hallgrimsson, "Do you have a first aid kit?"

Hallgrimsson stared at Lub.

"*First aid kit*," Lydia said. "Now, please."

"In there," Hallgrimsson said, and nodded to a cabinet next to me. I set the trident on the floor, then slid back the cabinet door and pulled out a big red tackle box. Lydia asked for gauze and bandages, then told me to cut tape into three-inch strips.

"You've done this before," I said.

"Once or twice," she said. She took off her jacket and dried his face with the fleece lining. Then she began to dress the wound.

Hallgrimsson increased throttle and powered us away from the cliffs.

"Just follow the GPS," I said.

He nodded. I wasn't sure what he was thinking. We might have pushed him one step too far, from Previously Understood

Reality to Crazy Town, Massachusetts. I could guess how he felt.

The waves grew steeper when we left the bay. Every time the ship nosed up into the air, or slid down into a long trough, I knew—*knew*—that in the next moment the boat would flip over, and I'd be thrown into the water, where, despite this bulky life vest, I'd sink into the dark.

A particularly steep wave hit us, and the trident slid forward and nearly impaled Hallgrimsson's foot.

"Would you stow that?" the lobsterman said.

I picked up the weapon. It was heavy, but well-balanced. Both staff and tip were made from iron, and every inch of it was engraved with strange symbols. Just holding it made you want to stab something.

"Where'd you get this thing?" I asked.

Lub smiled. "I saw it and I just couldn't pass it up." He winced as Lydia wrapped another layer of bandage around his head. I tucked the trident into the corner, behind the fire extinguisher. "It was in the Scrimshander's cave," he said.

"You found the cave!"

"Pretty much right where you said. In the deep end of the pool I found a huge tunnel entrance. I figure, this way to the Toadmother! That tunnel kept branching, but the main way was obvious—it was the only passage big enough for her. I was feeling pretty good until it ended in a big iron door. No way I could get through that. So I backtracked, and started following side tunnels. I eventually popped up into an air tunnel. From there I just followed the smell of old food. And . . . bongo."

He sat up to reach into his canvas bag. "Nobody was there," he said. "But I knew it was his place, because of what was on the walls. One thing in particular." He held out a length of white bone as big as an oval serving plate. "That's her, right?"

Mom.

The portrait was beautiful and terrible. With the minimum number of delicate lines the Scrimshander had captured the determined set of her mouth, the way she pursed her lips when someone was trying to bully her—or me. But her eyes . . . Her eyes were so sad. The overall effect was of a woman braced for a fight that she knew she'd already lost.

"It's . . . warm," I said. I turned it in my hands. "It's like a living thing." I could almost feel it breathing. No, not *it*. Her. Mom.

"Can I see that?" Lydia asked. She took the scrimshaw carefully. After a moment she said, "I don't feel anything."

I shrugged. She said to Lub, "Were there more down there? More portraits?"

"Oh yeah," he said. "Lots."

"We'll have to go back there," she said. "Rescue them all."

"How did you get to the *Albatross*?" I asked.

"I just followed the tunnel. Eventually I heard the ocean, and I saw that little wooden boat—the Scrimshander and another man were rowing for the *Albatross*."

"Montooth?"

"If that's the big guy who walloped me—yeah, him."

I was still mad at myself for thinking Montooth wasn't involved. We'd focused all our attention on Waughm.

"When they got to the ship," Lub continued, "the Scrimshander threw your mother over his shoulder—she was lying in the bottom of the boat, it turned out—and carried her onboard. I started swimming, and that's when I nearly ran into the Toadmother."

"She was in the water?"

"Oh yeah. Swimming like a natural-born First. She didn't see me, though. I held back while she climbed into the net and they winched her up to the deck. Then I—well, you saw the rest. Is he going to stop staring at me?"

Hallgrimsson looked back at the window.

"It's okay," I said. "He's on our side."

The lobsterman grunted.

"Can we catch the *Albatross* again?" Lydia asked.

"Not unless she pulls over and waits for us."

"How long till we get to the GPS coordinates?" I said.

"In this sea? Another forty-five, fifty minutes at least."

"And how long will it take them?"

"A lot less."

Great. Very helpful.

Hallgrimsson got on the radio and tried to raise the Coast Guard, authorities on the land, other boats . . . anybody. All we heard back was static, so there was no way to know if we were getting through. "The storm's interfering," Hallgrimsson said. "Never seen anything like it." He kept trying for another ten minutes, and finally tossed aside the microphone.

Lub got to his feet. Hallgrimsson glanced at him but didn't say anything. He was still in the Reality Adjustment Period. But then, after a few minutes of silence, the lobsterman surprised me.

"My pa said he seen you people," Hallgrimsson said. "Nobody believed him."

"We don't usually show ourselves," Lub said. "Humans might whack us in the face or something."

"It wasn't good luck for him, either."

That was the second time Hallgrimsson had brought up luck. I said, "Your dad took my parents out, didn't he?"

Hallgrimsson's gaze remained fixed on the windshield.

"Thirteen years ago," I said. "My dad, my mom, and me."

"It was supposed to be a three-hour tour," he said. "Your dad wanted to see a certain spot, way out on the water. In the middle of the night. Made no sense, but he convinced my pa to take you. A storm came up out of nowhere. A storm like this. That's when he saw *them*. Hundreds of 'em, he said, their heads poking up out of the water like seals."

"Hey," Lub said. "We're not as ugly as *seals*."

"That would have been enough to convince everyone Pa was

crazy. But then he said that a sea monster flipped his boat."

A memory flashed into my head: a huge shape underwater. Tentacles. Tentacles and teeth.

"They wanted to blame Pa for the accident. Tourist drowned, little kid almost dead. Your mother said he had nothing to do with it, that it was all the storm. But Pa . . . he wouldn't stop talking about those fish people and that damned monster. The more he talked, the less people believed him. Just another crazy old sailor. He started drinking hard. I used to have to go pick him up and drag him home." He shook his head. "He never recovered from that trip."

"Yeah, neither did mine."

Hallgrimsson looked at me, and his face clouded. "Tragedy all around. That's where it all should have ended between your family and mine. And then your mom called out of the blue."

"She needed to charter a boat," I said. "It made sense to call Hal. She wanted him to be the one to take her out."

"And that fool wanted to go. Said he wanted to track down that monster. But I wasn't about to let him go out like that. I told her I'd take her out, for one day. *One day*. That was it."

"She was pretty mad at you when you wouldn't go back out."

"Oh, I know. Marched down there to yell at me. I left her shouting on the dock."

"She's pretty . . . forceful," I said.

"I didn't expect Pa to hear about it and come down to the dock. And then . . ."

"Yeah," I said. "Tragedy all around."

We bucked the waves for another half hour, and then Lydia said, "Lights!"

Up ahead, the rain had stopped. A hole had opened in the sky, and the clouds rotated around that void. The eye of the storm. The water below gleamed with moonlight. The running lights of the *Albatross* were faintly visible on the far side of that clear patch of water.

"There something else out there," Hallgrimsson said. He raised his binoculars. "A small boat. No, a raft, and there's . . ." He lowered the binoculars, squinted, and raised them again. "There's a person on it."

I pushed past Hallgrimsson and stepped out of the pilothouse. I gripped the rail with both hands and forced myself to move toward the bow of the ship. Lub came up behind me.

"That's her," I said, though we were still too far away for me to see the figure on the raft clearly.

Lub said, "The Elders are here. Hundreds of them." He pointed at the water, but I saw nothing but the gleaming surface. His eyes were so good in the dark.

"We're not all like this," Lub said. "The young ones of the First, we don't want to—" He made a noise in his own language.

"Yeah, well, they don't seem to be bothered by your lack of participation," I said angrily.

Lub frowned, and his gills flapped tight to his neck.

The raft floated perhaps two hundred yards away now. I looked back through the rectangular windows of the pilothouse. Hallgrimsson was at the wheel, Lydia beside him—and now she held the binoculars.

"Get closer!" I yelled.

The pilot nodded. Then suddenly the boat lurched. I grabbed the rail again.

The engine had cut out. I'd grown unconscious of that diesel throb until it was suddenly gone. In the pilothouse, Hallgrimsson had his head down, doing something I couldn't see. Lydia was saying something to him.

We'd stopped moving forward. The *Muninn* drifted sideways toward the raft, then backward. Lub and I ran to the back deck. The high stacks of lobster pots, strapped down with ropes, had somehow survived the wild trip without tipping over or sliding off the boat.

Through the windows at the back of the cabin, I could see Hallgrimsson's hand moving on the control panel. "What's wrong?" I called.

"Working on it!" he yelled. "The prop's been fouled."

The raft was farther away now. "Lub," I said. "You're going to have to swim to her. Can you do that?"

He grinned. The bandage gave him a jaunty, piratical look. "I can do that."

"*Can* you do it?" a voice said. "Perhaps."

A man-shaped figure seemed to pour over the top of the back rail. It straightened, and water ran from its dark gleaming coat.

"But *may* you do it?" the Scrimshander said. "That's the question."

21

Under the keel nine fathom deep,
From the land of mist and snow,
The Spirit slid: and it was he
That made the ship to go.

"Go get my mom!" I shouted, and shoved Lub away from me, toward the bow.

The Scrimshander moved so fast. In an eyeblink he was past me and upon Lub. He seized the boy by the back of the neck, then threw him against the wall of the pilothouse. Lub's head smacked against a window, and then he slid to the deck, limp.

"We have rules," the Scrimshander said. He looked down at Lub's body and shook his head. "The First stay in the water. The humans stay on the land. Only a few of us are allowed in both realms."

He twitched his fingers, and the long knife appeared in his hand like a magic trick. Perhaps a dozen feet separated us. The Scrimshander stood on the bow, and I was at the stern with the wall of lobster pots behind me.

"Soon, though, we'll have new rules." His smile, in the lights from the pilothouse windows, gleamed like a box of razors. "And new rulers."

He walked toward me, gliding along the narrow deck. The tip of the knife flickered in the moonlight like a flame. "Urgaleth will soon be—"

The pilothouse door slammed open, into the Scrimshander.

Erik, son of Hallgrim, closed the door and planted himself between me and the Scrimshander. In his right hand he held Lub's trident. "Get off my boat, Scrimshander."

The creature looked surprised. His hand was empty now; the knife had been knocked from his grip. "Oh, northlander." His sly smile returned. "I've always admired you. For your bone structure."

Suddenly the wind roared, and the *Muninn* spun like a toy boat above a bathtub drain. I was thrown to my knees.

The Scrimshander lunged at Hallgrimsson and batted aside the trident. The two of them crashed to the deck. Hallgrimsson yelled, "Run, Harrison!"

I jumped to my feet and ran, skidding and swaying, to the other side of the boat. Lydia stepped out of the other side of the pilothouse, the wind whipping her hair, and pointed.

The water under the cloud break seemed to boil, churning with white tops. The *Muninn* was caught in the outer rim of a huge whirlpool, circling at great speed and rotating at the same time, like a spinning planet caught in the orbit of a sun.

The center of the whirlpool was a circle of smooth water like the center of a roulette wheel. The raft floated in that eddy, spinning slowly. Mom lay on it on her back, unmoving and seemingly unconscious. She still wore the clothes I'd last seen her in, two weeks ago. But her arms and legs were splayed, tied down. If the raft flipped, she'd drown.

I ran past Lydia, circling around the front of the pilothouse. The Scrimshander's knife lay on the deck. I picked it up.

Lydia caught up to me. "Look!"

The *Albatross* was stationed well back from the whirlpool, Montooth standing at the bow. But that wasn't what she was pointing at. Between the *Muninn* and the *Albatross*, on the outer edge of the whirlpool, the water seemed choked with fish.

No, not fish. Dwellers. Hundreds of gleaming bodies swam with the wheel-like current.

Lydia put her mouth to my ear. "Can you hear them?" she shouted. "They're singing!"

Somehow, the strange pitch of their voices carried through the roar of the wind. I thought I recognized the song.

"It's 'Rise, Oh Rise'!" Lydia said. Right. One of the hymns from Voluntary.

The *Muninn* spun again, and my mother's raft skidded into view, then just as quickly zipped away again. I looked at the knife, then jammed the hilt under the straps of my life vest. It would have to hold. Then I grabbed the rail and levered my non-meat leg up over the side.

Lydia grabbed the back of my vest. "What are you doing?"

"I've got to get out there!"

I looked down at the churning water. It was impossible to see below the surface.

"Help Erik!" I said. The *Muninn* spun like a compass dial. I hung on, and then the raft appeared, perhaps a hundred yards in front of us. My vision narrowed. The night curled in on me until I could see nothing but the raft and the length of water that stretched before me like a silver-black road.

I gripped the hilt of the knife, and jumped.

The freezing water crushed me like a fist. The cold squeezed shut my throat, burned my nostrils, roared in my ears. Then I popped to the surface and gasped.

I tried to take a breath, but my chest had seized up. My jaw felt like it was trying to grind my teeth to nubs. I pawed at my chest and was relieved to find the knife still there.

A wave carried me up, and I looked around frantically. The *Muninn* was less than ten feet from me. Then I spotted the raft, much farther away, and my mother, strapped to it.

Breathe, I told myself.

Swim.

Mom always said I could swim before I could walk. A real water baby. Somewhere, down at the muscle level, I must have remembered something, because my arms churned, my legs kicked.

Don't think about what's under the water.

Waves slapped me in the face. The *Muninn* was somewhere behind me, the *Albatross* even farther out on the edge of the whirlpool, but I didn't look for them. I blinked away the burning salt water and focused on the raft. I needed to power through the rough water at the edge and reach that smooth center.

Something tugged on my leg. I would have screamed if I was capable of moving my jaw.

Then I realized what was happening—my carbon-fiber leg was filling with water. I stopped swimming, letting the life vest hold me.

Detach the leg, Harrison.

But it's really expensive.

Detach the leg!

Okay, but Mom will kill me.

The snaps were under my jeans. I bent at the waist, trying to reach my ankle, and dunked my face into the water. A strangled noise escaped me. There was no way I could lift the jeans high enough. I'd need to kick off my shoes, then peel off my jeans.

Or . . .

I pulled the knife free. With one arm I stabilized my position, then jammed the blade into the side of my "calf." The blade tip stuck into the carbon fiber. I tugged upward, splitting the denim. A wave knocked me, and the blade jumped up almost to my knee.

Easy there.

If I hit meat, I'd bleed out in the water. Though I might not feel a thing in the cold.

I moved the blade down, across the point where the nylon strap should have met the plastic lock. I couldn't tell if I was there or not; it was like trying to tie my shoes while being thrown around in a washing machine.

I reached down with my other hand and pulled. The leg resisted me, then popped free of my stump. I pulled it out from the leg of my jeans and let it go.

Goodbye expensive leg. Goodbye cheap shoe.

Where was the raft? The current was twisting me.

Many yards away, the *Muninn* lurched into view. The Scrimshander's arms were wrapped around Erik. He'd lifted the man off the deck, and seemed to be squeezing the life out of him. A few feet away from them, Lydia stood with her feet apart, gripping Lub's trident, but the man and the creature were too entwined for her to strike. Then just as quickly the tableau spun out of my view.

I couldn't see the raft, but I could see the cloudless patch of sky at the center of the whirlpool. I'd aim for that. I pushed the knife into its makeshift scabbard in my vest and began to swim. A few seconds later, the *Muninn* came around again, farther away from me. The Scrimshander still had Erik locked in that bear hug. But then Hallgrimsson yelled, a war shout that carried over the water and wind, and brought his forehead down into the Scrimshander's face. The creature released his grip on the man, stepped back—

And Lydia stabbed him in the spine.

The creature screamed—a high, gargling squeal. He bent almost backward, then twisted to face Lydia, as flexible as a snake. The trident was still embedded in his back. The *Muninn* slid away to my left. I spun to follow its movement.

The Scrimshander leaped toward Lydia, and then froze in midair, his arms outstretched in a strange paralysis. Then he began to levitate. His feet twisted in the air, and then he rose higher.

Hallgrimsson had grabbed the trident, and the Scrimshander was impaled on it like a fish on a fork. The lobsterman raised the creature above his head, and with a heave sent him flying over the rail behind him—away from me, thank God.

A thrill ran through me, a hot jolt of energy better than Aunt Sel's tea. I turned about, spotted the patch of clear air. When the next wave came, I dove into it. I kicked hard with my meat leg, and then the buoyancy of the vest pulled me to the surface.

Swim. Don't think.

Some time later I realized that the wind had ceased howling. I stopped and treaded water. The surface was as glassy as a lake, and the raft was only fifty feet away. It was a flimsy thing, just a bundle of logs barely wide enough to hold her. My mother's face was turned away from me.

The voices of the Dwellers called across the water. The circle of black storm clouds still surrounded me, but the sky directly above was a deep, cloudless black, bristling with stars. The moon was a bright crescent. Tucked almost inside the cradle of the moon was a bright star that seemed to pulse with a faint green light.

The horned moon. And the star within its nether tip was the evening star—Venus, glowing with the Ashen Light.

I threw myself across the final yard to the raft. The fingers of my left hand smacked against the wood.

"Mom!" My voice sounded faint even to me. She didn't move.

My every muscle shook. I'd never been so tired. I took a deep breath, then another. Still holding on to the raft with one hand, I let myself sink until my arm was almost fully extended. The black surrounded me. My brain suggested, in a reasonable voice, that I could just let go. Wouldn't that be more relaxing? Suddenly frightened, I drew the blade and hauled myself upward.

I broke the surface, and the raft tilted toward me. I pulled myself a few feet out of the water, and before I could slip back I plunged the blade into the wood.

I hung there for what seemed like a full minute, clinging to the raft and the knife handle, breathing hard. Then I worked first my left shoulder, then right, onto the surface of the raft. I threw one arm over my mother's stomach and used her body to climb up.

I lay beside her. The raft bucked and dipped, as if trying to throw me off. Her face seemed so pale in this light, her lips almost blue. I put my hand on her chest, just below her throat. She wasn't breathing.

Don't panic.

Her chest rose. Or else it was my hand that moved? I waited, my brain thudding, and then her chest rose again. She was breathing. She was breathing.

I went weak with relief and almost collapsed on top of her. But I had to free her before the raft tipped. Her wrists and ankles were tied to the timbers with thick ropes. I reached behind me, found the handle of the Scrimshander's knife, and yanked it free.

I started with the rope binding her right wrist. The rope parted with an ease that made me newly frightened of that blade. I leaned across to her other wrist—and saw a shadow move over the water.

No, not over.

A shape rose out of the depths. The raft tipped up, and I plunged into the water.

The thing filled the sea below me. Its body was too big to see at once; I only sensed its size, the way the shadow of a mountain tells you of its mass. The body moved beneath me, a vast expanse of dark flesh just under my left foot.

And then it was past me. Still my limbs refused to move. I sank into the black depths, lungs burning, ears pounding.

And then, a sliver of light to the right, like the reflection of the crescent moon. I stared at it, and the crescent swelled, filled with white, and became an alabaster disk: the milk-white eye of the beast. The tentacles bloomed in front of me, then wrapped around themselves again, as if hugging themselves in excitement. The great eye drank me in.

I recognized it. And it recognized me.

The knowledge shuddered through me. This was the thing that had touched me. The thing that had taken my father. And it somehow knew that I was that child.

I should have felt nothing but fear. I should have sunk into the dark, or been swallowed by the beast. But then static roared in my head, and the black hole of rage I'd carried with me my entire life—that rage that I'd stoked ever since my mother disappeared—blossomed into something like heat.

I screamed at the creature. Or maybe not. Maybe that was a false memory generated by an oxygen-starved brain. Because how could I scream when I was out of air?

My paralysis, however, was broken. I kicked for the surface, and it seemed as if two legs propelled me. I swam blindly, instinctually, not sure if I was moving in the wrong direction. Then my face broke the surface, and I gulped air.

The raft was a dozen feet away. I took another breath, and swam to the raft, to *her*. My hands slapped against the wood, and this time I hauled myself onto it with idiot strength. The knife was gone. It must have been knocked from my hands when the raft tipped.

Mom was still unconscious. I got to my knees, scanning the water. The raft still stood in the center of a glassy lake. The *Muninn* still orbited at the edge of the whirlpool, along with the scores of Dwellers, their heads still visible, singing in those warbling, disturbing voices. Behind them, safely outside the whirlpool, was the white bulk of the *Albatross*. I could see a huge figure on its front deck: the Toadmother, taking in the show.

A hundred yards from me, the glassy surface of the water swelled, becoming a great dome. Then the shell cracked, and Urgaleth thrust upward. Water poured from its knuckled spine. Gripping its back was a lustrous oil-black blob the size of a man.

It could have been some tumor, or a weird external organ—but somehow I knew that it was something that rode *on* Urgaleth, like a lamprey. Or a parasite.

Urgaleth had delivered its precious cargo. The Blood Pilot had made it to our world.

The bulk of Urgaleth surged toward the raft, and the black thing leaped from its back, or was flung from it. It seemed to glide through the air, flattening like a manta, a blot of deeper black against the star-fuzzed sky. Its arc would take it to the raft.

I cried out and threw my arm over my mother. Then the blob splashed into the water, inches short of the raft.

The wave of Urgaleth's surfacing rose like a wall. The raft went near-vertical. I latched onto Mom, thankful that she was still tied down by three limbs, and then the front of the raft dropped, skating fast along the back of the wave. My mother's free arm flopped like a bronco rider's. I couldn't do anything but hold on.

Another wave, smaller than the first, tossed us up. The raft bucked and slid, but did not flip. The next wave was smaller still. Were Urgaleth and the parasite gone?

I moved across my mother and felt for the ropes that held her left wrist. The knot seemed like a solid lump. I'd lost the knife. How was I going to free her?

The back of the raft dipped, and water splashed over my ankle. I glanced back.

A trio of blue-black tendrils rose out of the water and latched on to the logs between my mother's legs. The creature rolled up out of the water. It seemed to change shape with each movement, growing and absorbing limbs as it needed them. A globulous head formed, then fell forward, as if bowing in prayer. A new tendril extruded from its side and caressed my mother's foot.

"No," I said. "She's not for you."

The Blood Pilot rose up. A hole opened in its surface, and the interior was ringed with teeth.

I recognized it now, as I'd recognized Urgaleth. This thing had taken a piece of me when I was three years old. Its bite had been poison, and had put me in the hospital for months. But it had never left me. Some of the infection stayed inside me. It roared in my head when I was angry. If I had let it control me, I would have killed someone by now. It would have liked that.

A second tendril reached for Mom's other leg.

I screamed. I don't know what I said, or in what language. All I heard was static. But I do know that it was a *command*.

I felt the same rush of power I'd felt when I forced Professor Freytag to solidify, when I'd made him speak despite the Scrimshander's hold on him.

"She's *mine*," I said.

The Blood Pilot shrank back, recognizing a fellow predator. And like any hunter, it understood territoriality.

"Go!" I shouted.

It oozed over the edge of the raft—at first slowly, and then all at once.

I dropped onto my butt, shaking. After a moment I realized that the *Muninn* was under power again, and churning toward me. Good. That was good. I'd need that trident to cut through these ropes.

Lydia was at the bow. She was pointing at me. No, not at me. Past me.

I twisted to see. The *Albatross* floated on the other side of the whirlpool. Montooth and the Toadmother stood on the deck, and the huge woman was screaming—not in fear, but in rage.

"COME BACK HERE, YOU STUPID CREATURE!" Her bellow carried across the water. "DON'T YOU LEAVE ME! BRING ME THE PILOT! BRING IT TO ME!

Fifty yards from her, Urgaleth surfaced again. Huge flukes like charcoal wings swept up and crashed down, loud as thunder. The sea buckled. But this time Urgaleth didn't dive. It coursed along the top of the water . . . heading straight toward the *Albatross*.

Perhaps they had time to say a prayer to whatever gods they worshiped. Certainly the god rushing toward them wasn't listening.

Urgaleth, the Mover Between Worlds, slammed into the *Albatross*. The ship exploded like a matchstick model, timbers and shards pinwheeling through the air. I crouched over my mother and ducked my head. When the waves subsided, both ship and beast were gone.

22

O dream of joy! is this indeed
The lighthouse top I see?
Is this the hill? is this the kirk?
Is this mine own countree?

Mom lay in the center of a large bed. She'd become a switchboard for a dozen tubes and wires, all connecting her to a choir of beeping, hissing machines. Her skin was pale, her lips colorless but strangely glossy from the Vaseline the nurses had applied. But what disturbed me most was that she was lying in a way she never did at home. Mom was a sprawler and a twitcher, and this person was as still and compact as a mummy.

But she was warm. I gripped her hand, and talked to her to convince myself that the machines were not lying.

The nurses weren't happy that I was out of my own bed. I'd been checked in last night, after passing out in one of the emergency examination rooms, and had woken up in a room with Aunt Sel asleep in a chair beside me. I'd insisted on seeing my mom, and had tried to hop into the hallway. Aunt Sel and the nurses had calmed me down by getting me into a wheelchair and taking me to her. As long as I stayed in the chair and didn't unplug the IV from my arm, they let me sit beside her. Aunt Sel told me to take as much time as I wanted and left me alone.

The doctors didn't know why she was in a coma. They'd taken CAT scans, sampled her blood, monitored everything they could think of. Besides the fact that she was a little malnourished and very dehydrated, they could see no reason for her continued unconsciousness. One of the older doctors said he'd seen this before, a spate of similarly unsolved cases in the area, the most recent one from ten years ago. Then they'd suspected a new type of virus. Their unofficial name for it was "the Dunnsmouth Disease."

I didn't try to tell them about monsters and mystical scrimshaw. They wouldn't have believed me. But I did try to tell Mom.

I told her everything, from the night she disappeared until the moment Erik Hallgrimsson had cut her free from the raft: meeting Lub and Lydia, spying on the Toadmother, outing Professor Freytag. Every new detail sounded more and more insane. But I told myself that Mom would understand, because she'd lived through half of the story herself. And someday she'd tell me her side of it: what had happened the night Dad drowned, and the night Hal Jonsson's second boat went down, and even, if I could bear to hear it, what the Scrimshander had done to her. That would come later, when she woke up. But for now, I talked and talked, because I was afraid to say the one thing I most needed to.

Finally, I was out of words, except for those. I held her hand in both of mine, and laid my forehead down on the bedrail.

"I should have found you earlier, Mom," I told her. "I'm so sorry."

All those days we spent searching the wrong stretch of coastline. All those days of following Waughm instead of Montooth. If I'd been smarter, I would have found a way to make Montooth turn her over to me. Or called down Detective Hammersmith to search the school, top to bottom.

But it was too late. Now she was a vegetable, turned into a living ghost, exactly like Lydia's parents. We came from a family of scientists, but what could science do in the face of this?

The door opened behind me. "Harrison?" It was Aunt Sel.

"There are some officers who'd like to talk to you."

I released my mother's hands and sat up. I wasn't ready for this.

"But there's someone who *insists* on talking to you first. Would it be all right if she came in?"

That could only be one person. "Sure," I said.

Lydia closed the door behind her. "I'm pretty sure she thinks I'm in love with you."

"Yeah." I couldn't think of anything more witty to say. I lowered my voice. "Is Lub okay?"

"He's banged up, but fine. Turns out he's a little hard to kill."

"How about Montooth?"

"Still missing. But I don't think anything could have survived that crash. Waughm's in charge of the school now. It turns out that he never got on the *Albatross*."

"Lucky him," I said. "But your uncle Micah?"

"He was steering the ship. Also missing."

"I'm so sorry."

Her face held no expression. "He brought it on himself."

"Okay, but—"

She handed me a piece of paper. I could tell by the off-kilter letters that it had been typed on an actual typewriter. "I had the Involuntaries bulletproof this," she said. "We think it's solid."

"What is it?"

"Our story."

"I'm supposed to *memorize* this?"

"The details, not the sentences. That would be an amateur mistake."

"It says that Garfield heard Montooth tell Waughm to 'get that Harrison woman' on the boat." I looked up. "Waughm will deny it."

"Sure. But we're going to implicate him as much as possible— Waughm and Chief Bode. Let them squirm."

The rest of the story was almost the truth. After getting the word from Gar, I convince Erik Hallgrimsson to follow the *Albatross*, he tries to radio the Coast Guard but fails, and then when I see my mom tied up to the raft, I instinctively dive in to save her.

"No mention of Lub," I said. "Or Dwellers. Or sea monsters."

"We thought it was best to keep it believable."

"So what's the explanation for how the *Albatross* blew up?"

"Not your problem. Don't speculate."

I looked it over one more time, then handed the sheet back to her. "There's one thing that doesn't make sense, though."

She raised an eyebrow.

"You. Why were you on the boat with me? Why'd you do all this for me? This was my problem, not yours."

"Because we're in love," she said flatly. "Everybody thinks so."

"You're a criminal mastermind," I said.

"We're not finished breaking the law yet, Harrison Squared."

A week later, I was standing with Lydia at the edge of the arena pool in the middle of the night. She was uncharacteristically nervous: pacing, playing the beam of her flashlight over the pool's surface, hands moving in fingercant as if she was talking to herself. I leaned on crutches and watched the water. It would take weeks and a trip back west for me to get a new leg, and I'd outgrown all my old models.

Lub's head popped up out of the water, and he handed me his canvas bag. "That's it," he said. "Those are the last ones."

We helped him out of the water. The cut on his forehead was still visible, but he looked otherwise unharmed. He said no one among the Elders had even noticed his wounds—they were too busy celebrating. Evidently, they were all excited that Urgaleth had surfaced and that the Blood Pilot had been delivered. It didn't seem to matter to them that I'd kept the thing from inhabiting the host. They were all sure they'd fulfilled their holy duty and that the destruction of the human world was nigh.

Cults. They always thought the glass was half-doomed.

Lub and I began unloading the bag, and Lydia began stacking the scrimshaw according to some scheme I couldn't work out. There were over fifty pieces, and each one I'd touched was blood-warm, almost moving in my hands. The arena seemed to be filling with voices murmuring to each other.

Lub and Lydia, however, felt nothing. To them the scrimshaw were just engravings in tooth and baleen. Artifacts.

Then Lub handed Lydia a piece and she grunted as if she'd been punched.

"You found them," I said.

She nodded. I leaned close and saw the gleam of tears in her eyes. The portrait was of a man and woman with Lydia's wide eyes and dark hair. They bore little resemblance to the graying, unmoving people lying in the living room of her uncle's house.

"They're alive," I said. "I can feel them in there."

"Don't say that," she said. "I can't stand it if they're trapped in there."

"At least they're somewhere, right?" Lub asked. "Some of these people don't have bodies to go back to."

"And how do we do *that?*" Lydia asked. She turned on me. "You have any answers for that?"

"I don't," I said. "For neither of us."

She looked away, and then nodded. For a moment she'd forgotten that we were in the same situation now. Both of us were artificial orphans.

"So where do we store these?" Lub asked. "I've got room at the lighthouse."

"We return them to the families," Lydia said. "As best we can."

That made sense. The portrait of my mother was hidden in my bedroom. I didn't want the police to seize it as evidence or something.

I squatted, balancing on one crutch, and picked up a portrait that I'd set aside. "I'll take care of this one."

The door to the library was unlocked. The lights, hanging high above the shelves, were still on. Maybe they were always on. Inside, it was never day or night. It was always Library Time.

I stumped my way through the stacks, not bothering to call out the professor's name. I knew he was in here somewhere. Instead, I enjoyed the quiet, and the presence of these old tomes. Books were always waiting. Hoping, silently, that someone would take them from the shelf.

I turned a corner, and there was Professor Freytag. He was looking at a high shelf, frowning in concentration. I waited for him to notice me. When that didn't work, I quietly cleared my throat.

Even that sound made him jump. "Harrison!"

I was pleased he could remember my name. "How are you doing, Professor?"

"Terrible! And you?"

"I was just thinking, it's like the books are watching me, wanting me to pick them up, but they're too polite to ask."

"Of course," the professor said. "The best books are always reserved."

I laughed. "Good one."

He looked at me quizzically, then broke into a smile. "Oh! Yes! Ha ha!" He removed his glasses and wiped them with his handkerchief, clearing ethereal dust with ectoplasmic cloth. "You know, I used to love jokes. Made them all the time. At least I think so. And very recently I began to feel . . . lighter. More free."

"The Scrimshander's dead," I said.

"Oh, many men have thought so."

"No. I saw him die."

"Well then. Perhaps that's it. Still . . ."

"Still. You're looking."

He gazed up at the shelves. "Oh, yes. I'm sure it's in here somewhere."

"I was thinking. Maybe it's not a book." He looked at me quizzically. I set my crutches against the shelf and took off my backpack. He watched as I unzipped the pack and took out a plate made of bone.

"I think this belongs to you," I said.

He placed his glasses back on his nose and leaned over. "Oh," he said. "Oh my." It was a fine likeness. The Professor Freytag before me was exactly like his portrait. Unlike Lydia's parents, there was no living body to continue aging.

He turned away from me.

"Professor?"

"Just give me a moment." He took off his glasses again and wiped at his eyes.

"I'm sorry if I upset you," I said.

"Upset me?" He turned, and put on a smile. "My boy, you've delivered to me a pearl of great price."

"Tell me what to do with it, Professor."

"What do you mean?"

"How do I set you free? Do I smash it?"

"Oh, don't do that! There's no telling what the consequences could be!"

"Then what am I supposed to *do*?"

His expression softened. "Tell me what's happened," he said.

"There are other portraits," I said. "One's of my friend's parents. And there's one of my mother."

"Ah. I see. Come, my boy. Sit down. Let's talk through the situation."

I sat in the armchair I'd found him in on my second visit. He stood patiently as I talked, not even pacing. I told him everything that had happened out on the water, and everything I'd since remembered about my childhood.

"First of all, let me congratulate you," he said. "Lesser men, upon seeing the things you have seen, might have gone mad. Oh, I've witnessed it myself. Two colleagues of mine glimpsed the mere *aspect* of a creature from another dimension and lost their heads. Both ended their lives in asylums. But you, my boy, seem to be remarkably sane."

"I don't feel that way."

"I understand. You've got one foot on the Other Side now."

"I think I stepped across that line a long time ago," I said. "I just didn't know it."

"The Blood Pilot, yes. You were bitten as a child, and infected. But you survived. You've obviously developed a sensitivity to the Other Side."

"Just tell me what to do," I said. "How do I get my mother back?"

"I haven't the faintest idea."

"I hate this!" I said. "*Magic.* The *supernatural.* Before Dunnsmouth, I thought the world was a rational place. I knew how things worked, and if I didn't know, I could figure them out with logic and a little research. I knew the difference between fact and fantasy. But since then I've made friends with an amphibian, fought an ancient serial killer, and faced down a god."

"And talked to ghosts."

"Exactly! None of this makes any sense! I want science back!"

Professor Freytag seemed amused. "When the supernatural turns out to be real, it's not *super*natural anymore—it's just nature. Yes, it may be strange, uncanny, or frightening. It's always scary to find out that the world is bigger and more complex than you thought. But that doesn't mean you *give up.* What if Galileo had given in to peer pressure? What if van Leeuwenhoek had thrown away his microscope when he discovered that there were tiny animals living in our bodies?

And does anybody *really* understand quantum mechanics?

"But think of how much you've already learned about this 'nonsensical' field. One: Consciousness can exist outside the body. I'm unliving proof!"

"Uh . . ."

"You see what I did there?"

"Comedy. Right."

"Second: The Scrimshander has discovered a technology by which to transfer consciousness and store it in another medium."

"Like a hard drive," I said.

"I've never understood baseball metaphors," he said.

"No, a hard drive is a—never mind. Go on."

"Third: Technology can be *learned*. There must be a way to undo what has been done, and move the consciousness to its proper location. We only have to find the right instruction manual." He nodded at his portrait, now lying on the floor. "In the meantime, let's find a place to hide that. On a low shelf, mind you, where I can see it. I'd forgotten how handsome I am."

The day my mother was released from the hospital, Aunt Sel threw her a welcome home party. Amazingly, she did not have it catered from Uxton. "This is a Dunnsmouth affair," she said. She cajoled Erik Hallgrimsson and his wife, Andrea, into providing fresh lobster, and Lydia made something called dagon chowder, which involved many ingredients I'd never heard of. Saleem made a dessert from an ancient recipe he'd learned as a child from his Persian mother: pineapple upside-down cake.

"Where are you from, again?" I asked.

"Minnesota."

"Right."

I was pretty sure Lub was lurking outside the house—we'd made plans to talk later that night—so I made a show of carrying the cake past the window.

We ate our meal in the living room, where Mom's high-tech hospital bed had been set up. Aunt Sel had thrown herself into the task of taking care of Mom, and Lydia had helped her create a daily calendar and care chart. After all, Lydia had the most experience of any of us in taking care of the victims of "the Dunnsmouth Disease." Aunt Sel, though, promised the best care money could buy. A nurse was scheduled for every morning and night, a physical therapist would visit every other day, and a Reiki specialist would come every Thursday "to maintain energy flow." We already had an appointment to drive Mom to see a high-powered neurologist in Boston. It was great to see Aunt Sel so focused on someone other than herself, but there was still something about the elaborate charts that made them a bit about Aunt Sel, too.

After supper, I started to clean up, but Aunt Sel told me my job was take care of the guest of honor. The others went to the kitchen. I hopped to my bedroom, retrieved my backpack, and sat next to Mom.

"I want to show you something," I told her. I held up the scrimshaw. "See? Your body's all right. And *you're* all right. We just have to put you back together again." I placed the scrimshaw on her chest, and placed her hand over it. Skin and bone were equally warm.

I'd have to come up with a story to explain the scrimshaw to Aunt Sel. And I'd have to somehow convince her that we absolutely had to stay in Dunnsmouth. Lydia would undoubtedly have some ideas. Maybe I could pit the women against each other.

"Don't worry," I told Mom. "We're scientists. We can figure this out."

EPILOGUE

The Toadmother lay upon her stone bed, breathing and thinking of food. She could tell by the stains on the floor that parts of her were still bleeding. When she moved, shards of wood and metal shifted painfully beneath her skin. The explosion of the *Albatross* had turned her into a pincushion. Her dress was *ruined*.

The swim back to the shore had been exhausting. To add insult to injury, when she'd reached her chambers, all the food buckets were empty, and her chambermaids were nowhere to be found. True, she'd told the girls to stay home until summoned, then had sealed the doors so that she could not be disturbed during the anticipated rituals—but that was before everything had gone wrong and her boys had abandoned her. She'd sent her eldest son to do a simple job—disable a boat, kill a few people, then swim back—and what had happened? He'd disappeared. Then, when she was almost killed herself, where had her youngest son gone? Davy Jones' Locker, probably. He'd died without even saying goodbye.

Oh, she was so hungry. She'd tried to remember the last time she'd gone this many days without a meal. The only way into her chambers that was still unsealed was the secret passage that led to the sea. She tried to remember if anyone except her sons knew about it. Probably not. That was the problem with secret passages.

If someone didn't find her soon, though, the consequences were dire. She'd have to get out of bed. She'd have to find food on her *own*. The thought exhausted her. How had everything gone so wrong? Hundreds of years of waiting, and now two failures within decades of each other, both brought on by the same family—the same *mixed-race* family! It defied explanation.

A scraping sound came from the direction of the secret tunnel. The chambermaids! The Toadmother pushed herself up to a sitting position.

"Where have you been!" she said. Her voice, now a dry croak, was still loud enough to set the air trembling.

A figure appeared at the tunnel entrance. The man was on all fours—though "all threes" might be more accurate, because one leg was bent at an odd angle and dragging behind.

It was her youngest son. The glossy black mass of the Blood Pilot rode upon his back. Its black tendrils roped around his lower jaw like reins and disappeared into his mouth.

Eston Montooth, principal of Dunnsmouth Secondary, had become the vessel.

"Come to my arms, my boy!" she cried.

Montooth crawled forward, then collapsed on his stomach, moaning. The Toadmother, with new energy, pulled herself from the bed to meet him at the center of the room.

"You brought it back!" she said. "Good job!"

He lifted his face. The Pilot had filled his mouth. It very well could have been breathing for him when he was in the water. It was the only explanation she could think of for his survival; until now Eston had never shown any talent for amphibiousness.

The black inside his mouth trembled. "THIS VESSEL IS NOT EMPTY."

"Oh," the Toadmother said. It had figured out how to

speak. "We had someone else lined up for you, someone completely vacant."

"IT FIGHTS ME."

"My apologies," she said. "Eston. Stop fighting the Blood Pilot."

He moaned. His eyes were wide and pleading. Such a baby.

She reached past her son's head to touch the Pilot's oil-black skin. Her fingers sank in to the knuckles. She pulled back, and her fingers came free with a *bloop*.

"So," she said. "When do we start building the gate?"

ABOUT THE AUTHOR

Daryl Gregory is an award-winning science fiction author. His first novel, *Pandemonium*, won the Crawford Award, and was a finalist for the World Fantasy Award. *The Devil's Alphabet* was a Philip K. Dick Award finalist and was named by *Publishers Weekly* as one of the best books of the year. His third book, *Raising Stony Mayhall* was a *Library Journal* Best Book of 2011. His most recent novel, *Afterparty*, now available from Titan Books, was a *Kirkus* Best Fiction Book of 2014, An Amazon Editor's Choice for April, as well as a *Library Journal* Starred Book and a *Kirkus* Starred Book and Best Bet.

AFTERPARTY

DARYL GREGORY

In the years after the smart drug revolution, any high school student with a chemjet can print drugs... or invent them. A teenaged girl finds God through a new brain-altering drug called Numinous, used as a sacrament by a Church that preys on the underclass. But she is arrested and put into detention, and without the drug, commits suicide.

Lyda Rose, another patient in the detention facility, has a dark secret: she was one of the original scientists who developed the drug, and is all too aware of what it can do; she has her own personal hallucinated angel to remind her. With the help of an ex-government agent and the imaginary, drug-induced Dr. Gloria, Lyda sets out to find the other three survivors of the five who made the Numinous to try and set things right...

"A great giggling psychedelic trip down the big pharma rabbit hole."

Paolo Bacigalupi, Hugo and Nebula Award-winning author of *The Windup Girl*

TITANBOOKS.COM